REX

ALSO BY JOSÉ MANUEL PRIETO

Nocturnal Butterflies of the Russian Empire

REX

A Novel

José Manuel Prieto

Translated from the Spanish by
Esther Allen

Grove Press / New York

Published simultaneously in Canada
Printed in the United States of America

FIRST EDITION

ISBN-13: 978-0-8021-1879-0

Grove Press
an imprint of Grove/Atlantic, Inc.
841 Broadway
New York, NY 10003

Distributed by Publishers Group West

www.groveatlantic.com

09 10 11 12   10 9 8 7 6 5 4 3 2 1

Esse *is* percipi.
To be is to be perceived.
—Bishop Berkeley

ACKNOWLEDGMENTS

There are many people I want to thank for the support they gave me as I wrote this book. First among them is Francisco Goldman, who has been an invaluable promoter of my work. Many thanks, as well, to Beatrice Monti della Corte, who offered me a home at the Santa Maddalena Foundation where I wrote the first chapters of *Rex*. Alma Guillermoprieto read the book in manuscript and had many insightful observations. The Guggenheim Foundation gave generous support. Finally, I finished writing *Rex* as a Fellow of the Cullman Center for Scholars and Writers at the New York Public Library and am very grateful to everyone there. Special thanks, as well, to Esther Allen, for her excellent translation, which is in fact a rewriting of this book in English. Thanks, as well, to Amy Hundley and to the rest of the Grove/Atlantic family, especially Morgan Entrekin.

Finally, I want to express all my gratitude to my family, my daughter, Alicia, and my wife, Elena Bezborodova, for their many years of support and understanding.

PART ONE

First Commentary

I

I've been reading it for years, the one Book. Over and over without stopping. Beginning again whenever I reach the final description of the vast party, the inaugural ball, returning immediately to the first words, when he's dozing off in the house in Combray and dreams of stopping time in its tracks, solidifying it. I've opened it at random in ship terminals (Helsinki), English pubs, Istanbul cafés. Each and every time, without fail, I've been stunned by the intelligence, the penetration, the unique capacity to perceive things that escape every other writer. Always the right words, flowing out miraculously, as if he never had to stop and think about them, as easily and naturally as someone randomly humming syllables, nonsense noises, tra-la-la-ing a tune.

Language, an aqueous thing, foundationless, a river of words. Yet how rapidly I sail along it, the mass of that river flowing beneath me: no mere suspension of sediment washed along by chance but the immense briny depths of a living liquid. And we can peer down and scrutinize its surface, see it at work, discover its life, watch its cells move and exchange information and energy without ever ceasing to transmit an idea. A profligacy of means, an expenditure far beyond most other writers. Not simply piecing together a more or less coherent story—making the sun come up, in the novel, over that red sea—but reducing the incredible life of that prose or song that lies beneath our own to its essence, as if the Writer had used blood where others only water, simple sea water. And the same astonishment when, turning your gaze from the adulterous woman, the fraudulent scientists, the aristocrats of dubious lineage, you discover that all of it moves and glides upon the very finest material, the bodily fluid, the lymph of an immense animal, the earth itself a gigantic living being that easily, shockingly, secretes blood. In a single, sudden, galactic rhythm.

To such a degree that when the manuscript reached the publishing houses—pages of this new substance placed beneath the microscope for the first time—its editor, M. Van Leeuwenhoek, could see nothing but platelets, red blood cells, and pushed it away in disgust, deeming it no more than a polluted liquid, devoid of human beings, storyline, any resemblance to the patterns of life. He quested across that vast sea—which in itself was an unprecedented extravagance, a technique from somewhere beyond the skies—in search of the skiffs and galleons of its characters and found very few of them, and those few as if becalmed. And he thought, "Can this be a story? Is it a book, even?" And it was the final book!

2

It startled, even frightened him when I spoke that way about the Book, this **being without fixed age**—at first I'd thought that was me, that the Writer might be referring to me, but on an instant's further reflection I realized the phrase applied rather to the man who had greeted me, Batyk. A man bearing a perfect resemblance to a peon, someone fetched from the depths of the darkest, sootiest oil painting.

I am concerned, he announced, with the infinite cunning and unction of Norpois (in the Writer); I am concerned, I fear that your manner of teaching, an education such as the one you propose, based on a single book, may not be the correct or appropriate one. So distorted an education, its vortex resting upon a single book, cannot, by all rights, amount to much. Didn't you list the classes you were to give him on my behalf? Spanish, mathematics, geography in Spanish? Hadn't you also mentioned physics? Didn't you assure me you were well grounded in physics, *extremely* (sarcastic here) well grounded in physics, didn't you agree to cover the entire sixth-grade curriculum and the seventh, as well?

And yet all I did in the first class was talk about the Book, and in the second I talked only about the Book, and in the third read aloud selected passages from the Book. That drew him closer.

To deny, like the Commentator, the greatness, the usefulness of the Book. To begin, like the Commentator, from his own terrible incapacity—the Commentator's—to speak in a frank and direct way about something that truly interests him. Abandoned, instead, to his zeal for denying all good books, ignoring the many that have been written, his particular vice of paying attention only and almost exclusively to minor authors, names in an index. The unwarranted fixation with which he studied them, reducing them to their elements, vivisecting them. Not *vivi*secting but *mori*secting them, for they lay there lifeless before my eyes. The satisfaction of a gambler who watches a machine, a miracle of engineering, busily revolving. The little wheels of his citations spinning in their niches, toothlet locking into toothlet, but a machine—you know?—devoid of human warmth. Perfect—but a machine.

Who hasn't felt that to be so? I invite any reader to write and try to refute me with the story of how he or she closed one of those commentaries in a state of agitation, moved by one of the dry commentaries that the Commentator sought to pass off as literature. Any reader on earth, ever.

And such a man, such a horror, in your house. His surprise when I spoke to him of the Book and he asked me for it, wanting to take a look. He held it up before me, rocking on his heels, moved it away from his eyes, as if farsighted, pretended to read it. He wondered, in a very loud voice replete with falsity, "And why doesn't it mean anything to me? Why doesn't this book speak to me and tell me what you say it says?" (The character who appears on stage in the second act wearing Moorish slippers; the instant we see him, his socks drooping, the djellaba thrown over his shoulders, we know he'll behave badly, perfidiously.)

As indeed he did, opening wide his arms, as wide as arms are opened in Syria or Istanbul (not in Angarsk, in Buryatia, where he came from), and pretending that the Book had slipped from his grasp. His whole malevolent being in that gesture. Falsely conciliatory at first, but then he threw the Book down on the corner of the table. From which, under the momentum of its own weight, it slipped and fell on its spine.

3

I didn't move or change expression, Petya. True, I did inch away from the wall, white with rage, but I regained my calm before making any further move. Then I walked to the middle of the room, forcing my feet to the place where the Book had fallen, and picked it up from the floor. I regretted having given it to him, having made such a miscalculation; how right the Writer is when he says: **the faculty of becoming in a few seconds.**

Words that mean or allow for this reading: as I bent over to pick it up I kept my face down and my intentions concealed, aware that there was only one person in your house I could go on talking to, only one person whose company had any appeal. The day of my arrival—horrified by the heavy tassels on the curtains, the ghastly luxury of every aspect of the decor, a garish statue of a turbaned Moor at three-quarters scale perfectly in keeping with all the rest—a change of plans suddenly occurred within me, running precisely counter to my earlier notion of abandoning the whole project. Like a liquid that polarizes, reorders its crystals in a new direction. At the exact moment I met your mother, and after our conversation in the living room, the blue water of the swimming pool sparkling at her back. She opened out before me like a strange new device, deploying all its antennae, setting its vital systems at their highest levels, and then emitting signals to me across the marble tabletop; the consistent breadth of her conversation, the isotropic structure of her intellectual armature sending out a strong signal in any direction you cared to go, an unvarying quality of lively intelligence, penetrating mind, open eyes.

The dress she was wearing that night without expecting any guests, the sobriety and intelligence of everything about her. The Italian furniture and carved ivory had led me to expect an overweight, slack-faced housewife in flowery poplin with enormous breasts at 8:00 p.m., the sort of pampered lady who goes out to buy cigarettes two blocks from her house and you stare at her, thunderstruck with horror, as she steps out of the car and lights up: the lacquered helmet of her hairdo, the antique cell phone on which she gives instructions to the distant executors of her idiotic will.

But no. Quite the contrary. The knee astutely concealed beneath the smooth fabric of the pale dress, the breasts discreet, youthful, the arm farther extended by the pen or pencil she continually pointed at me as she spoke, instructing me on the nature of my pedagogical undertaking, the education she wanted for her son.

And the light source on the index finger of that hand—an enormous stone, all the more tasteful and intelligent for its size, intentionally huge and disproportionate—could be seen, I think now, as the only point of contact between her and the dismaying lady buying cigarettes at the corner store. But she was fresh, without a single false note: the thin, oscillating blade of a clarinet theme introduced in a first movement. That was the tone—slightly masculine, not a flute or a harp doing arpeggios, but steady and delicate, addressing its questions to the heart . . . And not for one second was I tempted to tell her the truth; I lied as promptly as a chorus of strings and brass responds to the first violin.

4

Which is where the Writer, to whom no error whatsoever can be ascribed, says, **a pool.** In the sense that those houses, seen from the sky, had seemed mere appendices to their swimming pools, places from which to understand the more important fact of water in the garden. A cliff overlooking the sea, the highest point on the coast, and along it a row of beautiful houses with swimming pools. As if connected, the swimming pools, to the blue mantle of the sea, the wellspring that secretly nourished them and toward which, before ringing the doorbell, I turned back, for another look at the water breaking against the coast, the mist over the beach, the distant cypresses, before returning to the shards of blue ceramic over the gateway. Nothing about that wall spoke to me of the kind of house I feared: people you wouldn't want to sit next to on a plane, watching them take out their cell phones and petulantly mutter their final instructions before the doors are locked, shooting suspicious looks at your hands on the armrests, openly bellicose. Or, in another scenario: a voice warily inquiring from behind the video screen, a man looking up and down the street in both directions in case I've brought along an accomplice, currents of ill will, a graying muscleman ceaselessly tickling the ivories in the shadowy bar, flashy suits swarming across the garden.

But no: the best impression. The sight of the pool sparkling across the lawn stopped me in my tracks, amazed. Not only connected among themselves, those pools, by some subterranean aquifer, but also in constant communication with the sea: the same slow ebb and flow, the same majesty. The striped bathrobe my first paycheck would buy me, a small percentage of my first paycheck. A lifestyle with ample space for the sea, striped bathrobes, the servant or butler who waited, motionless, with pronounced courtesy, for the two halves of the gate, pulled by the mechanical arm mounted on the wall, to move back into place, that second or two, without polite phrases or words of any kind, while the heavy iron plate rolls along its tracks and the five bolts are locked once more, your host checking them by sweeping his open fingers across them. Turning back toward me now, asking me, perhaps (I don't remember) about my trip. Feigning friendliness and good manners and reawakening my distaste, my fear of objectionable companions. And then the horrendous luxury that inundated that house when I reached the glass wall, pushed back a curtain the breeze kept throwing in my face, and wondered, once inside, whether to put my bag down on the carpet, my bag containing the Book, which I hadn't stopped reading the whole flight until we began our descent and I looked out the window and discovered that there were blue circles next to the houses instead of the patches of cultivated green you see farther north.

5

None too sure, true, that I could do anything to diminish the idiocy television had wrought in the child's mind, like a vinyl disk scratched by an oversized needle, twenty-five inches wide: that was the width of the shaft of light the TV set projected onto him. Though I hasten to add: **the time within which he has lived.** Words to be read here as meaning: I would be able to tutor a child. But not, for example, an old man, walled up within habits acquired in the navy (the loathsome navy)—you leave the service thinking you'll never again tap the key or probe the heavens for a signal, but then you see an advertisement for a Morse code operator at a base in Fiji and circle it, and there you are three weeks later in shorts and a Hawaiian shirt having a lazy smoke in the radio shack as you shuffle along in Vietnamese flip-flops, rubber soles slapping the floor.

An intelligent boy, a clever boy, Petya: you. Who after letting me talk for a moment immediately understood what was up. Understood the method I'd chosen to educate him. Was able to understand instantaneously when he saw me linger over that phrase, in a passage, I told him, that illustrated to perfection what I had to say. Because somewhere the Writer explains that human ignorance, or, rather, human stupidity, is like the ocean cleaved by the keel of a ship, which is intelligence. And when traveling on that ship, one has the impression that something, a path, is opening up through the mass of stupidity (and human ignorance), but behind the ship the waters rejoin in an embrace that bears no trace of the ship's passage, no more than a light tremor, the white froth of the wake, and then, a quarter of a mile later, nothing. He looked at me, then: he understood that only thus, with the Book.

I was a young man of some self-possession, not a governess cast adrift in the world with all the amorous disappointments of her short life heaving in her bosom. The wisdom, in my case, of a reader of the Book: I was a calm and balanced man, very stable and aware of his place in time, the most recent watermark at the level of twenty-nine years—my age when I appeared at your door with the Book in my hand and a clear mission to save you, Petya, to save the boy I found sitting cross-legged, Turkish fashion, the whole of his insides intricately wired from his blond head to the pads of his fingertips. Pushing the right button and toppling the monsters without blinking, without a second's hesitation. The flautist (in the Writer) replaced here by an abhorrent being, a perverse dwarf with the deceptively simple-minded look of a mustachioed plumber and an unnatural way of leaping, as if about to levitate, when he tried to smash his big monkey wrench down on the small points of light circling through the air in the illuminated kingdom of Nintendo. And always another of those points of light emitting sparks over the doorway or in a hollow of the wall, showing the way forward to the next level of complexity.

Confronting, that first morning, the tremendous difficulty of teaching the class: how, by what method, to tell you about geography, history? I opened the Book I'd brought upstairs with me for no particular reason, without knowing, when I picked it up, what use I might put it to, and began reading you one passage or another. For example, the passage concerning the Verdurins, where the Writer describes the horror of the furniture throughout their house, which seeks to give an impression of wealth and succeeds, but of an execrable newly gotten wealth, not a mark or a wrinkle on the upholstery, every finish perfect and all the more horrible for its perfection. The constant impression of running into a wall of bad taste, a mirrored surface, to the point that sometimes I couldn't make myself go inside, hesitating, thinking: if I don't slide open the glass doors.

Surer now that I would know how to teach the boy. A flexible pedagogy, not forcing him into any subject, any particular branch of knowledge. It was, for that matter, what I'd have wanted for myself: not to have wasted months making my way through mathematics and algebra. To adopt the Writer as the sole basis, transmute the knowledge the Book contained into wisdom. A boy who was happy when I met him because he didn't have to go to school—and what boy wouldn't be, Petya?

6

A sense of having arrived finally settling into me, the impressive view beyond the garden wall, the highway parallel to the bay that I'd driven along that first day, gazing up, trying to guess which of the houses it was. Without, of course, ever imagining anything like this: the magnificent layout of the rooms, the bedspread stretched taut to a degree I would be incapable of achieving, ever.

The excellent idea of these houses with swimming pools, the days I would spend swimming, reading until all the light had gone out of the sky and the ones inside the house were coming on. The perfume that wafted up from the rough fabric when I leaned down to drop my towel in a movement that brought my eyes close to the deck chair. So strong a scent that I could visualize her, the lady of the house, walking along the edge of the pool in the same dress she wore that night, pale cream with a green patterning, the fabric stretching across her legs as she walked toward where I lay. Precisely the abandoned wife I would want for a house like that, undoing her hair before lying back onto the deck chair and impregnating it with her perfume.

Enveloped from that first day in the sound of the sea and wondering from the beginning how the waves could be audible, a thing quite impossible at the distance we were. Until I discovered a few silver columns in the living room that didn't look like, couldn't possibly be, but, on closer inspection, proved to be speakers, a very slender, very expensive type of speaker. Impossible to say which speaker it came from, of course. I couldn't tell if it was the one under the gem-encrusted lamp or another: the whisper of surf barraging the coast.

A thing I'd not heard of before, a new style for that type of house, rich people's house. But why the stereo? Why not simply, and better, the real sound of the air, the trill of the birds? To what end the plasma screen's aquarium of tropical fish I'd watch rise through their water, shifting from side to side like real fish, with the slight movements and trailing bubbles of real fish?

The cool breeze that greeted me the next day when I opened a door by accident, taking it for the door of my room, and air came wafting across enameled mosaic, afternoon light softly illuminating the tessellated sea of a floor. A design I couldn't take in without moving several steps back into the hallway to study from there the whole effect, the tub at floor level, the hard, clumsy head of a marine animal affixed there. Revolving, twisting its tentacles as I circled the tub in amazement. So much money! A simple bathroom transformed into a sanctuary! At the end of each looped tentacle: a three-paneled mirror, a rosewood chest of drawers, an enameled scale—like some sea monster in an engraving holding a sailboat, a bit of broken mast, a sailor in the air.

Ignoring all the other details, the many-eyed sponge, the nebulizers with their perfumes: my eyes on the faucets, gleaming at floor level and over the sink, plump as birds with puffed-out plumage. The delicate, unmistakable sheen, the doubloon glint. As I drew closer, the radiance intensified along with my certainty that yes, gold—but it cannot be! (I drew even closer.) Gold! Gold faucets in the bathrooms! How could it be? All the astonishment of finding chamber pots and spittoons wrought of finest gold on an adventure in some mythic kingdom. Nothing to draw attention to the fact, though, no sign attached nearby to explain the faucets or point arrows at them, the labels carefully peeled away that first day, the ones that said eighteen-karat gold. Without dwelling on it for a second, or maybe so, in the early weeks, tilting the head and half closing the eyes to the bright gleam, happy at the touch of the precious metal's smooth patina, but then dipping one toe into the tub to check the water temperature, immersed in the flow of days, without a thought for the faucets. Cool water splashing against green porcelain. And now there I was, standing at the edge of that tub as if at the mouth of a well, staring, hypnotized, at the bubbles.

7

Because the Writer speaks, finally, of a young man (right away, when he says: **many years younger**), almost a child, a late-blooming adolescent: me. Who goes on to fall madly in love, yes, I concede that, stupidly in love, which makes it all forgivable, even the very reprehensible abandonment—how I condemn myself for it!—of the Book. Younger that afternoon than I am now, Petya. I'd gone down every hallway of that mansion, finding bolted doors, daggers in the air, like a knight dragging his feet laboriously along in his blued armor, the tree in the window blue as well, the birds on its branches turquoise blue. Knowing I would never leave that place, at least not through the same door I'd come in by, knowing that, with every step I took, the configuration of the castle's corridors was shifting behind me.

In love, Petya, and prepared to distort the spirit of the Book, to wrest from its pages all that my heart and the heart of the woman I loved were seeking. Anything: a man hoisted upon a coat of arms, the most outlandish plan anyone could imagine, and the greatest danger, as well. My face turned toward those pages without knowing, the day I first arrived at your house, that it would all turn out this way: the text's meanings passing over my face, their colors iridescing.

Happy, Petya, when the man I might have taken for a Filipino butler, had I been a character in some California noir thriller, opened the door and I discovered, before taking a single step, the blue gem of the swimming pool sparkling in the distance. How to understand it? All that money? How was it come by?

Dishonestly. Certainly not earned, as your mother tried to make me believe, from the sale of a unique invention patented by your father. Because that was the first thing she told me, but then, as if she were someone whose **level were constantly changing,** she spoke of a sale of military surplus, mutually exclusive and contradictory versions of the (illicit) origin of that money. Multiple interpretations, Petya, infinite meanings. Pausing before one explanation, exploring it, then moving on to another. Without suspecting that I would spend hours in the middle of your room trying to gather up the various meanings the Writer placed in the Book and find a way to leave that place and the tangled mess that I myself, of my own free will . . .

8

Or as it appears, magisterially, in the complete passage: **For man is a being without fixed age, a being who has the faculty** (the faculty, Petya!) **of becoming in a few seconds** (in just a few seconds!) **many years younger, and who, surrounded by the walls of the time in which he has lived, floats there as if in a pool** (isn't that beautiful? as if in a pool!) **whose water level is constantly changing, placing him within reach now of one period, now of another.**

Isn't it incredible that he can say so much? Isn't it astonishingly precise? Because I see the day of my arrival, Petya: how the slow emerald wave swells up and I swim along its crest, the whole story laid out inside it. Not buried in its depths, but encrusted along its surface so that I can scrutinize different portions of it at will. The morning I spent several hours in the garden, wondering at the blue of the swimming pool. And how I stopped for a long moment in front of the doorbell: the little camera that bore my face to the eyes of Batyk, the "Filipino butler," the Book deep in my backpack, its radiance emanating from there, the center around which my work as a schoolmaster would be organized. A profession in which I had no prior experience, Petya; well aware that I'd be lying if I took that first step toward the garden's lawn, the blue of the swimming pool, and that I'd save myself from lying if I turned around and retraced my steps. But going in nevertheless, becoming someone who deceived your mother that same night, who spoke to her in lies, like the Commentator. To such a degree that in my story I emerged from the sea in the semblance of a

Greek doctor cast up by a storm between Kasos and Knossos, regaining the coast by swimming all night, water dripping all over the living room floor. Muscular as a cyclops, phosphorescent jellyfish clinging to my shoulders.

An image that struck her with all the force of a holographic projection: a man mutely embodied in the air before her, shaky as an old movie. And I had a book, a single copy of a book that I managed to save from the shipwreck, carefully wrapped in plastic. A horrible night, all the water in the world under my feet, my back, my belly. Precariously suspended over the abyss of the sea, as if on a wobbling stack of chairs. How did I avoid the reefs? How did I keep from smashing my head against a rock? I overlooked her questions, returning insistently to the image of the strong, cyclopean body emerging laboriously from the depths, bearing the Book. Because I'd managed to save it, a volume in octavo that I studied, standing there on the sand, the plastic that enveloped it, droplets disappearing in the morning sunlight as if by magic.

Second Commentary

I

Your papa held out his hand without taking his eyes off me for a second. I studied his face from below, still pretending to be more daunted than I actually was, though I was, in fact, slightly daunted. The shadow of a tan, hair ranging in color from wheat blond to the ash blond of more recent years, sleeves rolled halfway up the arm, the glass of orangeade in his hand (no alcohol in it, even more dangerous that way, I thought). His eyes drilling into me, which had about half the desired effect (the other half I feigned). He held his head to one side, opened his lips, inquired mockingly, "The tutor?" And then smiled because he was grasping my hand now and could, if he liked, abruptly twist my whole body around or shake me like a rag doll. I pretended his grip terrified me more than it actually did (though it terrified me) and returned his greeting with an affable expression, offering no resistance to the relentless spin of his drill bits: just an inoffensive person with no other thought in mind but to take advantage of his money and relax in the sunshine. A simple person, like any speaker of Spanish, an aborigine with certain skills—in this case, Spanish—summoned to serve in his house.

Full of prejudices, your papa: against foreigners, against Spain, against us, the Spaniards. I read it in his eyes. It didn't bother me, nor did I have any thought of changing his opinion. I didn't say to myself: I'll show him, with my work, my erudition. I waited for him to release my hand, which he did right away because he could feel the strength in my eyes, in the effortless way I removed them from beneath his gaze.

With a sweeping gesture, familiar from some movie, he motioned me over to the tawny sofa. My fear, real and feigned, was rapidly giving way to a deep conviction that he was insignificant (my papa? yes, listen), that all the valves in his chest were about to open and he would go soft, deflating after the long journey.

His little show, the way he greeted me, was like the involuntary performance of an actor who meets an admirer on his way to the dressing room and can't keep from continuing to play Mithridates, accepting the bouquet with the august expression of the character, not of the old, tired actor that he is. He invited me to be seated, still within that same impetus, as if preparing to speak of the great benefits conferred by an education within the home, the deficient instruction offered by schools. But the moment his back recognized the living room sofa, all the energy went out of him, and he sat there a moment, blinking and switching gears. When he opened his mouth again, he turned toward his wife with a sob: "A disaster!" Her displeasure was a very real and hard surface off which the black point of my gaze rebounded. I turned and asked their permission to withdraw. I said: "I think it's best if I leave; you must have things to discuss."

She didn't thank me for the sensitivity of the gesture, your mama; her expression didn't change. The two of them remained there, in suspension, a quivering freeze-frame that, the moment I'd gone upstairs and they heard the door of my room shutting, rushed forward as if some play button had released the image, the remaining twenty-three frames of that second tumbling out en masse.

2

Something had happened, Petya, but there are two ways of reading the passage, with opposite meanings. First: I should leave the place immediately and not wait to become an involuntary witness to even more terrible confessions. Because something had gone wrong for your father, so wrong that, the previous night, he couldn't wait for me to leave the room before telling his wife that the operation had been a "failure" (without my knowing precisely what operation). The hand he raised, with which he said—the fingers of his right hand slapping his palm—I tried there and . . . nothing, and over there, too, and . . . nothing again. Despite the luxury that filled my eyes, Petya, despite his unbelievable monogrammed slippers, the gold watch revolving on his wrist, the way he rose to his feet and shrugged on his plush bathrobe, the way he walked along the pool, past the row of orange trees, followed by the borzois, so slender they were like the silhouettes of dogs. The black sheen of the Mercedes in the breezeway. Despite all that.

And another reason I should leave: because I felt the same way. A failure! All the times I would go into the boy's bedroom—your bedroom, Petya!—and see how little headway you'd made in your education. Reproaching myself for wanting to hit you, as when, in Septimius Severus's house, the Writer breaks his pointer in despair over his pupil's head—that diabolical child who was beginning to manifest, whose blue eyes were beginning to show the early symptoms of the disease that would eventually kill him, to the great jubilation and delight of the Writer who did not take one step in his sandaled feet to clasp the child in his arms, run away with him, save him. Watching, instead, from the height of his eyes, the progress of the disease, the worms that entered through the nasal passages, perforating the hard mass of the brain. Not the infinite patience and honeyed words of the magister: no. Instead, those water snakes, thick and lustrous, made their nests in that unreceptive brain, almost entirely closed to knowledge. A boy he had come to hate, conscious that all his pedagogical art, all his zeal, would be incapable of penetrating that indolence, passing through the armor plating of that yellow hair into his head.

Or else—the second reading—I should stay. Divided.

I would watch your mother emerge from the water, stroll through the garden. All her innocence in the way she stood at the gate, warily scrutinizing both sides of the street, then come back toward the house with the spontaneity of Albertine appearing on the Balbec beach, that beautiful passage in the Writer, full of the charm of the group of young girls, each one different from all the others as she comes along the promenade. As if a bird were making its way across the grass, though have you ever seen a bird walk? Nothing clumsier. Not at all like flight.

But your mother was flying across the garden with infinite grace, hair brushing against her shoulders, thighs gleaming beneath the fabric of her dress. A courtesan and a murderess was Nelly—easy to see that in her way of walking, her calves speaking to me, her shoulder blades.

Standing at the window, watching her go by.

Like the peasants the Writer speaks of, their faces pasted to the great window of the hotel dining room in Balbec, gazing inside without giving away their thoughts, their terrible conviction that the bourgeois fish inside that aquarium would look better in a forced labor camp, working spiritedly toward rehabilitation, pushing heavy carts along and calling out to each other by their first names. Furtively observing: this or that fish, this or that form of conduct. Noiselessly sliding open the fish tank's sluice gates, toward which each swims of its own volition, the eyes of one filled with dreams of women, jewels in another's. And thus tricked into leaving the aquarium, they're forced to shovel earth and push carts.

The discovery I made that midday, the day after your father's arrival, and which changed everything I'd thought until then about the house, the porcelain elephants, the Asiatic luxury. A find whose décor or backdrop was the rainbow the "Japanese" gardener's sprinklers flung into the air from one end of the garden to the other.

For there was a treasure at the end of that rainbow, one drop twinkling among the blades of grass, immobile as a planet amid a flight of twilight stars. A drop of water artificially enlarged to the size of a garbanzo, though its walls had not collapsed. Blue.

3

This is what I'd been doing: I'd gone up to the boy's room to teach my class, as I did every day. I would go into the room, I would open the windows wide, I would shout into his ear: "For what purpose? Why so much time, Petya, between these sulfurous walls, these illuminated screens?"

Or was it to your advantage that you'd never read anything? A blank mind, ready to be inculcated with a love of reading, even if it was only a single book? I opened the Book, seeking an explanation there for your stupid fixation on the TV, and also for the other enigma that had been occupying my mind: What made them stay home all the time? Why didn't they go out, ever? Batyk's way of checking the locks throughout the house before going to bed, like a shadow, and the dogs, the borzois, brought from Russia expressly for the purpose, always panting at his heels. The wind that blew through the square garden, the low wind that blew in from the coast and enveloped us all there, next to the swimming pool after the boy's classes were over, and I would be thinking: Well, I've worked, I've done battle with his obtuse brain, why not go out? Go for a stroll? Go, all of us, down into the Marbella night? (I'd heard the phrase "Marbella night" somewhere; it wouldn't have occurred to me to call it anything else when I saw the streetlights along the Paseo Marítimo go on, a garland of light along the water.) A discotheque to dance in, a woman, Nelly, your mother, who would, at her age, be the prettiest, the most luminous on the dance floor. But no: they spent hours next to the pool, drinking orangeade, lying in the sunshine without making any move to get up, without saying to each other: Look, it's getting dark, the heat of the day is past. Put on your green dress, Nelly, why don't we go to that Portuguese restaurant, that Cambodian place? Yura and Natasha will come along, Juan and Arantxa.

Never.

They had no friends, no one ever called them, no one visited the house. They never went out. Sometimes I cast a look out the classroom window and saw her, your mother, leaning against the gate to peer through the little door at eye level—to catch sight of her husband coming back, I thought, after he left again, two weeks later. But no, because she'd also done the same thing, I'd seen her doing it, when he was there, perhaps studying the cars or people who went by (very few people along those streets, all of them in cars). Only Batyk ventured out, I saw him coming home from the market with loaded bags and sometimes Russian newspapers.

At that point I would go back to the lesson, I would think for a moment, or I would open the Book, cradling its spine in my hand and allowing its pages to fall open heavily, with the same weight as all the pages of the Bible, like a bibliomancer using the Book to prophesy, read the future. And on the morning I'm telling you about, my eye happened to fall on the beautiful passage that speaks of the sea, is full of the blue air of the sea, all its breadth and density reaching up to the sky, where the blue lives, Petya, every other color in the spectrum filtered out.

He fills those pages with a quivering group of girls (**in flower,** as the Writer enchantingly describes them), a scene that reveals the life, the promise of a better life, outside, throbbing, moving forward across the whole width of the beach. The Writer's unique method, writing in slow motion, calm seaside strolls like these, Petya, some day:

From the far end of the sea wall, where they formed a singular moving shape, I saw five or six young girls approaching, as different in look and gesture from the people usually seen in Balbec as a band of seagulls disembarked from out of the blue, and executing in measured steps—those left back catching up to the rest in quick bursts of flight—a stroll along the beach, a stroll whose purpose was as obscure to the bathers whom the girls appeared not to see as it was clearly determined in their own avian spirits.

Then I saw it beneath the sprinklers' fine mist: a drop of dew, an artificially enlarged formation, big as a garbanzo. Blue.

4

I walked all morning toward that flash, making my way through the blades of grass beneath the weight of a terrible suspicion. I reached it laboriously, picked it up, that sparkle, that solidified spot of light between my thumb and index finger. A blue stone, some type of crystal that I examined as I crouched there, which lost its sparkle in my body's shadow. Which diminished and was absorbed into my feet as I stood up without taking my eyes from the crystal, the sun at its zenith. I moved it then, the stone, turned it slowly to make it emit the sparks I'd noticed from above when I was turning my head and the stone was still, my eyes zeroing in on its blue.

In the garden, lying in the grass. How? Fallen from whose pocket? I knew instantly, as I gained velocity and my proportions diminished, whose pocket. Not from Lifa's apron, not from the Buryat's white nylon shirt or appalling gray pants, but from your father's immense trousers. The night before (a starry night? a starry night) arriving at the house, and once inside, past the wall, throwing down the stones clenched in his fist. Certain now that he hadn't lost his way back to the house, which he could almost touch, stretching his hands out in front of him like a sleepwalker and heading toward the illuminated living room. But before that, letting the stone drop, his strength gone.

The living room curtains blowing in and out all the while at my back, feeling the curtains there, no need to turn and see them. Should I walk in the opposite direction, through the gate, out into the street, lean back against the wall and study this object that serrated the air around it? Or turn and shout, "A diamond! Here in the grass!"? The air lapping at my pants, the sea breeze (or it came from inland, I don't know) blowing at my back, the light touch of a god, the zephyr. To understand it, assent to it: "All right, but, how? Flee? Run away because of a diamond in the rough? Because of an uncut diamond in the grass?"

That question in my eyes, pulling myself up over the wall without taking my eyes off the sea, the sea that moved slowly toward the coast, time and again, a secret hidden in its folds, starfish and sea creatures seen in cross-section in its blue mass. Rolling across that mass, inside it, was the answer to my question: Who were they? What had I gotten myself into? What should I do now? I knew what to do. I understood immediately. Leave, Petya, leave your parents' house, get out of there and go far away, taking care not to trample on the other houses. Like a giant striding away across the line of the horizon. Without looking back, without stopping to find out who they were. Contract killers. International blackmailers.

5

False, therefore, what the Commentator says. As if the Writer could have lacked the subject matter for an original or primary novel about anything at all, ancient or modern, a young man's arrival in the south of Spain, in Marbella, at the home of some Russians (or Russian mafiosi) where he takes a position as a child's tutor and comes under the spell of the owner's wife and finds himself involved in the most incredible of stories. Isn't that enough for an original book, a straightforward book, written out point by point, without flashbacks or commentaries, should anyone, a primary writer, be disposed to do so?

There was enough there in the story to fill several slim volumes, blonde women on their covers with eyes round as dinner plates, smoking guns. Seven paperbacks could easily contain it, there was matter enough to generate seven thrillers, or a series of seven little novels, each a hundred pages long, about the question of all the money the two seemed to have, the strange figure of the Buryat, the father's frequent and inexplicable trips away from home, and Nelly, the chatelaine, the abandoned beauty.

All of it told from the tutor's point of view, easily and comfortably, as if written in the 1920s when tutors were commonly employed (though still today, even now, I myself), with complete innocence and no need for commentary or any weight given to the detective stories and thrillers already written. Setting out to write it, should anyone ever try to write it, would he really have to eschew the frontal, vehement, and direct narration that the Commentator claims, or seems to claim with the whole body of his work, is now impossible?

I could write, for example, that I did not know the source of that money (the gem in the garden!). I imagined various possible pasts, your father's fists pumping in and out of a stomach, a man flying back, doubled over by the blows. Your mother had told me, had lied to me, that both of them were scientists: "Vasily, my husband, is a scientist."

In the sense—I suppressed a smile—that a famous bank robber is nicknamed "the Professor" for his habit of arriving at heists, bank vaults, long after midnight with a white lab coat over his shoulders and a leather case in which the security camera records not Herr Professor's stethoscope but the lock picks and rubber gloves of his trade, though there is a stethoscope, too, which he speciously applies to the iron chest of a Mosler with ten combinations. In that sense a scientist. The pair of con artists who, after years of sustaining their performance, have been completely swallowed up by their roles: the big strong man and his delicate wife, the ermine stole and suitcases with reinforced corners that the hero of a bad novel stumbles over in the hotel lobby, a detail the Writer would never have introduced, though he does have the passage—everything is there in the Book, everything!—where the narrator thinks he's detected a thief, a dubious character, out in front of the casino, and it turns out to be the Baron de Charlus.

He describes him in alarm and in minute detail: a thief! He wants to warn the hotel's owner. And then, no: it's the Baron de Charlus.

But with your papa and your mama I'm certain of it—no unexpected transformations. Your mother had the eyes of a thief, the long arms of a thief, the swaying walk of a thief: the way your papa had heaped the side table with remote controls was precisely the way a mafia kingpin, maybe a hit man, accumulates expensive audio and TV equipment and moves his hand without looking across the pile of remotes, picking one up at random and pushing a button to see what comes on. And if it's music, fine, and if the enormous screen lights up, that's fine, too. Like a mafia honcho on his day off. His wife, his inexplicably slender and lovely wife, stroking his hair against the arm of the sofa, fingers entwined in her husband's hair.

Like two big mafia honchos.

6

I left the house that same night, Petya, and walked all night beneath vast leaden clouds in a sky illuminated by bolts of lightning. Carried along by my feet and my despair at missing out on the vacation I'd anticipated next to your parents' swimming pool, hating and fearing my employers, your mother and your father, asking myself over and over what I'd gotten myself into and whether I should proceed immediately to the nearest FBI office and turn them in, like the deplorable citizens in certain deplorable Hollywood movies, who think that informing on or betraying someone in any way—that a snitch can help his country, save it from danger. Lamenting having taken the job with them, those Russians.

Careful! I had to tell myself as I walked toward Marbella, toward the Marbella night. Careful with them! Given all the money they had and how dangerous they were, and of course: the gem! Going toward the night, and in the night, though I didn't yet know it, a discotheque I hadn't imagined was so close by, an edifice immense as a castle, huge as the Ishtar Gate.

Without having planned to go in, Petya. But the spotlight sweeping across the sky, a movie theater, I thought at first, the beam of light announcing a premiere, and I stopped and saw it was a disco, the massive stone blocks of a castle's walls handsomely inflated, larger than life. Every color applied to it, the whole palette, on the battlements, the buttresses, the fake drawbridge. A structure that would have gladdened the heart of Bergotte (in the Book), his discovery of color fully comprehended and painted onto the building's gigantic walls, the discovery that thus, with **various layers of color.** The **dense yellow** he finds in Vermeer, to which other more Disneyesque hues had been added: phosphorescent greens and acrylic reds, the magenta doorway at which two Nubian slaves kept watch, ponderous and muscular as a pair of winged bulls. Understood: a rest, a place—when I'd gone inside and looked around—where I could leave the whole question of the stone to settle into the air as I moved, letting it flow freely around me without thinking about any spot or niche in which to place it.

Swinging across the dance floor with a thousand levels of freedom, spinning at any angle, not merely reaching the four cardinal points, like some medieval machine, but touching any and all points on the sphere. Behind, before, making stops at sonorous stations, my arrival marked by the beat, my hips and shoulders at a precise spot in the air. Smooth as a machine cunningly articulated on tiny ball bearings, endlessly spinning to the sound of that music, my head taken a thousand different places by the undulations of the dance. Tunes I could dance to perfection, tunes about which, Petya, I could have taught classes, entire, extensive courses, for I was vastly erudite in the secrets of dance, expert at moving back and forth with an ease conferred by early apprenticeship.

Or, as the Writer calls it (with reference to Swann): **the elementary gymnastics of a man of the world.**

7

But then a triumph and a truth on the Commentator's part, Petya! The surprise in store for me at the center of that sphere. A thought that forced me to stop in my tracks, my arms falling toward my body like the flywheels of one of Watt's machines. I drew near in astonishment the moment that evening's group started playing and watched their performance, stupefied. Never having suspected a thing like that. The way the singers, young black men, were moving across the dais, reaching the edge and retreating, as if tired, weary. The spirit of commentary permeating and making its nest in their innocent souls, the soul of the Commentator speaking through their mouths.

Songs I myself used to hum a few years ago, a tune which, that very autumn, earlier that autumn, had filled me with happiness each time I heard it sung (by an Englishman, a young Englishman), now commented upon by these musicians with all the disdain and profound sordidness of commentary. Hardened and old as commentators, the young black musicians, not moving toward us like the kind of singer who seeks to convey something to the audience and might even leap into the air, full of emotion. Shifting, rather, from side to side, without ever leaving the floor's level plane, barricaded, incredulous, with nothing to say about themselves, about their own lives, but something to say, apparently, about the song they were commenting on, as if intoning a Gregorian chant. First a passage, cited in scholarly fashion: author, year, and place of publication. Then they proceeded without pause to comment upon it, words weakly mouthed, in murmurs (or something like murmurs). Having lost, generationally, their skill, their faith in new songs, melodies that could make them run to the edge of the dais and put their hands to their chests in a burst of passion. No, never that: *cool*, you know? Arms dangling, peering up from beneath their eyebrows, faces turned toward the floor.

As if the Commentator himself had waited for me outside the disco to stand up and say: "See? I was right. Even these musicians here . . . All stories, all combinations of notes, all original melodies having— make no mistake about it!—run out. Nothing left but commentary, as these boys from America have grasped."

I didn't give it a second's reflection. I saw, outside there, across the whole width of the beach, that this truth was not his. That perhaps there was only this one justification, one principle, for commentary: peda- gogical purposes. Only for that reason important. My career as a tutor, all my work as a teacher, running on commentary. And didn't that make sense? In this case? Rather than hiding it, pretending I had bet- ter things to say, something better than teaching you every day about the Book, the gold mine of wisdom that is the Book?

Though only as a pedagogical method or procedure, I repeat: the method of commentary still execrable in itself. You may be thinking: a certain intelligence, a certain good taste in that, in commentary and the Commentator. The portions of text he ripped steaming from books and spoke about with subtlety and in detail, about the peculiarities of those books, the peculiarities of their authors. This is good; even, at times, praiseworthy. But never acknowledged, as I did from then on with you, declaring openly: yes, this is commentary; yes, these are commentaries. On the contrary, he always tried to seem like something more than a commentator and always avoided citing or commenting on any text by the Writer. In the medieval tradition of never, or only exceptionally, citing the moderns, or so he said.

8

The reception your papa gave me when I'd cleared the garden wall as the sun rose. Looking, whenever he would approach the kitchen window, like a gigantic monster: an eye that glanced outside, enlarged by the glass, and then immediately diminished in size, racing from one point of the kitchen to another like a toy car (a Hot Wheels? a Hot Wheels), growing larger and smaller in pulses, nervously.

Orbiting around me, your papa, like a binary system, two stars of different brightness and intensity. The hemispheres of two different men at work diagonally behind each eye, moving toward me at an angle to put me off guard with whichever eye was commanded to scrutinize me at that moment, the right eye being the good cop. A better blue, this eye: his scientific side, let's put it that way. The fathomless benevolence of that iris capable of disarming any observer, anyone who didn't notice that then, immediately, he would lower his shoulder and head transversally to scorch you with the terrible blink of the left eye, receiving orders, dilating on orders from his bad hemisphere, that eye.

Looking for a break in the light, a flaw in my shining, transparent self. He inspected my farthest corners and found nothing but my good intentions, my crystalline density, the excellent disposition and exquisite preparation of a reader of the Book, a man with clear ideas about the horrors of being educated in a school and the innumerable advantages of a private education in the home. All of which my lips had made audible from the first day. Without the slightest incongruence between my nucleus of goodness and the phenomenalization or external projection of that nucleus. None of the lace curtains, hateful partitions, cunningly placed screens for other people's eyes to slide along, baffled: no one had hired me to take the child—you, Petya—outside and place him, bound and gagged, in the hands of his abductors. I was not sent by the local mafia to spy on them, open the door, let anyone in to the walled enclosure of this house. None of that did he find in my bosom, in my arms crossed jauntily over my chest, no guilt (the stolen gem was mine, mine! I was the one who found it!) weighing on my shoulders to reduce my cyclopean size.

How great I was. How convincing. I convinced him.

But having brought his eyes so close to mine, I took advantage of the moment to cast a single glance, a fulminating bolt of blue lightning, inside his concerned father persona, seeking to read all at once, and not bit by bit as his gemologist's or jeweler's (or whatever he was) eye was doing, who he really was, to see the images of however many corpses had imprinted themselves at the back of his iris. But some barrier protected the dank, murky depths of his life and kept me from reading anything. And I withdrew immediately, having achieved nothing, no news whatsoever as to the provenance of his fortune, the money that had metamorphosed into his Mercedes 600, the Italian furniture, the Chinese porcelain, the fabulous sum that lay over the rainbow—silver-plated two-seaters, miniature yachts, perfect little airplanes precisely to scale—when to my surprise he mentioned the physics class he wanted me to give you. Bringing it up like this: "Batyk told me he's already spoken to you about this. Will you be teaching the boy physics at some point?" Obstinate in his farcical portrayal of a physicist and crystallographer.

He surprised me. I didn't know what to say, I stammered yes, soon, and wanted to clarify (but kept myself from doing so): that Batyk hadn't spoken to me, no, that he had tossed it away, the Book, had thrown it down and tried to dance on it. And yes, of course, some day I would teach him physics. Any kind of class can be taught with the Book, everything is in the Book.

Seeking by this absurd and misplaced request, I understood, to forget his fear, the terror he'd allowed me to glimpse, of a massacre or whatever it was that was keeping them hidden, your mama and your papa, in the worst place for it, a site they never should have retreated to, Petya, if they were afraid of robbery or assault. Which was why they'd never let you go out, in all those months. Six months there without ever having gone down to the sea, without ever having touched it, wet your hands in it. And wasn't I right to yield to my impulse, take you by the hand, lead you to the gate, push back the heavy bolt, and step through, the air hitting us full in the face when we were outside and heading, your hand in mind, down toward the sea?

To stroll along the beach, take out the Book, let the air ruffle its pages, open it up to any passage at all. To go out, I thought: a tiny incision. Letting the sea air rush in with a whistle, the real birds of southern Spain.

9

It was an impulse toward the sea, Petya. All those years I'd been moving toward the sea. Irresistibly attracted to the edge of the earth from the deepest heart of your country where my feet had taken me in an earlier part of my life to lock myself in behind kilometers and kilometers of land with no sea. I learned to love rivers, unknown to me until then, and sometimes, looking out a train window, an endless line of blue-green pines in the distance, tightly and evenly packed, would leave me speechless, for it looked like a sea! A deep nostalgia for the years spent near the sea, afternoons when I felt I would never again have all the sea—you know?—all the sea to myself. And I began, without being fully aware of what I was doing, to move, slowly, like a tectonic plate that begins to migrate. Toward Spain, I thought, and once in Spain toward the sea. To bring an end to all the false moves, the blue-green pines, the signs, the water dreams where I would sometimes see myself on the edge of a great lake and walk in amazement toward the undulating water, its movement thick and heavy, a primitive reproduction, a mental construct. Like a man on Solaris, an earthling, who never for a single day stops dreaming of the earth.

Sometimes, in the middle of the night, I would feel an urge to get up and take a train, a plane, walk with my rucksack on my back, wear out the soles of my shoes, eat cold food in roadside bars, sleep outdoors, fall in love with the girl in the post office, wake up one day with birds flying over my head. They, too, heading south. On my way to the sea.

What wouldn't I have done in order to take a job in your house, enter it like a young tutor in the nineteenth century who loves the lady of the house (not your mother, the sea) and finds work there so as to have occasion to see her every day? I read the advertisement. I lied in my response, endowing myself with pedagogical experience I do not have. All that so I could live, spend a summer, near the sea, let the sea come in through the window and in a single night displace the leaden sea of my dreams.

I asked Batyk if the house had any sea, any view of the sea. I'm not going anywhere, I told myself, unless someone brings me certain news of the sea. I interrogated him very thoroughly on that point. The advertisement read: "Young native speaker of Spanish wanted as schoolmaster of a young boy, private tutor, on the Costa del Sol." A small square advertisement, in Russian, published in *El Sol de Málaga* (this newspaper exists and that is its exact name: *El Sol de Málaga*). I called and didn't have to wait more than two days: Batyk rang me back to arrange for the interview. When, what day could he come and see me? It turned out to be a scorcher, an afternoon I spent walking barefoot across the tiled floor of the little apartment I was renting. An urban horror, a visual horror: a circle of bald hills, barren lots without green that I gazed out at and cursed bitterly.

My surprise when I opened the door and, with a step back, let in a man who looked . . . Russian? No: a man whose looks and manner were completely Buryat, whom I pegged easily and immediately as a Buryat. I told him so, and his surprise was so great he almost turned and left on the spot. As if I'd seen through his disguise. It gave him doubts about hiring me, a person with such minute knowledge of your country, but something in me, the sincerity and goodness radiating from my eyes, the exquisite fluidity of my manners, made him reconsider, change his mind. My duties would consist of giving classes to an eleven-year-old boy. Basic subjects: Spanish, geography, physics in Spanish. How to imagine that those classes would become the magnificent thing they are now, Petya? Magnificent, isn't that true? Or am I lying?

What was my profession, he inquired, what had my studies been? I lied, just as I've always advised you to do in such a situation. I would be able to teach an eleven-year-old, prepare him to begin going to school six months later. I didn't tell him, stopped myself from telling him, that a child didn't need Spanish classes, that a child would learn the language in a few weeks by repeating obscenities, clumsily swearing on a school playground. What need did he have of a professor all his own? A tutor who wouldn't even tell him what he most wanted to know, would avoid teaching him obscenities? Well, anyway. That's how it happened, Petya.

10

Or, to put it another way: there is no point or portion of human experience that did not affect the Writer and is not reflected in the Book, complete, clear, understandable, humanly comprehensible, and stunningly beautiful. Passages that require no commentary because they overwhelm the soul with their pristine force, Petya. The motives a young man might have for remaining in a house like your parents' house, after that first month. I might allege an explanation and convincing motive in my encounter with your mother one Monday at noon. I'd already seen and understood her to be a woman of overwhelming beauty, but then I watched her come into the living room that morning, her face illuminated by the stones of a necklace. Dressed as if to go out, though she never did, and for that reason I was doubly perplexed, trying to decipher where on earth, dressed like that, so beautifully attired, and with that string of stones at her neck. This time a cluster of immense diamonds, big as pigeon's eggs, cut smooth and round (cabochons, your mother would later clarify), all the light of morning inside them.

Everything is in the Book!

Paralyzed, not taking my eyes off the necklace as her legs bore it across the room, until someone—Batyk, undoubtedly—made her go back upstairs and take it off.

Without my being able to take a step or rather drop to the ground, return to earth, my feet a handsbreadth above the carpet, then falling slowly back down onto it, still plunged in my astonishment. All right:

I'd noticed, I knew they were fabulously rich, but . . . that necklace! Diamonds, without a shadow of a doubt. Because if once in your life you've paid attention, if ever you've seen a diamond, you won't mistake one for anything else, Petya. Just as it's enough for me to read a single page by the Writer, a single paragraph: how it glows, how it scintillates! And I'm not the type to say—as I know some people would, affording themselves the pleasure of stupidly proclaiming: So what? Diamonds? What do I want diamonds for? Why would I pay for a diamond if it's all the same—you know?—as a piece of cut crystal. I, a reader of the Book, was better prepared.

Terrible, that necklace. How much was that necklace worth? A fortune. The pink diamond, a fortune, the blue diamond, two fortunes, the red one, four fortunes. And so on. Not a king in distant India could come up with enough wheat to place on each successive square of that chessboard in exponential sequence. Indecipherable, the sum they'd carried off with them, and their fear all too explicable. Terrifying, Petya, that necklace: another level of complexity I wasn't imagining and that neither the blue of the sky nor the lily white of the clouds had foretold. The grace with which she then began wearing it every day, the disturbing poise with which she came down to breakfast with it glittering around her neck. And then she would go for a swim in the pool, and I would follow her progress with the attention of a sentry watching a submarine's red and blue navigation lights in the dark waters of an estuary.

Third Commentary

I

I went on reading to you: **They didn't generally dine at the hotel,
where the electric bulbs sent floods of light across the great dining room, making it like a vast, marvelous aquarium beyond
whose glass precincts the working population of Balbec, the fish-
ermen and petit bourgeois families, invisible in the darkness outside, would press against the windows to watch the luxurious life
of the people inside, gently rocked on swells of gold—as extraor-
dinary to the poor as the life of fish and strange mollusks . . .**

But you interrupted me, Petya. You asked: "What is it about?
What's the subject? The subject of the whole Book?"

"I've never thought about that . . ." I had to confess.

I had never thought about that. I stopped looking out the window,
turned around. What is the Book about? I had never thought about
that, can you believe me? I've read it thousands of times, I've entered
its pages at random, at any point, like a child who learns to go into
the house through the windows, familiarly. But once within I'd never
asked myself the question you had just posed. You forced me to pause,
having no clear idea of what he found a need to write about, a thing
that could be enunciated thus: The subject of the Book is. But now that
you ask, I can tell you. I know! It's money. The Book deals entirely
and exclusively with money. Because when the Writer takes a job as
the tutor of the sons of Romanianus and the weeks go by and he is
not paid, he stands at the window and asks himself a singular question: Shouldn't they be fabulously rich? Shouldn't they have money

in little leather cases, hidden away in vaults, shelves full of glittering gold, all that money emitting a sense of calm and security?

The Writer was able to address this with complete frankness, a whole chapter dedicated to the subject. For doesn't money figure at the center of all experience? Don't we need money for almost everything?

The way he pauses and speaks with exquisite delicacy of the beneficent influence of money, the detailed description of the ruby ring the narrator's grandmother leaves him at her death. A constellated ring: when the stone was turned downward, the flow of money dwindled; when turned upward, wealth came gushing in. Golden doubloons, antique florins with which he buys Albertine an airplane, a nice little one-seater with tarred wings that he, the Writer, uses as an introduction to the sections of the Book about flight.

Albertine—whom he never held prisoner nor kept with him against her will as so many commentators and myopic biographers have claimed —loved to fly. Obviously, if those claims were true he'd never have given her the airplane, for she would have been able to escape, to fly, literally, from the room, where she always returned, nevertheless, and where the Writer waited for her, avid for her stories, the herds of animals she saw grazing from the air, stampeding at the roar of the plane overhead. Dry lake beds imprinted with the cuneiform script of gnus. And sometimes she felt, he says, in pages brimming with a unique lyricism, like a friendly Count Ferdinand von Zeppelin sailing upon the ocean of air, or a Baroness Blixen, raised to the heights, transported by a genie from the *Thousand and One Nights* to the distant wildernesses of Africa and then back that same afternoon to the airport in Buc, on the outskirts of Paris. Though in that same plane she would crash into the sea and meet her death: Albertine, drowned.

The Writer never stops weeping for her or remembering the times he drove with her to the airport's green meadow, she in her ski helmet and driving gloves, attentive to the silvery circle of the propeller and the lamps of the stars she would fly toward, leaning out over the edge of the plane, letting her honey-colored eyes, like unfathomable quartzes, fill up with the green of the forests, the blue of the sea, the red of the sun on the horizon. The beauty of that passage filling my heart, certain that when the time had elapsed I would leave that house with all the money I'd been promised. Or was I deceiving myself?

Or was I deceiving myself, and had I not fetched up in the house I imagined?

2

Now, how to think of Nelly as a great lady? To see her through the Writer's eyes when, in the third volume, he gazes at his neighbor. A great lady like the Princesse de Laumes? Yes, I was sometimes inclined to believe that. Despite the vulgarity of the house, the shady business I imagined going on there, which the unbearable furniture hinted at. A woman on whom I could confer all the natural elegance of the Guermantes. Where the Writer says: **beneath a mauve hood** one day, a **navy blue toque** the next morning. And throughout this passage: **One morning during Lent . . . I met her wearing a dress of pale red velvet, cut quite low at the neckline.**

Alone, her husband away again.

The way she would focus her gaze fixedly on the tablecloth, her eyes inclined or falling at an angle like a shaft of light. And in the interior of that shaft the tiny figures of the false rich ancestors she never had. Obsessed with the idea that they'd been aristocrats at some point, that Vasily Guennadovich (your father) had grown up in a family of nobles, dispossessed, stripped of everything and excoriated around the year '17 and through the years '18, '19, and '20. The factories they'd owned in Finland—she was lying—all stolen. To the point that I told her, that first time in the kitchen: You should write a letter, go to Tampere, find those papers.

And she smiled to herself and gave me two quick glances.

Having sought out and hired me, I finally understood, as one more element of that deception, which would permit them to say: "A tutor for

Petya, just like the one Guennadi Nicolaevich, Vasily's grandfather, had. A certain level of instruction—you know?—a knowledge the boy would never have had access to in one of those schools, those prisons or warehouses for children, really. Although the one we hired is crazy or has had his brains scrambled by a writer he never stops talking about"— and she looked at me smiling when she thought that—"but he is good and generous and we have trusted him from the first moment."

With that facility for the third person so natural in intelligent women, which she used to downplay her obsession with the subject of nobility, speaking of herself as a more ironic, more observant person would, acting like a girl on a visit to someone else's house.

"She is, I confess, obsessed with the matter of nobility. And sometimes she'd like to fly away, escape from here. She'd love to pay you handsomely, to thank you for all that you do for her son . . . You don't wear rings?"

"I'd like to, you know?" I lowered my head toward her hand. Admirable, that blue gem, set high over the finger like a hard flower of stone.

I said nothing about her necklace, pretended she wasn't wearing the most fabulous necklace I'd seen in my life. Without taking my eyes off it, powerfully attracted by that necklace, fascinated and held by it, leaning toward her throat, with my feet firmly on the floor, imbibing the light her necklace radiated. Incredibly beautiful there on her breast. Obsessed with that necklace to the point that I'd searched through the fashion magazines they had lying around the house as instruction manuals for life in the West, scrutinizing the jeweled breast of every fashion model, Spanish or Greek, burnished skin glistening over the clavicle, neck tendons taut, for a gem like that one, the same size as that one. And finding not one, ever. Most of them, the best of them—it was easy to see from the design and the very bright colors—were just cut crystals.

I could think of nothing to say to her. I said:

"And yes, Nelly, it is something I have thought of. To surpass the objectives of a princely education, or rather, ignore them entirely. What sense in learning a foreign language if, once within that other world or universe, you'd only be fatally drawn in again by the magnet of the Book? Better to focus on it, for it's the same in all languages, impervious—as the Commentator perversely affirms, though of course without referring directly to the Book—to the fire of translations. Constructed on the solid foundation of a universal language, a primordial speech. All nuances, all distinctions, all subtleties within it. A Theory of Everything, Nelly, a Book for all days. I don't wish for, could never have wished for a better education for myself . . ."

"*Solntse*," she interrupted me. She went over to the window and set her hands on the frame like a bird alighting there to await her husband, who was not coming, scanning the horizon from there. "Wouldn't you like to go out for a stroll?"

And she turned toward me.

Her face.

Having stood back, the maker of that face, at twenty weeks' gestation, to study the precise placement of the cheekbones' brief elevation, the almond frame of the eyes. Rotated one second of arc downward at the inner corner and one second of arc upward at the outer, like wings. I was afraid to look her full in the face: the dangerous fascination voltaic arcs exerted on me when I was a child. But I couldn't help throwing a look at the white-hot point, the acetylene flare hurtling toward me, the nucleus of a star expanding outward in a sphere. And in the center of that sphere, birds and bands of angels.

Her throat.

The stones around her throat.

"A walk? With all my heart!"

3

I imagined, Petya, that we were off to withdraw some money, that our little jaunt had to do, finally, with matters related to my paycheck. Progressing happily down the Paseo Marítimo. Without a monocle, it's true, to bounce along on my chest. A monocle that would speak as clearly as the Writer of the happiness that suffused me, the soft purity of the morning. The hotels along the beach, the yachts with their colorful banners, the blue and white striped awnings of the beach clubs, the money we drew in with every breath, that perfumed the air of that city by the sea.

But picture this, Petya: a gentleman with a lady by his side and, with them, a dwarf. A rather different image from the one I'd had in mind, an image that can be read or glossed with no other significance but this: the dwarf was Batyk, who'd insisted on coming with us and whom I call a dwarf in the literal sense of a physical dwarf, not a moral dwarf. And not at all, never, in the allegorical sense to which the Commentator alludes with deepest hypocrisy in order to justify his own imposture: the sense of newcomers who, however small or dwarflike they may be, can see farther because they're perched on the shoulders of the giants of the past.

The same went for Batyk, on my shoulders, though it would be more correct to say on the Writer's shoulders, feeling him walk along behind me, paying attention to what he was seeing from that height, without understanding a thing. As when, to my disconcertion, your mother stepped into a jewelry store, with me all unaware of what prompted her to stop in front of the display window (the jeweler's name etched in a semicircle on the glass), study some of the gems there, and then go inside for a closer look . . . Sensing that we'd be standing there for some time, I positioned myself next to the doorway in a patch of sunlight which was exactly that yellow color the Writer devotes such beautiful words to in the Book, but which now, in the aim of bothering and confounding Batyk, I used as the pretext for an odious discourse on Ferragamo: how that color, mingled with a lovely blue, would be perfect for a pair of Ferragamos, which is what we should have been looking at, not jewelry, Nelly. (I felt Batyk leaning over my shoulder, stretching out his neck—what shoes? which shoes?—stooping lower myself to make him stumble and fall on the slope of my false interest in fashion, inexplicable in a man like me, as if a matter of such little importance as a pair of shoes could occupy my mind, turn my thoughts aside for one second from what we had gone into that store to do.)

The adorable dress of layered red muslin your mother wore that day, her hand palm down on her thigh, the better to scrutinize a pink gem in the display case. She raised her eyes, shooting me a meaningful glance beneath another client's elbow: a diamond, innumerable tiny facets that light could go into and then not find its way out again for one beat or two, until it flashed once more against my eyes, my astonished eyes. I looked up into her eyes without knowing what I was supposed to be seeing there, as if she were a botany teacher who goes on ahead and waits for you beneath a tree on an excursion through a garden. You reach her out of breath, you want to tell her something about the day, the view, but she puts her finger to your lips and asks you with her eyes: "Understand?"

Yes, Nelly: stones, diamonds, gothic diamonds, marquise diamonds, star diamonds. I don't want them, have no money for them. Or else (I suddenly stood up straight, looked back into her eyes), or else: "Hand over the stone, motherfucker, hand over the stone before my husband gets back and makes you talk. I know you've got it. No use pretending . . ." And I saw in the red of that stone, its blood-filled interior, how easily Batyk could smash my head against the counter, the iron grip of his fingers around my neck, or send me crashing against the reinforced glass. How the shopkeeper would shout, and not because of the glass (bulletproof), which would never break. Giving vent, in that moment of danger, to his anger and indignation, in Korean or Tamil. Meaning: Get out of here you Russian pigs, go kill each other outside.

I'd give it back. I'd run back to the house, fly up the stairs, take it out from under the mattress. Here you go, Nelly, I never wanted it, you know that, don't you? Never the slightest intention of keeping it, always meaning to give it back. And I had thought about doing that . . .

Easily comprehending, at that moment, my mistake: the mistake of having wanted to steal from the mafia.

"That's not true. My mama is not in the mafia."

"No, it is true. Just wait."

I regretted everything in that fearful moment, entering cold regions full of fear and leaving them for warm regions full of fear. Having taken a position as the tutor of a child as wayward as you, Petya, having focused my thoughts on the wife of a mafioso and spoken of warps in space with your father. All that as I stood at the counter without daring to open my eyes and look at her, without seeing that she'd moved to the back of the store without any of this in her mind, that she hadn't even noticed the stone was missing. So many stolen diamonds—if a single one fell down and was lost, what did it matter?

Were there, I wondered immediately—horrors! Petya, horrors!—were there many more of those diamonds lodged along the edges of the staircase, hidden between the sofa cushions and under the living room rug?

4

I must amplify the previous commentary. I had just returned to my room to flop down, not bothering to pull back the bedspread, lying diagonally across the bed, still trembling, when I heard music that someone had put on, and lowered the Book to listen.

The stereo's silvery columns filling the air with a melody that made me think of the Writer, of a breeze and the shimmering surface of water that is exactly what the Book is about: the days you discover from your window without there being the slightest gap between the vision of the sea lapping at the coast, the cypresses in the distance, and your mother, her soul, the way she had of gazing gratefully up at me, the way she squeezed my hand when we'd returned to the house, happy to have gone out. As if I, as if my chest were armored with metal plaques that bullets would rebound from. Or as if the Book, placed between my heart and the gun barrel, could miraculously stop the bullet that was tearing through its pages with a single line, this line: **one is a count or one is not a count, it's not of the slightest importance,** as Mme. de Villeparisis notes, and with good reason.

For she didn't stop talking, all the way there and as we went from store to store, nervously talking about the mafia, the many Russian mafiosi who'd taken refuge there, the whole coast crawling with them. And I stared at her in amazement, thinking: But you people are the mafia, *maja*! What are you talking about? You yourselves are mafia! And as we went past, I signaled her with a pointed glance at a Guardia

Civil's lacquered bicorn. Look there, I meant to tell her. Why is it that you wouldn't go outside unless I was with you?

Bent over the pages of the Book without reading, or reading blankly, pages going past without the Book's allowing anything inside—a rare thing in the Writer who always grabs you, his pages like Velcro, your eyes like felt. Trying to decipher, suddenly lowering my eyes to focus on the explanation, first found in the Book, for their great fear. But then she appeared in my room, your mother: knocking, *tock tock*, on my doorframe.

"I have a gift for you," she said. "Though it's not a gift, it's your salary."

She came closer.

"Don't you love dancing? You should dance for joy. It's more than we owe you, but I wanted to reward you for your goodness to the boy. That's why we went to see the diamonds. I wanted to find out how much it's worth."

She left the center of the room and walked toward me without taking her hand out of her pocket. Certain of the effect it would (and, indeed, did) have to drop into my hand, rolling bumpily down from hers, a stone, a diamond in the rough, an uncut gem. The size of a pea or bigger still. The size of a rather large pea.

I didn't manage to say a thing, or rather I said, stupidly, pointlessly, "Ah, yes!" and thought: How does she know I love to dance? So much?

And then immediately: My salary! Finally! But in the form of a small diamond (one karat, three karats, not small). A capsule or sphere of crystal in which I saw myself diving off a dock into water, younger and thinner than I was then (than I am now), wearing Hawaiian shorts . . . The yellow silk of her kimono, the birds and vegetation embroidered on it. The perfectly unrumpled boughs exquisitely situated on the sleeve which lengthened, following her arm. Without managing to raise my eyes and tell her (which is what I should have told her): But Nelly! It's a fortune! It's a lot of money! Which is what I thought and was about to say, but then, already incapable of thinking straight, I imagined kissing her hand while my eyes remained on the stone, seeking there the words and explanation for such generosity and munificence.

There also entered my mind the idea, which I had not sought within myself, that this was the perfect twin of the stone I'd found in the grass. It kept me from lifting my eyes, that diamond, I gave it one more astonished glance and was about to raise my head, but Nelly had gone. Whether amused or annoyed by my surprise or apparent ingratitude, I don't know.

5

Has anyone ever given you a blue diamond, Petya? Extracted from a woman's kimono, the smooth glide of its silk across her skin? No longer thinking of her as the abandoned wife of a mafioso (she herself a member of the mafia: *psst*, quiet!), but as a woman I could seduce, my hands on her wrists, bringing her one, two faltering steps toward where I sat on the bed, the folds of silk coming toward my eyes in a rush. Surrounding her with my arms, letting them rest on her waist, breathing in the sweet fragrance of her body. What if she were a thief, what did it matter? What if she were a murderess? How many women do we watch in bedazzlement as they walk down the street, gazing at their legs, bedazzled, and those may well be the legs of a murderess, a thief— impossible to tell from the line of an ankle, the curve of an instep.

Have you ever found a blue diamond in the grass, Petya? I fingered the earlier stone in my pocket and pulled it out, the two more alike on the palm of my hand than my preliminary mental comparison had registered. Fearful now of being spied on by fiber-optic cables: anything was possible in a house like that. Batyk stabbing at my face on the screen with his finger and shouting for Nelly. "Look, aren't there two stones there? Isn't that one identical to the one you just gave him for a paycheck? Where did he . . ." Etcetera. Then, breaking off his reflections, he would leap up the stairs, his chest full of hatred, to hit me.

In one movement, supple as a thief in a hotel room, I switched off the lamp. Then, Petya, as the light slowly withdrew from the halogen bulb and went out, the stones began shining crazily, phosphorescing as if they were the last two points of solder a gigantic man were applying to my chest, sealing up the vacuum in that ampoule. Then, certain I was closed up inside, seeing me raise my bewildered eyes in there, he rubbed his hands in satisfaction, took a step, and was gone.

6

Those stones phosphorescing, glowing on the palm of my hand, trying to tell me something, foggily. That I'd been spied on! Suddenly I
understood: I'd been spied on! The memory hadn't come to me until
the moment I switched the light off and remembered those eyes, gleaming like carbuncles in the cave of a face. In the discotheque, at the back
of the discotheque, as day was dawning or almost dawning outside but
the corridors within were still dark. And in the darkness inside, someone, over by the wall, had been spying on me, watching me dance,
given over to the foul—and for me insane—diversion of dancing.
From the moment I stepped onto the dance floor until I went out along
the corridor to the parking lot and the sun hit me in the face.

And those eyes, which I didn't remember having seen until now,
which I'd buried among other impressions, bloomed before me at that
moment or were dragged out into the light by the maddening glow of
the stones on my hand.

The anguish, now, of having been watched, the anxiety of having
seen, as I twirled and spun, a pair of eyes gleaming from the back of
the disco and, I had only just understood: fixed on me. Like the terrible eyes the Writer sees flashing in a hallway in Saint Petersburg; he
realizes he's being watched because he sees a gleam, and when he turns
his head he sees it blink out. Hidden there, that man, knife in hand, to
kill me. And, in the Writer, I had to stand there like an idiot, or with
the magnanimity of a prince, seeking him out in the darkness, making
my eyes, brimming with goodness, illuminate the other man's, which

were cold and inhuman. I should have called out to him, told him, Don't spy on me, Batyk (for it was Batyk): Don't spy on me. There's nothing here for you to take back to Nelly or Vasily, nothing I would be ashamed of. Even if I did go home with great fear in my heart, the tremendous anguish of having danced like that, unstoppably, thinking: Dancing for what? With what end in mind? Dancing continually like a man possessed until the last song, whether commented upon or without commentary. God! When I had a house, a job, my pupil awaiting me. What if they could take advantage of my late homecoming, those who were spying on me (if it wasn't Batyk), the ones inside the house were so afraid of; what if they were waiting for me to open the door so as to erupt violently into the garden. Not Batyk, I repeat: the Russian mafiosi they were all so fearful of, the ones they never stopped talking about. Waiting outside until dawn in order to get into the house.

But no: it had been him, Batyk.

If not, then where did that comment come from, the one that stopped me in my tracks, asking myself . . . How does she know that I dance? Frenetically? (That was what she meant, your mother.) How does she know?

7

And then, two days later, back down to the city again. Your mother and I, arm in arm, strolling farther and farther from the little bay in search, I hoped, of a place where we wouldn't be seen. Then, at the end of that long walk, we sat down on a bench at the tip of a jetty and she kicked off her red moccasins and lifted her feet so that, after an instant of weightlessness, her calves rippled with a dense movement that touched me to the core. And I realized I loved her desperately and was full of tenderness for her.

On that dock, far out over the water, she was continually looking back at the path—in case Batyk were coming, in case he'd followed us, I imagined then, but now I understand: she was debating whether to let me in on the secret. The water pounding beneath us like the motor of a boat about to speed away, the first spin of the propeller. Gazing at me while the dock behaved as if it were about to move, all the force of that water, and Nelly calculating whether or not to get me involved in it. If only she herself had weighed anchor, told me, putting her hand on her heart, gazing into my eyes, "Stay here. I'll be back in two weeks, I'll call you." Or, rather: "Go ahead, what are you going to do all alone here? You'll get bored." Separated by the blades of water down there between the boards, the sun in the sky. Stripes of water between the jetty's planks and on her breast. And she was debating.

I saw that and was afraid for a moment that she'd actually say something. I said something, spoke to her about what I'd been paid. "You don't know how grateful I am. I will need, would have preferred cash, but no! Nelly, I'm lying: How can I tell you? It's more than I was owed, much more . . ."

"Let's go," she interrupted.

We'd be seeing more jewelry, I thought. She'd give me a few lessons on how to spend that money, the fortune it no doubt represented—a diamond! Then the rest of it seemed to happen under water, as if it was us flowing between the boards. The blur of beach-goers pretending to smoke in the sidewalk cafés, lighting a cigarette in an alley between two stores, the two of us sheltered from the wind, the narrow passageway with its service entrances and a man with a gun, visible for a second, before diving into the mist to fire at us from there, under cover. Leaving the shore at top speed, racing to a high point along the coast.

8

Like a pair of assistant directors scouting along the edge of a steep cliff for the right location to film a scene of love and complicity against the wide-open sky. The way she gave me her hand without looking at me, placing or lodging her moccasins in the grass, her calves flexing at every step. Without turning toward me when we reached the top, both looking out, both of us educated in the same antique (or primary) painters, our eyes seeing, and my legs feeling from the air that blew in through the bottoms of my trousers and swept at her skirt, that we had arrived.

I'd imagined for a moment that I would still be telling her about the hatred I harbored against the Spaniard, that painter ("the greatest of the moderns"—in other words, a commentator), and that she would listen to me without saying a word, only to suddenly turn and present me with her lips, rapidly revolving, pivoting on the axis of her neck, her eyes shooting out sparks, transformed by the sun into diamonds.

But this was what she did: she lifted her arm and stretched out her hand so that a ray of light reached my eyes, sweeping the meadow to its right, directing that light with dizzying skill or invisible diligence: the blue, the gold of the tardy sun, the green of the plants, the violet of flowers that seemed to grow larger as the beam of light swept over them.

And, revealed and concealed by the turning blades of the sun, which was simplified like a sun in a poster, its rays slicing the air into circles, her lips drew near and revolved before me, appearing and disappearing behind the beams. Pale pink outside the ray of light, shiny red within it.

Because the gesture of extending her finger had warped the surrounding atmosphere and as this magnifying glass developed in the air around it, the blue stone on her finger began shining brighter and brighter. I had only to lean forward a bit more to analyze its chemical composition (carbon, rings of carbon) and to marvel for the umpteenth time, now very close, at its unusual size: the disproportion between the size of that gem, the size of her necklace's cabochons, and the cheesy little stones worn by Silvia of Sweden and Margriet of the Netherlands.

And along the edge of that airy magnifying glass entered the words of a long explanation that I read as if in a trance, without being able to take my eyes off its surface for a second, the words distending as they reached the edges, then disappearing—but I had no need to reread them because their meaning was not escaping me. This was not a passage to comment upon, delve deeply into, and explore in order to extract some hidden message. All was expressed and stated with utmost clarity, golden words against a blue background. Without my ever having been able, without my ever having imagined anything like that, not the slightest inkling in all that time.

And when the words about the amazing size of the diamonds, their unusual coloration and, consequently, the money and Asiatic luxury of the whole house stopped emerging, the magnifying glass vanished, and I lifted my eyes and gazed deep into hers for a long second, throwing her a gaze of astonishment. Still more air entering my chest when she nodded her head several times, trying not to lose my gaze in order to transmit in that gesture the weight and gravity of her message. Which had the contrary effect of pumping even more air into me and making me continue on my upward trajectory with irresistible momentum.

9

To journey back into the past, set myself down at that point on the **walls of time,** walk through the garden, introducing myself into that moment as a wiser man, someone with the experience and exact knowledge of having already lived through that day, the late afternoon light in which we came back from the walk, went into the sun porch, and I was about to exclaim: "Synthetic diamonds!" To go over to myself and put my index finger on my own mouth, introducing a partition into the flow of that day. So that my words would flow down the opposite slope, at a wider angle, in order to extract them from my life.

And yet, no. I did none of that, none of it happened: we stopped for a second in front of the pool like two blank silhouettes, her hair rippling, my linen shirt loose. There was a moment when we reached the house and she finally turned to me and broke her silence, resolving to let me into the secret, moving me or roughly ejecting me from the safe and peaceful time where I was moving (or floating) into nights criss-crossed by white gunfire beneath a red rain. With blinding clarity. Only there, her eyes told me, only beneath that rain could I kiss her, only if I came to meet her there, leaving the island of dry air within which I walked.

Stopped there, having come full circle: on one side, my scant monthly salary as a tutor, my commentaries on the Book, the arid landscape of Spain glimpsed through a door in a wall. And on the other side, Petya, without words, without any need to use all the words I'm expending on you, a golden woman beneath a red rain. And even more diamonds among the garden grass. Diamonds revolving octahedrally in the air. Which one would you have opened, which door? Even if you knew a tiger was lurking beyond the frame, waiting to pounce?

Fourth Commentary

I

There are writers I *can* mention by their names, minor writers like H. G. Wells. A contemporary of the Writer, a man who also pondered and addressed himself to the subject of time. But in a clumsier, more mechanistic way, not like the Writer, who imagined a more subtle procedure for transporting himself into the past and recovering lost days. A state he summoned up—as everyone knows—by means of certain magic potions, certain mushrooms or fungi he kept in the pocket of his artist's smock and which, whenever he wished to travel back to his childhood and reconquer a day that was lost, he needed only to nibble, as if they were crusts of time itself (not madeleines as in the common misconception and not lime flower tisane, either) that took him immediately back to the segment of the past from which those mushrooms, those potions, came.

Not given over to daydreams, either, like an opium smoker luxuriantly sprawled on a cloud, as was fallaciously proposed by that predecessor of the Commentator (De Quincey), to whom the Commentator owes, let it be noted in passing, almost all of his tone, his subject matter, and his cynicism. A man cynically installed at the very height of a literature upon which he commented as if from the bottom of a barrel. Or like Diogenes, the cynic. And all of these opium eaters, all these minor writers or commentators, have claimed to travel in time or have pretended to travel in time and bring back smooth, round memories, rubies and sapphires, recovered without difficulty.

Only the Writer discerned, amid the blue-green mass of the past, between the sinuous, oscillating lines of lost memory, time itself. And saw that the past is made up not of hard, tangible memories that can be recovered at will, but of vague blue and violet memories—not red, not hard nuggets. And he conceived of writing a detailed report that he inserted into a chapter of the Book where he mentions in passing, without its being his primary concern, the solution he arrived at to the technical matter of time travel. And to ensure that it would more easily reach the minds of dull readers (that is, of the public) he used the words "lost time" (etcetera) in the title of his book. A book, he seemed to be saying, that also attempted to offer a solution to the question, so much in vogue during his era, of time travel. A man who wasn't afraid to resort to a small deception, a minor imposture, in order to advance a project, oiling it just enough so that it could be introduced with minor friction or noise into the minds of his contemporaries. Later the Book would be cleansed of it; the more intelligent men of coming generations would know that this, the matter of time travel, was not the subject of the Book, was only mentioned in passing. And what was his subject? Everything, all things, all men, the greatest book ever written, a summation of all experience . . . human experience? Human experience.

Nor did the Writer ever speak of or allude to any "time machine." For when Wells speaks of the "time machine," he's referring to an actual machine, a mechanical device that allows you to travel in time, enter the fourth dimension, physically. The machine seen or glimpsed as it makes its way through the puff pastry of the ages, biting into and pulverizing an enormous swath of lives, a wheel or plate of diamond that cuts straight through with perfect ease, never encountering a hard bone to gnaw at, a prince, a princedom, a particular year. All of it neatly reduced to dust.

2

I was left with a single woman, as the Writer was left with Albertine alone, among all the girls in the little band: Andrea, Rosamund, Giselle. Among the compulsive gambler I'd been imagining, the murderess, the international con artist, among the multitude that your mother—cloned into an entire band of bad and perfidious women—had been until that day, I'd chosen a single one. Just as the Writer chose Albertine. I listened to her, my eyes brimming with tears as I sat with her on the leonine sofa, entering into her tale of love and diamond cutters.

She told me everything, very animatedly at first. How they had to strip, in those workshops, and run in single file, completely naked, with the quick, awkward gait that women (not triathletes) have when they run: elbows too far from the torso, hands in the air in front of them, fingers open very wide. Watched at every moment by guards who kept them from hiding anything in their bodies, a half-cut gem, a diamond they could finish polishing at home.

And she, in her tale, coiffed, as in one of those films that touch my heart when I see them, with a lovely little white handkerchief. The modest attire of a young girl from the provinces who's never stolen anything, the simple dress beneath which, despite its baggy cut, the shape of her body can be discerned, the shoulder blades and delicate back of a very beautiful woman: who knows how she's involved, why she's part of this sordid story? Pure innocence in her thick eyebrows, her way of wearing the kerchief or babushka, her dress gray, the kerchief white.

She'd been cutting gems for years, allowing the blinding brilliance of certain stones, the real diamonds of Yakutia, to make their way into her eyes and groove thick furrows in her irises, which are striated now as I watch her from a distance boarding the factory bus, looking for a place to rest her poorly shod feet: a pair of some kind of round, heavy worker's boots. Without ever, for one second, she told me, gazing into my eyes, without ever for one second thinking of keeping or stealing any of the stones.

That, stooping low over the faceting machine or raising a cup of tea to her lips, garbed in the white lab coat of a cutter, was where she met Vasily. He approached without her noticing that she was being observed by that right eye of his with all the intensity of a gemologist. Or a monster, a giant cephalopod waving its tentacles, floating through the empty air of the factory restaurant one afternoon in E*.

From where, in the end, he scooped her up or abducted her and bore her down into the depths of an empty, provincial life. The hours he spent displaying his vast repertory of circus tricks to her, the way he could lift her with one of his tentacles, spinning her high above as she blushed and laughed, her hair falling amorously across your papa's horrible suckers (my papa? yes, your papa: listen), allowing him to deposit in her bosom a miniature image, the homunculus of an odious child who would grow up with his hair always too long and his ears always dirty. Such horror. The awful resemblance of Caliban, the child, to his father, horrid Prospero; the angelical sweetness of Miranda.

"All that in the Writer?"

"Not all . . . I can tell you where Caliban, Prospero, and Miranda are from. They're from another writer, but what does it matter? From another great writer . . ."

3

The fright I had, the fear I felt when I raised my teary eyes to your mother's, not wanting to believe, unable to fathom that her lovely clavicle, her soft shoulders, had born such weight, that your father, so inconsiderately, without calculating the pressure of his horrible embrace, had dragged her into that life of privations like the owner of a delicate alpaca who burdens it with a heavy load and drives it along a precarious mountain path with continual thrashings. And I moved nearer and spoke to her and told her I was there . . . to save her! (To save her? To save her!) With such vehemence that she could only smile at my impulse, first drawing closer to me, then changing her mind and standing up with a smile, touched or amused, I couldn't tell, changing a record, her neck and shoulder blades smiling at me.

She waited for the music to come on, making sure it was the record she wanted, and turned with another smile on her lips: months of goodness and dry towels on the bathroom shelves. The golden eyes of a woman no longer young, older now than the girl Vasily had swung through the air for whole nights. And I was older, too, you know? Than fifteen or ten years ago. All of us, necessarily, older than ten or fifteen years ago, and slower. But don't I like slower songs nowadays? Melodies that make my sandals speak with greater sincerity than the frenetic boogie-woogie of my dancing shoes? The way I went over to her, the drop of sweat that fell from my arm, inside my shirt, fell and left a discernible and isolated wet spot on my waist.

Afraid of frightening her, with a parsimony similar to Lifa's, in the kitchen, making her way among the copper pots, bending down, slowly lowering her torso to one side to check the height of the stove's flame. In which the two of us danced, Nelly's face and mine, our faces consumed by fire, the blue tongues of my passion, the impulse that led me to inhale the aroma of her hair, bewitched by the arc of her brows, revolving at the center of a slow song that astonished me when I heard its first chords because I said to myself: jazz, but without being able to tell you, you up in your room at that moment, to interject a rapid commentary, overlooking for the moment the commentaristic (or belated? or belated) nature of jazz. A song that now, each time I hear it, of course.

Intending this in every turn of the dance, making this clear: whatever she wanted from me, without a second's hesitation. Anything, so as to show her . . . Anything. The molecules of my soul arrayed in a unique pattern, through which would always blow, through those molecules, the same air, the same tune. Wherever I might happen to be, in whatever segment of my future life. Forever back in that same afternoon, the uproar and shock that first reached my central nervous system and assaulted me there before I understood anything fully, the horror of your father, the octopus, having watched us through many bars of the music now, from the other side of the glass. Falsely modest and all the more terrible for that: **Like a king standing in line outside a theater so long as the authorities haven't been notified that he's there.**

The light almost gone out of the afternoon behind him, the swimming pool's water grown denser. No one else outside, nothing to keep him from coming in, putting a bullet in me or dragging me out, paralyzed, not daring to move a muscle, to drown me in the pool like a puppy, transmitting that water into my eyes, my trachea: the inadvisability of having wanted to kiss the boss's wife.

But I hadn't kissed her! Do you hear me, Vasily? I hadn't kissed her, I hadn't taken, so to speak, my turn. I would die not only without guilt, but also without even having kissed her. Vasily!

Nelly was smiling, still dancing though she'd seen him now, her husband, in a turn of our ridiculous dance, halfway through that awful song. Yes, awful. I would be the . . . what number would I be, Petya? How many tutors had you had before me, how many of them had Vasily gotten rid of already after finding them, like me, seducing or being seduced by his wife? I can explain everything, Vasily! The fright, the terror, like a bolt of lightning scorching everything in its path, exploding everything inside me, soldering me with its fire, rewiring me for life, leaving only certain combinations of synapses activated.

And how is it that this doesn't figure in the books that someone—I, for example—someone sitting down to write, would write?

Inconceivable, unthinkable, always in me, from that afternoon on, Vasily's darkening silhouette, before he came in and threw . . . And threw nothing and no one out! Casually coming toward me as if only going to switch off the stereo and then, having gone past or pretended to have gone past me, turning back to slip a knife between my ribs with Nelly screaming "Vasily, the carpet!" (which she didn't do). The scream I was about to let out like the black slave surprised by Schahzaman, which echoed in my head, now wired or reprogrammed forever. I screamed, within myself: *Rex! Rex! Rex! Rex tremendae majestatis!* Overwhelmed with panic, as in Mozart. Can you believe me?

4

Now: if time is a discrete or discontinuous magnitude, then tiny spaces must exist between its smallest fractions, little gaps in which no time whatsoever transpires, minute spaces of eternity.

And someone, a man, who had reasoned out the intermittent structure of time, could take advantage of this, slow his body's revolutions, discover, beyond a certain point, those interstices, like windows in the air, passageways to eternity, a substrata of nontime in which the hours stand still. Catching up to it there, advancing toward the beginning of my stay in your house, the moment before my arrival, when I should not have knocked on the door, banged the knocker, rung the bell insistently. Or else flying in the opposite direction, toward the plot's denouement, with all mysteries resolved, its keys laid out in front of me, deciphered.

Or like the thief of the peaches of longevity, in the Writer, who impassively observes his pursuers, Forcheville and Andrea, hopping with impotence from the other side of the canvas, unable to lay a hand on him. A journey like that, immediate or sudden. Not the one in which I rode along trembling, from the moment Vasily asked me to get into the Mercedes, and we sliced through the air at a thousand miles an hour. Looking, he said, for a place to set me down, the cliff where I'd been with his wife hours earlier, an isolated spot where he could settle accounts with me, because his wife should never, in a burst of sincerity and frankness.

Let in now on the dirty secret, going to die now because of the dirty secret of that money. Trembling and hating myself for having allowed myself to be softened up and won over by his lovely spouse.

I thought of Lifa, the only person in the whole house who really loved me. Who, having seen me get into the car, hands behind my back, eyes vacant, would try to contact someone, call the Royal Canadian Mounted Police or the Guardia Civil (it didn't matter! whichever could reach me first!).

Out of a mistake on Lifa's part, a confusion, but that's fine, I accept it. For she'd taken the Book for that other book and I'd allowed her to retain that belief. The apparent devotion with which I pressed the Book to my heart made her notice it, believing she had discovered in my hands—in the volume in octavo I always held open, toward which I lowered my nose, over which, following the lines, my nose and eyes would move, my brain scanning page after page, tirelessly— a breviary, a Gospel I was reading, far from home, finding myself among strange people and bewildered by my fate.

No other book could be the object of such veneration, could be read with such devotion. She didn't fail to notice that I would skip pages, whole sections, that I put my finger in without looking, letting the settling of the pages (I was watching Nelly come into the garden instead), the sun shining on their gilded edges, determine my reading for the day. And when finally they (the pages) fell to one side or the other, I would lower my gaze and plunge into the passage, the minuscule figures of Gilberte de Swann or Princess Mafalda activated by their contact with my eyes, the whole scene in the Book coming to life.

The way she had of stopping things in midair, Lifa, and then moving about among them, dodging the frozen flies, the immobile birds three feet off the grass, passing through them like someone going past a hummingbird in a tropical garden. It was she who managed to save me from your father's wrath that afternoon: she slowed down the flow of the day, stopped the sun in the sky, made it give light for more hours, interfered in Vasily's plan and kept him from finding, as we traveled along that highway, any gulf of darkness, any cloud along the horizon to go into, the blade of his knife or small red dagger coming at me, glinting amid the cottony white.

Vasily peered out the window of the car several times, slowed down on several occasions, but then had to go on, accelerating with rage, the sun obstinately in the sky, the overabundant daylight. Still shining in all its splendor when he turned the wheel and we drove down the circular driveway of a mansion or enormous house, also on the beach.

5

I found her where a beauty of that kind should be. The Writer's description of those women in their luxurious Fortunys, like **ships,** he writes, with sails unfurled, floating lightly through parks and that garden-like forest in Paris. They're closer to us now, those women, we can see them without the impediment of a garment: easily visible on the beaches or next to a swimming pool. Larissa.

The way the sun played on her half-raised arms, her flat stomach, her manicured nails. Not a vulgar platinum blonde but a platinum blonde of the most sophisticated type. The way she spoke elegantly on a topic about which I could gain no clear idea (thinking still of the danger I'd just been through). Without understanding, I repeat, what the woman was talking about, but understanding the way in which she was addressing her subject: with absolute elegance and poise, someone from the same institute among the trees where Vasily had worked his whole life.

The way she stood up with total innocence, devoid of coquetry, walked in front of me, cutting through the air as she went for something, a hairband on an adjacent lounge chair, raising her arms to tie her hair back, still talking, holding it for a moment between her teeth, the hairband, muttering something I understood perfectly (and which did not amaze me: that Vasily had been there last week and hadn't flown to Amsterdam as he'd claimed), her breasts taut beneath the bikini top, rosy in the afternoon light, soft and round. The veins or blood vessels beneath her skin like those new telephones made of translucent plastic, designed to show the electronics running through them, and glowing, a red light coming on when someone calls (instead of a ring). And even if the afternoon light hadn't finally ceased to shine and the sun that had remained in the sky for so many hours (in answer, perhaps, to my prayer for more light, first to try to kiss your mother, and then for fear that Vasily would finish me off) had not finally disappeared into the deep darkness of a suddenly fallen night, this woman would have glowed like a creature from another world, from Epsilon Indi of the constellation Tucana, myriads of photons shining through her pores as if she were an angel or one of the stones that had phosphoresced in my hand. Equally disturbing, this effect.

A man, a giant, an immensely lucky man, whom I'd all too quickly dismissed as merely vulgar but who had the two most incredibly beautiful women, manufactured to conform precisely to the very latest prototypes for beautiful women, all the falsity of technology incorporated into their gleaming bodies. Calculated to make any man tumble and fall into them. My God, I said to myself: a goddess!

6

Psellus, I thought. I'd prefer that you call me Psellus, though my name is something else, as you know. But from the eyes of Michael Psellus, from that sphere, I will follow you with the diaphanous gaze of a sublime pedagogue, my hand on your head, feeling the Book's knowledge pass into you, seeing how you claim it for yourself, Petya. So that if this civilization with its exquisitely tiled bathrooms and your parents' solid gold faucets were to cease to exist and only my lessons, my readings of the Book, were preserved, these days could still be recuperated, the echo of my words holding fast in you like inclusions in amber.

You and me, beneath the slow spin of that spherical surface: you listening, me speaking to you. Fragments of the Book, commentary on its passages, floating around us, emerging from my lips, traveling through the air to you, your concentrating face perfectly visible. Blue letters unfurling across the floor, on your clothing, on the courtyard's paving stones, as the sphere turns and the text moves slowly up its walls.

Fifth Commentary

I

Neither a book whose infinitely thin pages contain whole libraries in a single volume nor a library made up of rhomboidal chambers where men—librarians—worship the books, venture on long peregrinations, interrogate abstruse combinations of letters, or are thrown into the void to die, etcetera. (Which, by the way, is a rather mechanistic simile now quite outmoded, a compression of the concept of a library). I've come up with something entirely different: a circumference whose radius is infinite, a spherical construction, a bibliosphere that has its Ptolemaic center in every reader and makes room between its thin walls (no thicker than a page of the Bible) for all books, including this one, and all commentaries upon them.

Though yes, strictly speaking, the commentary on a single book would suffice . . . But how can I describe or depict my distress, my despair, when I came back from Torremolinos to discover that someone had profited from my absence by destroying the Book, stripping me—or so I believed—of the source of my knowledge and pedagogical skill.

"What? The Book? Burned?"

"Burned . . . Destroyed by fire . . . But forget about that . . . First . . ."

"I know you're listening to me right now, Batyk; you haven't stopped spying on me for one second since I got here." Though never visible in the garden when I'm talking to the child, talking to you, Petya, Batyk always knew—I'd gathered from his way of retorting to things I'd never said to him—what passages we'd touched on, what subjects we'd covered on a given day in April or March (the subject of gravity, for example, so important) and the precise words we'd used. Until, overwhelmed by the force and wisdom and undeniable beauty of the Book, he conceived of doing away with it, depriving me of this public—not secret: public!—source of my power and pedagogical erudition.

The day I came back from that trip, Petya, knowing exactly where in the Book to find a passage about your mother's nervous collapse: the words of Cottard, the family doctor, words that would allow me to read the fear in her eyes correctly. I went up to my room for the Book and my fingers, fanning out wide, found nothing, probed only emptiness on my night table, and my eyes registered only emptiness. Without my ever imagining for a moment anything along the lines of: you in short pants and suspenders like a child from a bygone era, stopping in your tracks on your way to the Nintendo, then proudly turning your back on it, retracing your steps, pulled back, by my months of effort, to the Book.

I found in my mind a miniature representation of what must have happened, a replica of the passage, in the Writer, where a sultan approaches the mystery of a table and beholds a seeming chessboard on which small wooden effigies are arranged. And then, to his surprise, he perceives that they are all in motion: the horses prancing and curveting, the warriors brandishing their scimitars, the half moons of their helmets gleaming. And he sees it all from the surprised distance of his eyes, with a faint sound of drums and trumpets and the clanging of arms. Which was how I saw the Buryat lurking along the stretch of wall between your door and mine, his hands interlocked at his forehead, listening to passage after passage, sentence after sentence, and registering an important fact I'd mentioned in one of my classes: the combustion temperature of paper is 451 degrees Fahrenheit. Why Fahrenheit, though, when the Writer would have used Celsius, making it 232.77 degrees? I don't know, don't know. But Batyk understood and schemed what he would do to my copy of the Book at the first opportunity. Which did not take long to present itself during my two-day absence—and without your doing anything, Petya, to save it. To save the Book.

My outstretched fingers found nothing but air on the little table and only closed, hours later, on a blackened oval of stiff paper lying in the hedge next to the pool bar. The pages had been torn out one by one and consumed by the flames without a trace, while the harder and more flame-resistant material of the cover, the calfskin, was only charred along the edges.

I studied that cinder for a second, not a trace of the title's gilded letters at the center, nothing to signify the Book, the name of the Writer, the cursive of his signature. I understood immediately what the Book's fate had been and flung the cover away from me with a movement of the wrist, just as I throw the Frisbee to Almaz, the borzoi.

And it rose through the night to the back of the garden; it rose, caught and propelled by the turbulence its very advance and rotation were generating, and sailed neatly over the wall. Impossible now for me to walk into the house with that black cinder and throw it in the face of the Buryat, who would pale, etcetera. A cackle of laughter or the air that could have erupted into a cackle of laughter filled my chest without my actually laughing into the night, only my eyes: HA! And I turned around to present my face and my laughing eyes to the lights of the house, for at the moment the wafer of the Book went flying off into the night, my eyes had seen an illuminated stele of light advancing toward me through the air. Without any laborious searching, I'd come up with a passage from the Book about wild laughter. This one: **He picked up the turban and put it on all different ways until— oh wonder of wonders!—when he looked at himself in the mirror, he had disappeared! He gave the turban another spin and there** he was in the mirror again. He turned it again and disappeared. He took it off and could see himself in the mirror. Then he burst out in peals of wild laughter, bellowing, "All glory to Chernomor and his turban! Terror begone! May joy return to my heart!"

2

Allow me to stress this point: I suspected nothing. I hadn't seen it coming, never imagined it for a moment. Ersatz diamonds. There was nothing to foretell it, nothing in the Writer to help me understand. A subject unworthy of him, a matter to which he would never have devoted a sentence, not even as a joke, an exercise: never! The manufacture of ersatz diamonds, the double cross an ersatz diamond inevitably and almost automatically places in the soul of its creator: would such a subject occur to a gentleman? Would a gentleman devote himself to the manufacture of ersatz diamonds? Would a courteous young man—myself, for example—ever wonder for one second whether the diamonds his employer's wife, a beautiful woman with exquisite manners, had placed in his hands as payment for his educational efforts were in fact ersatz? Never. There are things about which it's best not to think, things upon which a limpid and upright soul never dwells. Allow myself to be invaded by your father's hammered gold chains and ruffian manners, the way the bottoms of his trousers swept his shoes as he walked? To what end? Toward what objective?

I'd been afraid, had imagined him shoving me along the top of a cliff, pebbles rolling beneath my feet, a question in his bad eye: Have you been seducing my wife? Giving me a beating that is precisely described in the passage of the Book that prefigures *The Matrix* (everything is there in the Book!), the scene in *The Matrix* when one of the agents catches up with Neo in a metro station and launches a series of quick blows, a wheel of fists hitting Neo's torso like the blades of a windmill—what a minor nineteenth-century writer might call a "hail" of fists, when it is in fact, as the Writer describes it, a **constellation** of fists, which fall by the simple force of gravity, breaking the torque at a certain point and then smashing down like pile drivers . . . All that, in this passage of the Book: **as an astral phenomenon appears in the sky, . . . two ovoid forms . . . with vertiginous speed . . . Saint-Loup's two fists . . . that enabled them to create, in front of** [Smith, Agent Smith], **an unstable constellation, etcetera.**

I'm sure of this. I cannot be mistaken about something like this: I hold the whole Book in my memory, its text incarnate in me. Nor should you be confounded by the turban and cackling laughter, which may appear to be a later addition, a corruption introduced in a subsequent era. The same goes for this passage with the unusual image of the constellation of fists.

Carried away with that image, I was imagining fists in the air all the way to Torremolinos and the whole time we were there with Larissa. But there were no fists. Quite the contrary: Vasily was friendly and indulgent, a scientist who entirely understands that a young man, almost a boy, in so luxurious a mansion, in the company of so lovely a woman. Surrounded by diamonds, this woman, not only her neck but her whole being, an entourage, a cloud of diamonds orbiting around her: how could anyone not fall in love, not fall madly in love with such a woman?

Your papa's demeanor had deceived me, I was thrown off, never having seen real mafiosi, only in the movies. I'd taken him for, believed him to be, one of those.

Now I understood: he was a defenseless scoundrel, a petty thief, a small-time crook, garroted by fear. His terror palpable in the way his eyes swept the top of the wall as he emerged from the swimming pool, putting his hands on the edge and pulling himself up, then quickly turning toward the wall as if someone might take advantage of his back in the water, a swimmer's vulnerability, to put two bullets into him, a sudden red stain in the swimming pool spreading out in a purple cloud, and Vasily floating strangely in the center, fixedly observing or as if fixedly observing the glint of a coin at the bottom, the bullets that missed.

But this, too, this thought yielding speedily to fear of an encounter with the windshield, even more terrible!

These people I'd believed and imagined to be fabulously rich, immensely affluent? Horribly poor, in reality! Bankrupt! He himself had confessed it: bankrupt! Catastrophically bankrupt! Nobodies!

Profoundly swindled, Petya. I felt profoundly swindled by your parents, deeply deceived by this couple who had so well, so consummately, so garishly played the role of supperrich. To the point that I'd believed them, presumed I was living in a castle, sucking deeply and directly from the udder of their wealth and congratulating myself upon it. And let's be clear about this: only to gain some time and make myself a little money (never enough) to save up for the hard days ahead and go on with my journey. True, I'd had moments of suspicion, sudden rushes of glimmerings, my hands and feet trying to correct the false picture, the mistaken perception my brain was constructing.

For example, there was the exaggerated tip I'd seen him give a few hours earlier on the way out of a disco even more luxurious and expensive than Ishtar. Indignant over it, angry at seeing myself forced to emend the error, wrest the bill away from the astonished doorman . . . And the worst of it was—my gaze fixed on a church steeple that I didn't stop watching until it disappeared around a bend in the road— they hadn't paid me! At all! Ersatz diamonds? They hadn't paid me!

How much is an ersatz diamond worth? How much money can an ersatz diamond be sold for?

He read it all in my face, Vasily; he didn't stop watching me all the way there, but without ever seeming anxious or cornered. Quite the contrary: a smile on his lips. A smile of aplomb and impudence, of smug self-satisfaction with the car he was driving, the lovely creature he had for a wife, and the beauty, the ineffable beauty, he had for a lover. I studied her again this morning, couldn't take my eyes off her: Larissa, standing there in front of her house, then walking back toward the door in her sequined jean jacket, thick blonde hair halfway down her back, turning and waving to me happily, her arm held high. To the point that I wondered, as in a nineteenth-century novel: Will I see her again? Ever?

3

I didn't open my mouth for several kilometers. Along that part of the road we ran into a cloud of insects that I took for locusts or African grasshoppers but that turned out to be tiny yellow butterflies. The Writer has a beautiful passage where Swann and Agostinelli enter such a cloud of butterflies and roll along pulverizing them beneath the wheels of their Hispano-Suiza, hearing them crunch and watching them pile up on the windshield until they have to stop the car and clean the small crushed thoraxes off the glass. The sun about to rise on that April morning, still a little chilly, and those butterflies, the golden dust from their wings.

And there was this: the relief that your mother was not a member of the mafia. Impossible that she could be evil, so sweet a woman with whom I'd talked over so many things during the evenings he said he was in Rotterdam. Married to a man who was cheating on her, a man I couldn't hope to control or set limits on and who was escaping me at top speed, his left eye opening a path for us a few inches above the asphalt. Not taking his eyes off the road for a second, laughing, his eyes surrounded by the bunching wrinkles of a man laughing gleefully to himself. He had a very beautiful lover (I'd seen her), a fast car, and his wrists had grown larger—how could he have failed to be in excellent spirits that morning? Sunrise over the Costa del Sol.

The wrists had appeared suddenly. All the force of his new look, his newfound internal security enlarging his wrists. But I, too, eh? I, too, could hit back at them, could reduce them to nothing, though they had to be taken into account, those wrists. They dovetailed without deviation into his arms or rather his arms fit with greater security and strength into the bridge of those wrists, wider now, more blood could pass along them, more troops, if needed. I could let him stand up, the muscles of his back rippling menacingly, and throw himself confidently onto me, only to catch him in midflight. By the wrists. Not grown so large, Vasily, that I couldn't encircle them with my thumb and index finger if I wanted. An optical illusion, Vasily, an optical illusion I myself was about to fall victim to. In fact they were not that large or thick, those wrists. Normal wrists. Piece of cake. One: (to the ground). Two: (say uncle?).

"How can you do this to Nelly?" I protested. "I wish I had the Book here, I'd show you; you'll end up saying to yourself: **To think I've wasted years of my life, I've wanted to die . . . for a woman who wasn't my type!**"

"Not true," he snorted. "I'm never going to say that," not taking his eyes off the road until he did move them for a second, threw a glance at me, and laughed. "No way am I ever saying that, *batiushka*."

"Yes, you are, I can't be mistaken about a thing like this. What's more, I'm saying it, too. I'm saying it to you: how can you do this to Nelly?"

(Although it wasn't true, undoubtedly wasn't true. How could she be **a woman who wasn't my type** when she was the perfect blonde, the Platonic ideal of a blonde, an iridium blonde, immune to any variation in temperature, a blonde who was the octagonal seal wrought of gold which, in heaven, imprints its form on all other blondes? How, in what way, could I ever come to regret or conclude I was wasting **the best years of my life** after dancing with a woman like that?)

And hold on, wait a second: I hadn't yet heard your father's proposal.

"They're counterfeit, aren't they, Vasily, the diamonds?" I said.

And waited, in the deepest part of my soul, watching through the car window as the steeple began to move, waited for him to answer: No, they're real.

"They're counterfeit," he answered, as we flew home. "But they'll sell with absolutely no problem, for thousands. There's no one else in the world who makes them that way, nothing similar."

"Sell them? How? I had to loan you money just now, back in the disco. Out of cash, Vasily? Washed up?"

"Yes, I noticed that, and allowed you to do it because I love you like a father would," he lied. "And you're wrong. I want to show you something."

4

What does it matter what you see with your own eyes if it isn't there in the Book, Petya? How to believe in any empirical fact, any phenomenon not sustained by the authority of the Book? Such a thing would cast down the whole edifice of your education and damage the key to my method, which is to supplant a reading of its pages with direct observation, only slightly displacing the Book from its well-deserved position as the one source of knowledge and understanding in the world, healthy and beneficial to our hearts, casting its light on all enigmas and offering us a glimmer of the divine inspiration that engendered it and without whose aid its existence cannot be explained. For how could it have been written by a mere mortal, a Frenchman afflicted with asthma, a man who spent his whole life literally gasping for air and yet produced one million words, 3,500 pages, the most magnificent Book ever written?

I had said to myself, had sagaciously deduced: here's a man who has invented the phantom menace of a band of gangsters for the benefit of his wife, to make her live in fear of being attacked in a foreign country, ensuring that she won't dare leave the house unaccompanied, or even accompanied. A city she imagines to be crawling with mafiosi, a nest and refuge of evildoers. All to keep her at home and thus go out with the other woman, a great beauty, Petya, a real pinup. Your mother must never come to understand that the people in the mansion next door are peaceful Jordanians, and the couple in the big empty house at the bottom of the hill are only caretakers, that the same tranquil decency, respectability, and wealth prevails along the entire coast from Algeciras to La Cala. Instead: urban guerillas, low-intensity conflicts, scores to settle—all visions deliberately nourished by your father. It was that simple.

He read it in my face in the way I leaned against the door and studied him incisively for a second, the false danger I, too, had believed we were living in all these months now deciphered. He didn't find it necessary to make any counterargument, no need to press the point. He bent toward the glove compartment and waited with marked calm for me to take my hand off the panel marked, in tiny letters: *air bag*. He held that position a moment as if to say: You see? You see how patient I am with you, young man, despite your being an unbearable know-it-all? His eyes laughing again. And he didn't say—though I'd been expecting him to come out with it all day—he didn't say: What were you doing seducing my wife? Dancing with her?

He took a case made of buttery leather out of the glove compartment, holding it between thumb and forefinger. The panatelas that a cigar aficionado takes along on a two-day trip in its ridged interior? He tossed it onto my lap and returned his gaze to the road, consulting the speedometer and the time, far too busy to occupy himself with a callow youth like me. Leaving me to the task of understanding why the case, what was inside.

A square of thin fabric that I took out and tugged on, extending its corners: there, rolling around in its depths, were a few small cubes, a few chunks of frozen light, a few diamondlike objects in all colors and forms. More of them and bigger than the ones I'd imagined and even more beautiful and incredible than the ones in your mother's necklace. Gems, precious stones, their color both intense and diaphanous.

Their light entering my eyes, the most genuine expression of astonishment on my face, as darkness fell along the coast. Emerald greens, blues like the finest sapphires, tender lilacs, ruby reds. Losing track of whole kilometers of the way as I rolled them back and forth across the cloth, unable to read this correctly, leafing through the pages of this book of stone without understanding what passage to delve into, whether, in this case, a literal exegesis of the danger would be adequate—jewels, beautiful women—or whether a more allegorical, Alexandrian interpretation was required: great danger, jewels, beautiful women.

I was about to say something to him, object to something and resist him, but just then his cell phone rang to let me know my time was up, my turn was over, and it was over to the next contestant now. I didn't know the answer and had no exegetical weapon at the ready, no passage of holy writ to cite or apologetic stab to make at addressing the question satisfactorily, understanding it. He raised the phone to his ear and his eyes stared into the air at something that had been said to him, panic transfiguring his face, reordering his expression from the eyes down, lowering the corners of his mouth, draining him of blood.

"I'm almost there," he whispered. "Hang up."

The Writer's monsters catching up with us, emerging in myriads from between the pages of the Book, lifting the immense machinery of their bodies into the air over the highway, their wobbling, spidery legs moving at top speed, the suckers of their grape-shaped mouths projecting in our direction. At the very beginning of the invasion, just arrived from Phobos, ready to snatch us up and crunch our bones. The viruses that eventually kill them in the Book not appearing yet, no trace of them.

5

If you receive nothing more from me than some knowledge of the details of the Book, if in all your adult life you don't manage to retain any more than a few passages, a few scattered phrases of the Book, that would be enough to give you a distinct advantage as you go out into the world. Only through the Book can you learn to judge men sensibly, plumb their depths, detect and comprehend their obscurest motives, sound the abyss of their souls.

Why am I not startled? Why did it not surprise me in the least that Batyk should turn out to be the author of so immense a con job? That it was Batyk—as he proudly told the story, taking a step forward—who'd first conceived of the deception that would force them to flee, alter the course of their lives forever? That he was the one to whom the monstrous plan of passing them off, Vasily's diamonds, as a set of real diamonds from Yakutia (in Siberia) had occurred? That it was Batyk who came up with, planned, and carried out the sale of those diamonds to a pair of mafiosi come to E* for the express purpose—openly declared in every bar and café in the city so that word would get out among the emerald prospectors and the thieves working in the gem factories—of buying emeralds and topazes?

Why didn't I find any of this strange? Not even the next bit of news, for which I was entirely unprepared, and which struck me as the craziest, wackiest, most delirious thing yet. What a pack of madmen, I thought. The truly impossible part of the story, which began with a conversation Batyk and Vasily had with the two strangers, the mafiosi (real ones this time), the four of them in a bar, sitting around a minuscule table with nowhere to put their elbows. We have—they were addressing Kirpich, the only one of the four to have put his profusely tattooed forearms on the table, their eyes drilling into him—we have (they maintained) a set of diamonds of the first water that we're looking for a way to sell.

Which was followed by the story, highly improbable in its fantastic absurdity, as if discovered in the work of the Commentator, of how they'd come by those stones, stumbled upon them by chance: a kimberlite pipe, a whole field.

Something had caught his eye, a spark in the underbrush, he told the mafiosi who were listening with gaping mouths; from among the pebbles he'd picked up a stone, a bit of glass, a bluish crystal, and the sun's rays, streaming through the treetops, broke into a million shards against it and made him realize what he had in his hand, what he'd found, and that he was presumably (presumably? that was the word he used? presumably, yes) standing on top of a whole pipe of kimberlite, and that this was a diamond.

He walked around it, measured it with great strides of his reindeer-skin boots (in fact there were never any reindeer-skin boots!— though they do wear that type of boot in Buryatia, too). He gathered that it was a large field, not previously exploited, the top of a pipe that trees had shielded from the satellites' sharp eyes. He'd jumped for joy, wept for joy—he lied to Kirpich and Raketa—and then immediately grown frightened, his pupils darting back and forth in the slits of his almond-shaped eyes, understanding that he'd need the help of a white man: this man, Vasily, a professor, a scientist, a white man.

That was what Batyk said, and Kirpich and Raketa believed him! Two lumpen proletarians, two big-city gangsters who'd never once, whose parents had never once in their whole childhoods taken them to visit Yakutia or Buryatia or anything that wasn't Saint Petersburg, or even to the Russian Ethnographic Museum where they might have learned how intelligent and crafty the Nenets, Yakuts, and Buryats can be and are most of the time—six months of daylight, six months of night. Fully capable of exploiting any pipe all the way down, extracting its diamonds and then traveling to New York City, dressed as they always are, in the reindeer-skin boots that were false in Batyk's story but are indeed worn by actual Yakuts, who would call ahead to arrange an appointment with Ronald Winston, licking their fingers in the Russian Tea Room, and Ronald not caring in the slightest; he, too, eating with his hands, sampling chicken fajitas off the plates of his dear Yakut friends Urutai and Bodonchor.

Such bumpkins, the Buryats, Batyk made them believe: incapable of taking an airplane, he lied to them, or of selling diamonds on their own. Vasily had forced him to raise the price, he lamented bitterly, but what did it matter? A big field, lots of money!

(Six and a half million dollars in cash? I gave a start and stared at them with question marks in my eyes. Six and a half million dollars in *cash*? I stifled a cry and didn't say "and my money? my salary?" Already up to my armpits in the nerve-racking quest for those diamonds.)

They told them their story in the bar, and a month later, without having loosened their hold on the swindle's reins for a second, took them to a spot fifty kilometers from E*.

To a forest that opened out before them like a realm of enchantment: the evening stars in the sky, the March frost still glittering gem-like on the tree trunks, the white snow they trekked across to reach a cabin. Once inside and seated around a rough wooden table, Kirpich dropped a leather case in front of them and took out a small hammer, ready to put the diamonds to the test.

And that was when Vasily began to be afraid, understanding how dangerous these two were and the real risks involved: when he got a clear look at the sun clumsily tattooed on the back of Kirpich's hand (this detail had escaped him in the bar), a northern sun casting its rays across the pink skin. Not a drop of regret in those eyes, full of hatred and dark schemes: Kirpich, eight times sentenced for rape and bloody crimes.

When your father pushed the diamonds across the table toward him, he chose one, picked it up, and started tapping on it slowly with the hammer. Each little tap unleashed a smug grin of satisfaction that ran across his entire face, which dimpled up like a child's as he perversely tapped his way through each and every one of the diamonds with the perversity of an ex-convict who for years and years, immobile in his cell, has dreamed of hitting, hitting anything. Faces? Fine. Diamonds? Better. Much better. He was satisfied (Vasily had created them in habits that prevented direct blows to any plane of exfoliation, where they were fragile) and raised his gap-toothed criminal face, laughing until the gold of his teeth illuminated the farthest corners of the isba. He said, "Tap, tap, just like that"—and gave the hammer a good bang against the plank—"just like that, if they turn out to be fake" (*which was precisely the case*). "Wherever you try to hide!" Then, his threat deeply imprinted in Vasily's and Batyk's minds, he got up to leave, went to open the cabin door. But a storm had broken out in those few short hours and dumped down vast quantities of snow. The door was blocked.

6

Had they really gone down into the cave where the forty thieves store their gold, into its deepest depths? I looked at them, not wanting to believe any of it. Were they sick in the head? Didn't they know that the gold was guarded by dwarves who would spring out at them, race after them the instant they saw them come out with the ingots? Nelly read the questions in my face and nodded ruefully, with a quick inclination of the head toward Batyk, the genius and mastermind behind so brilliant a plan (jeeringly). She picked up the story now and continued it in a voice of scorn, indignant over how bad an idea it had been and also because the story didn't end there, as you will see.

It ends months later, when those mafiosi (real ones, Petya, real ones!) went to sell the stones—having spent the intervening period taking them to Amsterdam in three lots—and learned the truth and realized that this man, a scientist, a weak man in appearance (without glasses, that's true, with excellent vision, the eyes of a gemologist, let me tell you): this man had swindled them! Right there in the jeweler's they let out a howl of pain, furiously twisting and turning and craning their necks high like young wolves as the Dutch policemen's arms encircled them. As if those arms were braided out of the same cords that in 1795 would have tied Kirpich and Raketa to the galleys to row their way across the seven seas (as happened to the Writer's Jean Valjean) but now, only a year and a half ago, had them assembling traffic lights in Bijlmerbajes. At least this was healthier work, their huge stumpy fingers battling with the tiny, fleeing screws. Dreaming throughout their prison sentence of throwing Vasily to the ground and jumping up and down on his legs with that false joy of criminals who seem to take all jobs as a joke, even the task of delivering a beating to someone, jamming the steel-reinforced toes of their boots into Vasily's ribs. They hadn't seen it coming (the traffic signal's red light blinking on and off during the final test sequence), they hadn't understood, and they'd fallen prey to that swindling scientist.

Top quality synthetic gems, though, it must be said, for they did succeed in selling a first lot in London's diamond quarter, and not a single one of the gentlemen with Victorian sideburns and knit vests took them for fakes. Quite the contrary: their accomplice, Senka, an amateur jeweler, collected the money and sent it to them along with the good news, and they used those dollars to buy themselves the fine aluminum briefcases and luxurious Italian shoes that must have been waiting for them in some storage locker at Bijlmerbajes.

During those same months Vasily (but not Batyk, whose strange preference was for kilims and Persian rugs and who had no eye for Italian clothing) was putting the first wrinkles in his first 100 percent cashmere suit, bending down to see if he could detect any new fold not foreseen by its designer and going out the next morning to buy himself another one, and more clothes for Nelly, and expensive little sneakers for the boy. Or inviting, as he told me he'd done, a whole table of relatives to E*'s top Chinese restaurant. The datable, isolatable moment when he acquired the bad habit of tipping 100 percent. Almost all the money spent in the same place as the swindle, at the very entrance to the forty thieves' cave, in E*.

But how, I asked Nelly at that point, how could they have imagined they could stay there in the city all that time after pulling off so massive a double cross?

They'd been frightened, quite naturally; they'd gone much too far, what doubt could there be? Trembling and sweating the whole night they'd had to spend in the cabin, Vasily afraid and Batyk terrified that with a scale model of a natural diamond continually revolving in their minds the two lumpen proletarians would suddenly figure out they were being swindled. But in the end they managed to get out of there, finally emerging the next morning across the same embankment of dirty gray ice, following the chrome fenders of the thugs' jeep.

"Friends?"

"Friends!"

Until the jeep went around the corner and they watched in relief as it turned and disappeared behind a wall of pine trees, and then said to each other: That's all folks.

But not shouting with glee, as in the silly movies where they throw money in each other's faces. Tense and keeping a tight grip on the steering wheel, a heavy feeling in the stomach that only diminished with the passage of days. Until your father stopped keeping an eye on the door they might come through at any moment, Kirpich and Raketa, the men he'd watched as they slept fitfully on the table's unvarnished planks, the four of them trapped by the snow storm, with millions stowed away under the table. And the two mafiosi had behaved themselves, they'd slept peacefully and hadn't swerved into another possible ending for the story that would have had them going out into the snow as day began to break, softly closing the cabin door behind them, the money back in their possession and two corpses left sprawling on the wooden floor behind them.

7

Larissa had already told me about it while we were out on the dance floor. I wanted to find out what all the talk of disaster was about (failure! bankruptcy! as your father had cried out that time, inadvertently confessing) and was about to ask her when she herself, during Vasily's momentary departure for the men's room, grabbed me by the arm and we made our way, continually moving to the beat, to the very center of the floor beneath the music's fullest blast. She told me everything, shouting in my ear, and my astonishment at what I heard was such that I stopped dancing and stood there petrified, at the mercy of the other dancers' momentum and the thrusts of their elbows. Seeking her ear wherever the movement of her dancing took it. When she told me, I stepped back and looked into her eyes, wanting visual confirmation for what I'd heard. And grabbed her by the shoulders and again and again yelled: It can't be! Impossible!

Amsterdam? I asked her immediately. And she answered: Of course not. I've had to push him sometimes, to get him to go home, because he has to do something. I've told him so, he can't just hide out waiting for them to put him to death (I overlooked the word, Petya, she couldn't have meant: **dead**).

Nor was what she told me about your mother true: that it had been her idea to move to that rich city, Marbella, that seaside resort where he was still bent on going ahead with a second plan, an even more fantastic plan. At the very mention of which Larissa, when she heard what Vasily was telling her, had burst out laughing. And laughed that night in the disco, again, remembering how she had laughed. A plan that involved the following: Nelly herself behind a counter, a small workshop in Marbella, specializing in jewelry repair. Where they would restore brilliance to cloudy diamonds—according to the sign outside—bluer now, redder, just like new. The real diamonds being, when the jewelry was returned to its owners, very far away, pried free of the little teeth that kept them in their settings and newly on sale in cities like Bombay or Tel Aviv. All due to the great skill of Vasily, who by then, two weeks later, three weeks, would have made stones in no way different from the originals. Twirling on their owners' wrists, gleaming in tiaras and Cartier bracelets, emitting flashes of sparkling light whose falsity was indistinguishable to the eye. Their owners would never know: gems of the same water, the same size. "And me?" Larissa giggled loudly. "I'm the queen of Sheba and the empress of Russia!"

Idiot girl! It shocked me to hear her talking about Nelly like that. I pulled my head from her shoulder to look at her and question her, about to retort: Nelly? No way! But that gesture took me out of the range of her voice, and I had to draw closer to her eyes (spheres of golden crystal, so beautiful) and thus could see, as I watched her speak, wherein lay Nelly's, your mother's, mistake.

Not because their owners or the alert eye of some jeweler invited to a party aboard one of those immense yachts might somehow realize. Anchored well away from the coast, reaching into the cooler and colliding with the bejeweled wrist or forearm of Rania (of Jordan), this hypothetical jeweler would never shout, "Hold on just a second there, my queen! Those stones are fake!" Never, though neither his etiquette nor his good breeding would prevent it: a jeweler can be just as vulgar as anyone else. But to begin with, no jeweler would ever be invited aboard one of those yachts; a simple jeweler would never be rubbing elbows with Fannia or Theodora of Greece, his index finger pointing to a set of tourmalines on the arm of Mathilde of Belgium. And even if such eyes, by some miracle or improbable chance, were present there, they wouldn't respond to the glint of Vasily's diamonds with any suspicion, blinded as they'd be by the similar sparkle of all the other stones, their corneas enameled by the intense brilliance, light hammering hard and fast at their retinas' rods and cones.

The danger would not appear there, did not lurk among the rods and cones. No, Nelly! (No, Petya!) The danger was this: how many chokers, how many rings, how many Van Cleef invisible settings—the stone seeming to float, trembling, upon a golden net—how many damaged pieces, how many stones blackened or made opaque by the years? How many? I shouted into Larissa's ear. Very few. How many Saudis, how many Russians, how many Englishmen would drop off their Carrera y Carrera, Boucheron, or Bulgari at a nameless work-shop? I could picture them going in, examining the pieces on display, and fleeing after one look at Batyk, his skinny arms crossed over his hollow chest, his sullen gaze.

Larissa had to be about my age: a franker nature and longer bones, a common sense her whole body exuded and a forthright intelligence that had made her laugh at their project. But Nelly had accumulated more sun in her cheeks, like a piece of Baltic amber which, closely scrutinized, held up to the eyes, contains little figures, inclusions, bio-graphical accidents, flies trapped in the fresh resin, insects that should never have flown so close.

And there was I, in excellent spirits between those two suns, like a compatriot of Skywalker on Tatooine gazing upon the two luminous bodies in its sky, one orange, the other blue. Turning to face one and then the other (mentally). A sect of sun worshippers on that distant planet: which of the two would it revere? What would Sir James Frazer have gathered from their ancient lips? Which of the two suns, Petya?

The question didn't trouble me; I didn't hesitate a second. I was more powerfully attracted by the sun that had shone in space for more years; my adoration was greater, and there could not be nor was there any battle within me between the sect that worshipped the young sun and the worshippers of the older sun.

Sixth Commentary

I

Indistinguishable from an original text at first sight, the words of the annotater, the Commentator. Which, if subjected to isotropic analysis by some prodigiously memorious savant of India and read from right to left, starting with the final word, would reveal no break whatsoever in their paragraphs, a clean crystal with no flaw to shatter the light. Knowing, nevertheless, having understood long ago that these are false and secondary texts, cunningly secreted around the grain or seed of a primary text, which he gradually surrounded with commentaries, building them up layer after layer from the prodigious decoction of his memory (that, yes). Cultivated pearls, muscovite micas, metamorphic crystals that shine, in the end, as if by a natural light and for which he had very beautiful texts at his disposal, other people's gems that he had no qualms about breaking into pieces in the depths of his study.

A whole public library at his disposal. And not by chance did he take refuge in a library, in the depths of its labyrinthine corridors, a room with a fake sign saying *Do Not Enter* or *Staff Only* where he examined those fragments or bits of text in satisfaction. A treasure, the rich copy of precious stones that could reach us and be admired only thus, truncated and inserted into his commentaries. Knowing that he would give them the full brilliance of the book they were torn from, so that entering into his work our eyes wouldn't see a single break in the light: an equivalent reaction coefficient set in an exquisite mounting, that was his aim. But to come upon one of these fragments of Baudelaire (page 133) or Maeterlinck (page 189) is to turn off a dirt road, a bumpy backwoods lane, and go speeding along the ideal asphalt of a superhighway. However bad this comparison or commentary of mine may be. Here's a better one: like Han Solo's ship after someone has taken a hand to it outside an intergalactic bar and suddenly, with a low hum, it shoots off effortlessly into space.

Always flowing better in those passages, but then back again to the feigned taciturnity, the mania for the right word, the con job of the precise adjective. Without ever a real metaphor or image. The Writer says of Flaubert that he never finds a good image in his work (nor have I). Only that dogged struggle with the text, the tireless polishing that finally dries it out, or perhaps it's not dried out but oiled to the maximum degree, to a high sheen, with a look of premeditation about it. Abstract gestures, paper frenzies, never a pair of hands raised to the breast in an outburst of true emotion, as when the Writer confesses to us that he has wept, that his hero, an alter ego of the Writer, Søren K., has wept.

2

The same astonished reaction from your father to the answer you gave him out by the pool one evening when I was watching the two of you from above, not knowing that you were talking about me. He asked you in amazement: Where? On hearing you muse over the reasons why no man can vanquish terrestrial gravity, why gravity cannot be annulled. "So much theory, such profound knowledge: from where?" he inquired. And you answered: "Do not be amazed by my learning, Papa, for I am receiving my education from a person who is the very incarnation of the intellect." And he raised his eyes then and tried to catch a glimpse of me from below, intrigued by these words: this young man, this foreigner, the incarnation of the intellect?

My turn to be astonished now, for the man I'd taken at first for a bodyguard (and with that flimsy build, not a very good one) had arrived two months before I did and was also in hiding. As I told you, as I've already roundly denounced: it was from him, from Batyk, that the idea of swindling the two from Saint Petersburg had come. And it was Batyk who had brought word that Kirpich and Raketa had been freed.

(Pause.)

But was he a scientist, too: that kind of scientist? Yes, no more and no less than a very gifted researcher, someone who had some knowledge of the subject to bring to bear and who'd provided indispensable help in the production of the first diamonds. Which Vasily had been synthesizing for years without ever achieving gem quality, always frustrated by the slow rate of growth, until one day, with a softer gradient and some refinement of the metallic solvent: larger and better diamonds than anyone else, ever, in the whole world. It wasn't one of those scientists in the West in their state-of-the-art air-conditioned labs with machines in the hall that dispense chocolate and cookies, no! He alone! In the deepest depths and from the deepest depths!

Confident from Petya's reply about my physics classes that I would understand (as indeed I did) the arduous explanation of his method for manufacturing diamonds, the procedure he first put into practice one winter morning. How he grew them in a Feielson press, following the advice of Batyk—he, too, an exceptional physicist (I wrinkled my brow again here, Petya, disbelieving). The corrections and improvements made to the design of the growth chamber, the—fabulous! —diminution in size, which made the press virtually portable, when taken apart into sections.

And the afternoon when the petals of the growth chamber opened and through the cut they'd made in the matte surface of the sleeve they saw it sparkling, they peered inside and glimpsed in amazement: a diamond, an intensely pink diamond. And understood that they were the first. Color diamonds, synthetic color diamonds such as no one else in all the universe (or perhaps someone, in some far corner of the universe: some minor god, Petya, busy at this vulgar task) had created. Large and blue, round and red, translucent.

"And you," he turned, in the same indulgent tone he'd been using when his cell phone interrupted us—"you. Such intelligence, a man who can explain Bohm's paradox of the fish to me, a scientist, with your fluency in Spanish . . ."

Should I have interrupted him, Petya, to explain, to clarify that Spanish was my native tongue?

"Of course it's going to be easy for you, though for me the situation has become untenable, a dead end, no way out."

Meaning: no way out for the diamonds. All the times he'd gone to those cities and stood before the windows of Böhmer and Van Cleef & Arpels without daring to go in. His silhouette reflected on the glass as in that extraordinarily sweet passage by the Writer when Odette de Crécy (the fragility of her arching brows, her lovely dark eyes) breakfasts at Tiffany's, feasting on the sparkle of the jewels on display at Fifth and Fifty-seventh, dreaming of all that money, the bracelets and pendants she'd buy if she were rich.

And then immediately, in terror: what kept me there, Petya, what kept me there, between your father's ineptitude and Batyk's incredible ill will? Your mother? Her shoulders? The money they'd told me I'd carry off with me some day in the end, before leaving Russia, that amazing, corrupt country, and the Russians, my amazing, corrupt friends?

3

He rolled this ruse or clumsy deception toward me, your father, like a tumblebug pushing its sphere of dung, like an Amazonian ant with its bubble of wet clay, his iris transfigured, enlarged by excitement, as he scanned my face, waiting for a reaction of understanding or consent to his crude proposal. Only one possible reading here: deception, a trap from which I would never be able to extricate my head and that I would lament for many winters to come, waking up freezing in fifth-rate hotels, wondering, how could I? How could I have accepted his commission that day and fallen into his little trap, descending irremediably, stumbling and bumping into every protrusion all the way down to this hotel room?

A decision that the whole of my life wouldn't give me sufficient time to regret. That would reach into and permeate each and every one of my future days. And I told him: no.

Of course not. Naturally.

Never would I agree to become the seller of your stones, the corrector, in essence, of your ineptitude, Vasily (thus, in those words).

Ineptitude I'd never heard of a few months ago and to which I have no connection or solid link. Why would I go anywhere near it now? Why would I turn off onto this branch of fate along which I'd have to scurry forever, hiding, giving the slip, a police sketch of my face in every branch of Graff, printed on paper watermarked with the forty-eight facets of a gem?

Who would decide, who on earth would make a plan to swindle the mafia? In what universe did they think they were living? In a membrane universe, whose porous borders would allow them through, loaded down with the millions, and leave Kirpich and Raketa behind on the other side, filtered out as undesirables? Incapable—or so they thought—of reaching them, of passing through the filter? But no: Kirpich and Raketa had sharpened their wits. They, too, had purchased beautiful shirts made of expensive fabrics, refined their manners, learned to move with subtlety, passing through the most minute pores of the West. And if seen, for example, in a hotel lobby speciously studying an airline schedule, they'd never be taken for killers, for individuals with automatic weapons tucked in their breast pockets. Cleanly erased, no longer visible on their faces, the suffering, the grimaces of pain of the frail old men they'd tortured, the tears of the shopgirls whose diminutive kiosks they'd entered and whose friends they'd pretended to be, forcing them to converse for hours and then to make room on their narrow straw mattresses, the money the girls— almost willingly!—gave them bulging in their pockets.

What had made them believe, what had given them the idea, how had they imagined that I could run off to some jeweler pretending to be a young African, an excombatant in one of those conflicts in Africa, pockets full of diamonds from Namibia or Zimbabwe? When it went without saying that I'd be thrown in jail in a heartbeat, no matter how fluently I spoke Spanish. And then no one, never. I'd be abandoned. Nelly wouldn't come to see me on Wednesdays, say, or Thursdays, in her red dress. Putting her hand on the glass and forming an *I love you* with her lips. I love you? Yeah, right. (Though she wouldn't do even that.) On the other hand, I'd be learning all sorts of Arabic words with my new friends from Meknes (in Morocco): *hatred, pain, loneliness,* and *idiot* (that's the one I'd really need). I'd shuffle along in line, holding my dish of soup at belly level and seeing reflected in it, as in a mirror of ink, the luxurious life of 4x4 jeeps they'd still be leading outside, laughing at me, at how stupid I'd been. Had they hired me only for this? The tutoring no more than a pretext?

Lying to me, moreover, during their visits: claiming they were in an identical state of despair, they, too. Though I'd see it all: more money, inexplicably; more jewels, more chokers around her neck, no reduction in Vasily's production levels, and had they somehow come up with a way of selling them, reached some sort of arrangement with the local mafia? Lying to me in their letters, too: "Dear Psellus, we still haven't been able to sell anything. I know we owe you (six months' salary? Six months, Petya!), but for now we can do nothing." And three more paragraphs of lies. Along the lines of: "We think of you always and if you could only see how well Petya is speaking Spanish now!" (in closing). Things like that, pure falsehood on your mother's lips, as if Batyk had been speaking through her mouth that day of the interview and from the pages of her letters, always.

And there was this, too, Petya: I couldn't condemn them, I felt sorry for Kirpich and Raketa. Whom I may well have seen or met in that city, Saint Petersburg, where I, too, once lived. Poor Kirpich and Raketa! Happily going home to their apartments on Pionerskaya or Vasiliostrovskaya, home to their wives, stroking the blond heads of their children, telling themselves before going to bed as I had told myself for many nights: "a good business, this!" Imagining, as I had imagined after a successful sale, the things they would buy with the money: beautiful thick gold chains (though I would never have imagined anything like that), furs for their wives, Nintendos for their children, houses with swimming pools in the South. All the things that Vasily, your father, had bought. All of them imagined with precisely the same bad taste by those gangsters in Saint Petersburg. And the awakening, Petya, the brutal awakening: how they tried to run away in Amsterdam, the two years they'd had to spend in prison, minting traffic lights and finishing them off by hand, while imagining, knowing, with chilling precision, how they would exact their revenge.

I could stop them, their entry into my room. Explain: I understand you, gentlemen. You were foully deceived; it isn't something I approve of. And me, too, at some point, merchandise in poor condition, a swindle like that. Not comparable, of course, with what was done to you: that moment when I took off my rucksack, loosened its straps, and said: You'll see, gentlemen, a quality such as you've never seen before— only to see nothing, to find nothing in there! But on very rare occasions, the times when, like everyone else in Russia, in 1991, 1992, those years, I sold things, a youthful dilettante, buying a pair of boots in Moscow and selling them in Saint Petersburg, right there in the train station, the difference in price covering the cost of the train ticket. Little things like that, Petya. So now just imagine, see them unfolding the black cloths, the little packets of diamonds, smug as thieves, to discover, with a cry of pain, with a wild beast's howl, that the stones were counterfeit!

4

Remember how I told you about that movie, *The Matrix*: how incredible that the Writer could have seen, dozens of years before, the chain of fists, the levitating men, miraculously sustained in the air? Though we are not going to go to the movies; the movies are bad. Consider, for example, the effect that Hollywood has had on your parents (their unbearable bad taste), as well as the fear that terrible scene of the beating in the metro installed in my soul and in my head. Imagining during the nights when I was piously bent over my desk—studying my notes in preparation for our class—your father's screams of pain and your mother's cries for help as she ran through the house seeking refuge. While I covered my ears, pretending not to hear. The door of my room wide open to say: me? No sirs, nothing to do with any of that. Come in, I'm the boy's tutor, just here preparing some classes, reading.

The panic I lived with for many days, the danger that filled the air until one afternoon looking out the window, keeping watch in case the killers were coming, I realized none of it was true. The tree growing out at a far point along the beach, which I hadn't seen until that day. Crystal clear: their story was made up out of whole cloth, for the manipulative, shady, dirty purpose of making me sell the diamonds.

All of it false, Petya, from beginning to end! There was no Kirpich, no Raketa, no one had swindled anyone, your mother's fear was pure dramatic performance, as in the movies! My love for her, my obvious love and deep feeling for her, used and channeled to force me to take this step.

They'd agreed on it, planned it out with Batyk, who had mysteriously disappeared the day we took the second outing. They were subtly winning me over, plunging me—a mere child, no older than you in spirit—into a dense cloud of ink and deception, knowing me incapable of correctly reading the twisted minds of three adults, allowing me to hold her close while dancing, the heat of her breasts through the dress. From her warm arms to the fear of being executed for having seduced his wife.

And then, without giving me time to come back to my senses, zap! —Larissa! The ultimate blonde, the most beautiful woman, the incredibly appealing young lady in whose delightful proximity I'd be softened up once and for all. Thus weakened, and previously addled by the revelation of the ersatz diamonds, I would agree to sell them, my eyes vacant, my pulse fluttering.

And should I fail to yield immediately, should they perceive some residual stiffness in my neck, there was the showy ploy of the cell phone call and their feigned panic that the monsters straight out of Wells and Welles were catching up to us.

Coming toward us, those men, and nothing could stop them.

I inquired: And if you gave them back the money, wouldn't they be satisfied with that? Wouldn't we ultimately gain the most important thing, Nelly, which is time?

They don't want it back, was her answer, they want us dead. What's more, we'd never manage to sell so many millions. Nor is that the plan; we don't want you out there selling that many stones, only what's necessary, just enough money to fly to South America and settle there.

I wouldn't go back there with them, Petya, repatriated by that strange affair and then suffering and regretting later, many winters later, in that hotel room.

And when I'd reached this point in my reflections, the tree out at the far point along the beach explained to me, rustling its branches: "Excellent! Very good! What you've come up with is the true explanation, the closest reading, the correct gloss of all that part of the Book, its first chapters or commentaries, no less." Or was I to read that fiction as real, the whole improbable story of the swindle, the tall tale about murderers? False, Petya! False, Vasily! And—forgive me!—false, Nelly!

There were no such murderers, no danger threatening us, no malevolent pursuit, only your father's infinite ineptitude, Petya. The times he'd tried to sell the diamonds and hadn't been able to, staying at Larissa's place instead, contemplating her alabaster breasts like a modern jeweler who selects mother of pearl, opal, and quartz where others before him had used only diamonds. But for what reason? Why diamonds? he must have said to himself, when I have garnet lips and cheeks of pearl right here?

No murderers. They could have refrained, Petya, from lying to me, your mother putting on that big show of fear. Dreaming up the whole thing entirely for my benefit in the sole—and now, in the branches of the tree, clearly discernible—aim of making me sell those stones.

5

Now, just as I took to be false the Commentator's claim that the ancients had no word for blue, that they didn't distinguish between the various tones of blue so that to them the sea really was a sheet of red, **the wine-dark sea,** I resisted believing in the reality of the murderers and took them for a tale ingeniously spun by your parents in the sole and obvious aim of making me sell the diamonds. Until one morning I heard it, the sound and rumble of the sea changing color. The machinery ground weightily to a halt; the motor in the depths of the ocean ceased to pump out blue, and the whole sea, its entire surface, took on that other, impossible coloration.

Perhaps I'd thought the wine color was some optical device, the sea studied through a prism, an uncut diamond. Or else colored by nostalgia, sadness, the words the Writer confides to his private journal in Balbec, sighing inconsolably over the Duchess of Sanseverina: **Why is the spectacle of the sea so infinitely and eternally pleasing? Because the sea makes us think both of immensity and of movement. For a man, six or seven leagues are the radius of infinity—an infinity in miniature. But what does that matter if it's enough to suggest the idea of total infinity?** An annotation in blue, *azul,* no red about it, and I wasn't tempted, even for a second, to look through the window for ocular confirmation. For that would be to put it to the test, to experiment. Far more efficient and unobjectionable to rely on the Writer's authority, pulverizing the **wine-dark sea** by the greatness of the passage in which he speaks of its unfathomable blue, of its **infinite spectacle.**

My fear? Vanquished, Petya, completely vanquished. Listening to music at night, growing calm, a single record. I slept better with that record, I managed to reconcile myself to sleep again after having believed them to be so close, the Writer's monsters, that I imagined them floating out there in the darkness beyond my window, peering in. And I would turn out the light and listen, before falling asleep, to a record whose story I've hesitated to tell you. In Dresden, in 1947, the ambassador plenipotentiary of Russia, a nobleman with a German family name, was suffering from severe insomnia (though there is nothing in Forkel or in Spitta about the reasons for his anguish). In the middle of the night, Johannes Goldberg, a disciple of Bach, would be summoned to staff headquarters on Vogelstrasse. His cab fare was covered, and I imagine he was rewarded afterward with generous tips. Goldberg would race up to the Count's chambers and sit down before the clavier in a corner of the spacious bedroom. He would begin by playing the Aria which the Commentator mendaciously attributes to an anonymous French author and not to the divine inspiration of Bach, the greatest ever, the musician who is to musicians what the Writer is to writers.

The cascade of the first variation emerged from the clavier into Keyserlingk's ears, and he listened attentively, without ever understanding its mathematical formulation. Perhaps he would close his eyes at the sound of the first chords, his knees quivering in agitation during some of the canons and fugues. Dresden and Leipzig both under his command, the Soviet troops billeted there trafficking in carpets and wristwatches, and he wishing ardently to go home—or not, I don't know. He would raise his eyelids and study Goldberg's emaciated back, his thin arms opening wide and closing in over the keyboard. A Jew, as his surname indicated, a survivor of Auschwitz, and the Count listened to him play, wiping away the tears, moved by the harsh fate of this young man, hundreds of kilometers from home. Until a deep sleep would overcome him, he'd succumb during the fifteenth variation, an inverted canon. I know he would because I never managed to make it past that one either, couldn't get out of bed to turn the record over. Once the sixteenth started, my sleep was guaranteed.

I didn't know—can you believe me?—that somniferous powers are often attributed to this piece. I discovered those powers by chance, and since I invariably fell asleep at the end of side one, I didn't know the latter variations very well for several years. Sometimes I managed to turn the record over, and I would always wake up again when the Aria resumed, just as in the beginning, the same slow and majestic air. I should have gotten up then to turn the stereo off, but I preferred not to, anguished by the darkness, in the disquiet of late night. The record would go on spinning, the stroboscopic eye tirelessly counting the grooves on the edge of the turntable (a model from the 1980s; they don't make them like that anymore), the needle advancing toward the center of the record.

What can he have meant by **total infinity**? Spinning in silence, turning his words over and over until suddenly: a tumult. Like the sound of a sea changing color, I thought. A roar, the machine of the sea first stopped and then set back into furious motion, a bitter dispute, as if in gibberish, unintelligible. I jumped to my feet, my eyes on the window: they're here, idiot—on a Saturday morning? A Saturday morning. They are here, you idiot: run for your life.

6

From the top of the stairs, trembling in the skylight's illumination, certain that they'd seen me, that it hadn't escaped their notice that I'd slipped on the tiles in the hallway and had now stopped in my tracks, aware that there was no other avenue of escape, the only exit to the street blocked. The voices of those men, brawny as Achaeans. One I could see from behind, the brief bronze of his right hand cleaving the air, wondering aloud who to leave alive and whose throat to cut: this head, this other head (Batyk's), the boy's (go right ahead!), but mine? The tutor's? To what end? What good would that do Kirpich and Raketa—for the hoplites with shoulders bulging out from beneath their chitons were none other than they?

The violent argument before the none too receptive ears of their victims, their throats slit, arranged in a circle on the living room floor like complacent spectators or enormous puppets they would later carry out to the trunk of the car without worrying about banging their heads on the front porch's flagstones or thudding them down the steps.

Without worrying about hurting them because they were dead!

Paralyzed by the noise of the violent argument, I didn't make a move, until they fell silent, and one of the killers, the woman, looked toward me, raised her eyes, discovered me at the top of the staircase, and asked without turning: "Which of us is right?"

I looked at her a second, still gripped by fear and without managing to conceal my surprise. I went down to her, seeking in her eyes an explanation. Then, removing her gaze from the figure that had so irritated her, the figure of her husband, Nelly settled her eyes on me. Eyes of a mauve tint now, like spheres containing an oscillating liquid, a miniature sea complete with waves, a sailboat rocking upon its silken waters.

A vision of a sailboat and the sea that makes the tutor fall to his knees and raise his enraptured eyes. Another tutor in another book, let's say. Not me. I held her gaze, though without daring to explain the source of that liquid to myself or from whence that sailboat . . . Nelly raised a hand toward me, raised the white circles of the palms of her hands to my eyes. She discovered, incredulous, the effect her words had had on me and burst out laughing.

About which the same bad writer, an epigone of the Commentator, a glosser of no imagination, would have noted that it had the effect of breaking the spell, undoing the enchantment, but which that morning, in the reality of the Book, made all the crystals that filled the garden gather in all the energy of her laughter and become even denser, frenetically multiplying, growing throughout the house. Imprisoning me.

Nelly asked me again: "You, you've been listening to us!"—I hadn't been listening to them, I'd heard her without understanding her, had made an effort not to understand her—"Which of us is right?"

7

The meaning of the Book must not be altered by facile interpretations such as those proffered by the Commentator in his insubstantial commentaries. Nor should it be distorted by the opportunistic interpolations he performed in the depths of that public library. Seeing her and hearing her argue in that tone of voice, and then understanding her question with absolute clarity and seeing myself compelled, unnaturally, to concede that she was right, made me understand how much intelligence the Writer put into that phrase of his, which mentions neither astonishment nor bewilderment, only the force of an ax that falls and strikes. Without my ever yielding to the temptation to add words, inclusions you would never notice, Petya. Keeping myself honest and at a respectful distance, using my lips to give voice only to the words of the Writer, without falling into the heresy, so frequent in the Commentator, so much to be expected from him and never any the less reproachable for that, of interpolating his own glosses, as when he twists and does violence to sentences by lesser writers in the deliberate and, coming from the Commentator, false aim of extracting a few drops of sense, interpreting.

Letting myself be taken by surprise, always, yielding to the greatness of the Writer's images. Because once or twice I, too, have wondered: like a fist, only a fist? However great the power with which it hits you, would I wake up, as in the Writer: **If the book we read doesn't wake us up like a fist pounding against our skulls, what are we reading it for?** Clear and beautiful, Petya, incomparably strong. But only one fist? I've approached that fist (in my mind), I've opened it, spread out its fingers and inserted that hand into an iron gauntlet. And then it goes like this: **If the book we read doesn't wake us up like a fist [*clad or enveloped in an iron gauntlet*] pounding against,** etcetera. You see? But this step was rendered unnecessary by his redoubtable intuition, because he glanced back over his shoulder, without need to take the fist away or envelop it in anything else, and this time hefted an ax which he raised and let fall with all the force that the first image lacked. And even more: **A book should be the ax that breaks up the frozen sea inside us.**

Which is to say, first this: **If the book we're reading doesn't wake us up like a fist pounding against our skulls, why are we reading it?** To which he wisely adds this: **A book should be the ax that breaks up the frozen sea inside us!**

How to write, then, simply: "Your mother's words, as I listened to her and instantly grasped her plan, the scope and (unquestionable) insanity of her plan, left me frozen, immobile, such was the astonishment, so immense the impact"? No—on the contrary: her words broke up and shattered all I had vaguely thought about her and your father, the mansion or castle. Shattered it absolutely.

As can always be said of the Book and its words about the **fist** and the **ax**: that not only is it clear, but also simple and restrained. Simple because it's not difficult to understand; restrained because it employs only those words that are necessary (he doesn't, for example, include a gauntlet, bristling with spikes). And unambiguous because it says and means a single thing (thus forestalling divergent readings). It means: absolute astonishment, total bewilderment on my part. It means: her words, the details of her plan, falling on me with the force of **an ax.**

"Which of the two of us is right? Whose argument is correct?" she asked me.

"You are, of course," I had to say. "Yours, naturally," I said.

8

Or else lie to you, Petya? Tell you I'd decided to leave the house that first afternoon, not twenty minutes after my initial inspection, as in the Writer, or else after the first week, put off by the unbearable sheen of the unbearable furniture, the fake swords and suits of armor—until I saw your mother next to the swimming pool and suddenly changed my plans? Just as in the Writer: the passage where he's given up trying to find lodging in a series of houses in a New England town and decided to leave when he sees a young girl, a nymphet barely twelve years old, on the lawn, a girl with a Spanish name, come to think of it.

Much has been made of how she, this girl, in all her irresistible candor, represents Amerika, and how the Writer, a fifty-year-old émigré in the Book, volume 4, is enchanted, transfixed by the vision of her **frail, honey-hued shoulders** (so he says) through which, through all her bearing, she transmits (or the Writer transmits, by means of her) the fatal attraction that the vulgar young American girl exerts on the soul of the ravaged and disenchanted old European.

I could lie to you, put my own clever spin on this passage, tell you I'd resolved to leave after the first week, disgusted by your parents' impossible furniture and the atmosphere of palpable danger, the daggers in the air, but that the vision of your mother in a bathing suit next to the swimming pool stopped me. By which—incapable of lying to you—I would be transmitting the following message: unlike the Writer's character, unlike Humbert, I, a young American, stood there paralyzed and ecstatic before legs that were still youthful and full of the wisdom of Europe. And your mother, with her hyphenated family name and the black moles on her breast, represented the enchantments of a civilization that was antique but still ripe for enjoyment and full of juice. And I, an inept young American, represented vulgarity and ineptitude, though full of drive and all that. As if I were showing you the reverse side of the plot (the Writer's plot).

And what had I just said to her, telling her she was right without yet having fully understood her plan or knowing precisely what she'd been talking about, moved simply by my feeling for her? But once she'd explained it to me (and I'd understood it), I told her:

"The Writer has a phrase for this, Nelly: a **harebrained idea.** An idea that even after being hit over the head with a war mace, let's say, can't be picked up and flung off the battlefield or dislodged from the place where it appears or unexpectedly emerges, so it stays there, **harebrained,** without any possible application because it slips from the fingers of all those who try to grasp it. You see? (We were walking through the tall grass and I showed it to her, her **harebrained idea:** the lips a vivid scarlet, emeralds for eyes, a brightly painted doll among the meadow flowers.) How to get it away from there, how to stand it upright so it would move and talk with all the resource and sagacity of a mechanical doll? Not possible, it eludes me, it slips away. See?

"Although only **harebrained** for that reason. The idea itself is excellent, your idea, the one you were arguing about with Vasily . . ."

Then she made a point which I understood and which left me speechless.

Left speechless by her intelligence. That's the passage where the Writer says, in the words that Appian of Alexandria used with reference to Cleopatra VII, last of the Ptolemaic rulers of Egypt: **He** [Julius Caesar] **looked upon her as a marvel not of beauty alone but also of wit.**

Or, and it amounts to the same thing: *get out of there right now*. Out to the garden and from there to the street and into a taxi that would carry me to Puerto Banús. Without a clear idea of what I would then do, but with the obvious, crystalline, sole, and unique meaning, Petya, of leaving, fleeing.

For what gives the Book its greatness, what makes it unique and unrepeatable is the fact that it is a machine for thinking, the greatest compendium of instructions ever written. And all of them in the exceptionally user-friendly form of a novel, with characters whose lives and vicissitudes concern and move us. And when your brain makes contact with the encoded surface of that paper, it will always give you the most fitting solution, the canniest response, the one most effective for your intelligence: *flee as soon as you possibly can, right now*. Without the money, but safe and alive.

9

My hands and feet connecting themselves with places where I could try my luck, safe from her insanity, places with sea. The swaying boat attached to the wall by a ring of metal. Taking out the stones and studying them over the foam. Regretting the money I could have earned, forced now to leave it all behind. The airplanes I saw descending in the distance to land at Pablo Ruiz Picasso International, and I'd have to board one of those planes and fly away.

Returning, then, after less than an hour, to a café on the Paseo Marítimo, the soothing pale cream of its tablecloths. Might I not be fleeing or thinking of fleeing, I said to myself, from the greatest stroke of luck, the most immense fortune, placed at my feet by the woman I love? As if, sitting there at the table distractedly sipping my iced tea, I'd seen your mother materialize in the air in front of me, heard her speak to me. The talking head that calls out to the hero from atop a crag and helps him unravel the mystery, predicting that by tomorrow a strong wind will finally swell his sails. Or as if, and to my infinite astonishment, I had noticed that I understood the song of the birds, the parliament they were holding on the café's awning. The knight who slays the dragon, bathes in its blood, and discovers to his bewilderment and wonder that he understands the lark's song and decodes its twittering with the speed and skill of a Morse operator probing the heavens, deciphering the cave's coordinates at top speed, the nonsensical password.

Running to save her, back to the Castle. Everything understood, having understood all of it, Petya, your mother's whole ingenious plan. The giant or colossus who is first seen sniffing a bunch of daisies and then destroys everything in his path as he runs, the diminutive globe spinning beneath his feet. Able, in no more than the life span of a sigh, to cover the distance that separated me from her face, from the enormous windows of her eyes, as if her head had been engineered by Dalí. And she was laughing, too, her hair snapping in the wind like a row of oriflammes, her adorable, darkly honey-hued locks. My euphoria, all the happiness of that night in these words which the pedant Bloch falsely attributes to Avicenna: **For love is a disorder resembling a hallucination, similar to melancholy . . . On some occasions it incites lasciviousness, on others not. The symptoms of this disorder are as follows: the eyes of the afflicted one are sunken and dry, the cheeks twitch constantly. Such a person laughs without cause.**

Laughing—me, too—without cause. As if a team of young men were hidden in the folds of my face, among the smooth muscles and undrooping cheeks, and, having received an order to pull, were making me smile despite my strong will not to laugh for fear that Vasily, your father, would find out my secret. But my brain, by that mechanical action, was receiving in its turn the neuroperception of a smile, at the same time as another team was pulling at the muscles of my back, raising me to my feet by a thousand ropes as if I were a fairground colossus or an assault tower positioned before your mother's face to throw across the bridge by which I would easily gain access to the city within, and enter. Certain that she had come up with the perfect solution, as if discovered in the Book! Laughing in great bursts, absurdly confident. Watching us make our exit like that, dressed as if for a Greek tragedy, attired in tunics, our faces grave, our fingers bejeweled. All of it in the Writer, easily understandable. Or as in Mozart.

A subject that Mozart chose for an opera; that must be a good subject, mustn't it? Imposture is precisely that: Mithridates, the imposter, in a land today called Russia. Vasily on high as King or Czar: pretender to the throne of Russia, no less! Only thus would we be safe from the danger that menaced us and had encased the Castle and all the Castle's gardens in ice. Which the Writer, with his enormous wisdom and strength, had to break up. Right now.

PART TWO

Seventh Commentary

I

And this other defect (I do not use that word in relation to the Book as it would be imprecise: there can be no defects in the Book). I've often thought, just as another great writer, Milton, once mused, long before the Writer, that a good book is the precious lifeblood of a master spirit, and I have meditated that the flaw in the Book, its one flaw, is to have built its story not around the life and great deeds of a king, but rather around the minor, lackluster life of Swann, a gentleman, and, still worse, around the anemic existence of Saint-Loup and the sterile life of the Baron de Charlus, mere bourgeois gentleman and minor aristocrat, respectively. Neither one a king—not kings. A flaw no scholar of the Book, however great, has observed.

For the subject of a great book . . . for only the life of a king, placed at the heart of the narrative—though for that to occur the book would have to be constructed very deliberately . . . Only thus should a literature be brought to a close, the cycle completed: not with the dry and tearless commentaries of the Commentator. In their place, a story tempered from beginning to end around the figure of a king, braided beard beneath eyes of stone: the distinction and gravity of a torso swollen with laws.

I could dedicate years of my life to it. In the noble aim of erasing all trace of the Commentator's work, so that those years, seen from distant points on the scale, would not remain years of coldness, written by a man who did not fall in love, did not have children, and saw himself brought by the very nature of his stories—their bloodless nature—to a dubious protagonism. Concealed (me, the person who took on the noble task) behind the figure of a king, a sovereign whom I could serve and who, in the Book, embodies all that we know is about to disappear. For there are still people living among us who knew the Writer in his lifetime, men (and women) who were born and lifted up their little hands in their cradles when the Writer was still throwing pages to the floor day by day (as his schoolmaster or private tutor, who was used to it, tells us he did). Gentlemen who chew soft bread with their bare gums today, but once watched him stroll out of the Ritz. This is the moment. A few years more, another generation, and it will be too late.

And a final commentary: let's imagine, putting ourselves in his place (which I, by the way, would not leave in Balbec, a beach town on the Norman coast, etcetera, but would resituate among the colossal Roman ruins of the city of Heliopolis or Baalbek, far better Baalbek than Balbec), that the Writer had written a Book whose central theme was restoration, the ascent to the throne of a fifth dynasty. Would that not be a superior book? Its pages magically illuminated by the purple glory of such a tale? Would it not simply be a far better book?

Another writer, whom the Writer placed among the greats and mentions in the Book (volumes 1 and 4), a writer who was also unique, felt this to be so. And in his final book he addressed—and placed at the central point in its pages, standing over them—a king. And an act of regicide. King Alexander II, who meets his killer, Alyosha Karamazov. He didn't manage to write it and it fell to—I was about to say to the better writer, but no, simply to the Writer—to do so. But some deep-seated internal weakness, something, kept the Writer from it. Nothing that had to do with his capacity for writing, his matchless genius. A certain absence, a certain secret failing that kept him from placing a king at the center of his Book, as in the very first book, the one about the king of Uruk.

For something happened to the Writer, something terrible, I suspect. I see it sometimes, as if a light source were illuminating his lines
from behind, casting a striped shadow, a fan of light. Which I observe
in astonishment, but without managing to discover the secret. There
must be something. I'll find out what it is. Ceaselessly concentrating
on the Book, extracting sense and meaning from the text, I will learn
it some day and come and tell you what it is, wherever you might be.
But—you know?—I'm afraid of discovering something terrible.

2

That same night I went back to her **brilliant idea.** Refulgent with a thousand sparks and with a thousand crystalline filaments by which to grasp it, a liquid and ever-changing mane in which the fingers of even the clumsiest hand could become entangled. A **brilliant idea.** That must be understood. An animal, a crystalline jellyfish, hard and supple in the red air of a helium planet. I stood there looking at it, stunned. At her idea.

"Excellent, Nelly, your idea: an excellent idea. I rejected it initially when I first learned what it was, but now I can't help but see that it's pure genius: a **brilliant idea.** A king! No more and no less than the immense, radiant figure of a king. As if taken straight from the Book, Nelly! O infinite subtlety and cleverness! Saved and protected by the legend of a king, a czar! Down there in Spain: a man who could be our king, who sees himself as king of all the Russians, but lives surrounded and threatened by killers who haven't scrupled to pursue him and threaten the life of his son. Will the nation, will Russia, permit such a thing? Will the very decent and patriotic godfather of the Moscow mafia allow it? Brilliant, your idea: not to flee from the mafia, but go even deeper into it. Only a woman . . . Nelly!" Fully perceived and understood: precisely how the mafia would accept this project, in the most refined and intelligent way. With quick and supple minds: how much good a king could do for the country, a monarch, and how profitable that could be for them! They'd think it over a bit more before getting into their cars, casting a final approving gaze across the roof of the Mercedes at another elder or godfather, the contained and august gaze of a mafia kingpin, the old-fashioned square lenses of his glasses.

3

A complete imposture; an assembly of nobles (all of them imposters, too), with well-tended beards and cavity-riddled teeth. Perhaps one or two with a noble ancestor, well aware of their own illegitimacy, their role as attendant lords, swelling out a scene or two, convoked to elect a czar, as in 1613, the first Romanov: youthful and weak, malleable and easily abused. Would the public wish for a handsome sovereign, the sideburns and trim beard of the last czar? Though *he* was actually a grotesque being, one of those prognathous kings, deformed by generations of consanguineous matrimony, the trace of many monarchs in him, mutations, overlong cellular chains accumulated in the nucleus of his being: impotence, lack of will, and incapacity for command. A perfect nullity.

Or would the public heartily approve of and clearly prefer Vasily's porcine roundness, the evidence of many potatoes boiled and bathed in butter and mugs of beer downed with smoked fish, the hard-boiled eggs whose shells he cracked open against the table, the pickles he fished out of the jar with his index finger? A man they would recognize as one of their own. The mutinous army of gladiators, having fled the circuses and united all together on the peninsula, elects a king who steps from his tent amid huzzahs—and we see that he's potbellied and wide-shouldered, with the manners of a caveman (a king of clubs? a king of clubs).

And at only a few meters' distance from your father, Kirpich and Raketa would receive the order from the Muscovite elders and without slowing their pace would begin to flex their legs in preparation for executing the dotted red line of a downward arc. To prostrate before Vasily the very knees that, back in Moscow, had been ordered, instead, to rise violently and plunge into his lower belly. Heads bowed, murderous eyes raised in devotion.

And Vasily, his hand extended, having discovered, the moment Kirpich and Raketa came in, that they were there to kill him; the gesture of one seeking to ward off men whom he fears, to keep them from approaching any nearer. And that hand, too, tracing a lesser arc now, pointing to the spot where they were to sink down, the moment he understood from the gaze of the two new arrivals that the elders had countermanded the original order. Meaning that they owed obedience to him, to their king.

Both assassins would stop and exchange astonished gazes, instantly understanding the sudden change in the intentions of their Moscow bosses and the rest of it, and would then proceed forward, but no longer to kill Vasily. To mutter, perhaps also obeying an order: *Our Father*. And then louder: *Our Father!* All their hatred, their infinite reserves of violence, transformed into wonder and devotion. With the facility and understanding that only the mafia can grasp, in its acceptance of a hierarchy: the total allegiance due a boss or godfather in the mafia. Orders understood and heeded without doubt or hesitation, without halting the smooth, slow movement of the red point of their knees which, borne downward by that order, appeared to glide and land softly on the cushion or royal footstool at the feet of Basil.

"At the feet of a pseudo Basil."

"At the feet of a pseudo Basil, then. Who cares?"

4

Even I, a foreigner, could handle this. As when a director is invited to the Royal Danish Theater in Copenhagen, though he knows no Danish, not a word. Well, maybe one word: perhaps he can say "bad," in Danish, to shake up the actors. But through the mouth of his assistant, his interpreter, comes his wise guidance on the lighting, the mechanics of a gesture, the wellspring of an emotion. And on opening day everyone is amazed by the brilliance of actors whose performances had until then been mediocre.

Guiding Vasily via remote control, like a puppeteer, making him raise the right hand and extend it forward, majestically caressing the head of the child bearing the bouquet of flowers. Vasily, moving within a sphere of crystal, an immense gem. Softly applying the bottom of his foot, moving it forward with care, the soft chamois of a soft shoe that makes it roll forward, applying its gentle torque to the entire sphere. Stopping, casting glances to both sides, as the Sun King did upon making his entrance into Versailles. Without passing through its walls, his eyes resting on the surface of the crystal, some courtier on the receiving end of that sight line, or the peasant bearing the summons. The careful spatial order, the pantomime that for well-known kings—Rainier of Morocco—generates a royal essence or substance.

The same thing in a man intent on dancing it. Liberating within him, within his bloodstream, the qualities of a perfect king. Which I can cite here extensively, in keeping with Valentinian's rule, always haughtily ignored (no, not haughtily, perfidiously) by the Commentator: to cite no more than five authors. A king, states Julius Pollux, a king must be . . . Or rather, he says:

5

"Praise the king with these titles: Father, benign, peaceful, benevolent, foresighted, just, humane, magnanimous, frank. Say that he is no money-grabber nor a slave to his passions; that he controls himself and his pleasures; that he is rational, has keen judgment, is clear thinking and circumspect; that he is sound in his advice, just, sensible, mindful of religious matters, with a thought to the affairs of men; that he is reliable, steadfast, infallible, that he has far-reaching ideas, is endowed with authority; that he works hard, accomplishes much, is deeply concerned for those over whom he rules and is their protector; that he is given to acts of kindness and slowly moved to vengeance; that he is true, constant, unbending, prone to the side of justice, ever attentive to remarks about the prince; that he is well mannered, readily accessible, affable in a gathering, agreeable to any who want to speak with him, charming, and open-countenanced; that he concerns himself for those subject to his rule and is fond of his soldiers; that he wages war with force and vigor but does not seek opportunities for it; that he loves peace, tries to arrange peace, and holds steadily to it; that he is opposed to changing forcibly the ways of his people; that he knows how to be a leader and a prince and to establish beneficial laws; that he is born to attain honors and has the appearance of a god. There are in addition many things that could be set forth in an address, but cannot be expressed in just a word or two."

6

Except—I noticed this difficulty immediately—that a man, a baker, let's say, in Padua, who by the most incredible fortuity receives an embassy of nobles come to inform him (to his infinite astonishment) that he is the lost heir of the House of Savoy! This man of austere habits, able to dine on a crust of bread, who, as he took sacks down to the mill and brought sacks back up from the mill, never once dreamed of a fortune, and when it was in his hands, was indeed **circumspect, no money-grabber.** But not your father. Not Vasily, who immediately, as soon as the bills passed into his possession in that cabin in the woods, saw miniature yachts, minuscule Mercedeses dancing before his eyes, and this house, here in Marbella, full-size, which he bought, ostentatiously, in cash, the briefcases stuffed with banknotes that he presented to the sellers who choked and salivated (they by no means free of the charge of **money-grabber** either).

A Russian! They'd quoted him an exorbitant price, which later turned out to be 25 percent more than the neighboring mansions, and he hadn't blinked, not because he was **no money-grabber** but because he was a money-lover and confident he would come up with much more of the stuff, that he possessed the infallible formula for making money. Out of keeping with his rank here, viewed from this angle, incapable of fitting into the mold of a king and less still into that of a perfect king.

Not **reliable, steadfast** either. For how to endow his figure with the greyhound sleekness of a Duke of noble blood, make him abandon his crude manners, his way of shambling across the garden to the swimming pool bar for a beer? Looking, as he moved, like a man who'd stolen a fortune, who perhaps was toying with the expedient of growing fat, eating fishsticks unceasingly in order to attain the objective of hiding himself from sight inside a hugely fattened body. Could this be called **reliable**? Could this be called **steadfast**?

Certainly not, quite the opposite: a brutally voluble person, changing his mind every second, who endlessly consulted the tiny screen of his cell phone throughout the night they spent in the cabin, continually on the point of standing up and confessing everything to the gangsters. And not **steadfast** either. Because he'd accepted the idea, it had struck him as good, and then, on the way to the cabin, when they had their goal in sight and while Batyk (pretending to be a Yakut) was rubbing his hands with gusto, your papa suddenly entertained and esteemed the idea of making a U-turn and racing back to E* in the jeep without selling anything. So how **reliable**, then? How **steadfast**?

Becoming aware of this difficulty and pointing her double error out to Nelly, on the basis of the Book's authority and of this argument, which was to my mind insurmountable: that imposture is intimately linked to commentary. The result would be impossible to sustain; we would not succeed in deceiving any reader with our swindle, just as I myself always react when confronted with the Commentator's falsity and imposture.

Without the words of a commentary scrawled ineptly across the foreheads of many of these imposters—such and such an opera singer, the "best" performer of Bach, so many painters—they would collapse. On closer view, it's easy to discover how diminutive the text that holds them up is: what a critic said about him, the most knowledgeable authority on Renaissance vocal music, the number one specialist in alfresco painting, men in their turn puffed out with words, repellant palmers off of citations, people whose words have no weight whatsoever, not even for themselves, if they can't manage to make them refer to an authority. Impossible for that reason, Nelly, and for this one, too: ranged against the feasibility of a new czar is the fact that there are already ten royal houses in Europe; the Russian house would make an improbable eleventh.

7

Or how about **has keen judgment, is clear-thinking and circumspect** when he couldn't stop admiring the ingenuity of the men who wanted to hunt him down, and was shouting, "Mother! Are you listening, Mother?" to Nelly (wasn't it absurd, that way he had of calling your mother "Mother"?). "But which is better? Huh?"

Explaining how there was once some Vanya somewhere, a man in Russia, coming back from an important meeting, walking with the quick steps of a young mafioso to the distant black point of his car (also a Mercedes), pulled up on a patch of lawn. Not on the sidewalk, not on the asphalt of a parking lot—why would he park it on asphalt, between the yellow stripes that frame a normal car? And he saw, drawing closer, that someone, that something was hanging from the handle of the door—a plastic bag, tied around the handle by some idiot. Easy to see it now: a plastic supermarket shopping bag.

Tied or left there by some mechanic from the nearby garage or some TV repairman, a man walking to his shop in the morning or on his way home from the night shift, unable to keep his envy of that car parked on the grass from making him tie up that bag there, in passing, as a stupid and out of place reminder: *Hey! There are still workers coming in or going out at these hours, while you, bourgeois thief, and not even bourgeois thief, big mafia strongman, go around robbing and thieving, leaving your car on the grass.*

The man standing at the car door saw all that, imagined the mechanic's gray overalls disappearing down the alley, leaving his stupid and inappropriate declaration hanging there, and thought of the many things he'd like to explain: how, for example, he himself had worked in one of those repair shops until not very long ago, but without time to argue or any desire to do so, very irritated and full of rage.

And he went to swipe the bag away with his hand and be rid of this impertinence, and it was a bomb—wasn't it, Mother?—a bomb that exploded the moment his hand ripped it furiously away. "Low tech, huh, Mother?"

As if, during a production meeting, some young fellow, a killer newly arrived at the Technical Solutions Lab, had listened to his older colleagues' meanderings about limpet bombs, motion-activated detonators, resins set off by remote control from beneath manhole covers (and how? with the car on the lawn?) and had modestly raised his hand and suggested this: low tech. A degree of acquaintance, a precise calibration of the sequence of thoughts triggered by a plastic bag left hanging from a car door. The final thought sequence of the man who ripped the bag away while still talking on his cell phone. "Russians! Huh, Mother? Russians!" Vasily grew animated as he told her about it, then lowered his eyes, defeated by the evidence of a multiform ingenuity that would hunt him down in the end, wherever he ran, wherever he hid.

Tormented not only by the ingenuity, but also by the perseverance of a sharpshooter, posted for many days at the top of a building. The attic where he waited patiently for the curtains to part in the house where, also patient, without ever going near the window, a father and son were hiding. Two men who'd swindled the mafia, two entrepreneurs who had robbed too much (millions), without succeeding in buying a better house, or without having had time to do so when their game was up and they'd had to run and hide in that apartment, never going near the windows. But one afternoon, the kitchen's yellow light bulb already switched on, the cold air of winter coming in through the window above, the older of the two, precisely the one on whom the godfather's order of execution was weighing, had approached, had wanted to see something in the courtyard, the scene that he knew from memory—snow flattened by cars, children playing in the vacant lot—and had taken the bullet before the curtain had fallen back into place, the finger withdrawn. One glimpse. An H & K abandoned next to a mattress in the attic of the neighboring house, its three-thousand-dollar price tag amply covered by the payment guaranteed under the contract, no fingerprints or cigarette butts or sandwich wrappers anywhere nearby.

"No one could shoot you, Vasily: we're on a cliff, there are no houses higher than this one," I told him.

Your father repeated my stupid words: "*Boooo, boooo!* No one could shoot you, Vasily, there are no houses higher than this one . . . *Booooo!*" And turned his head from shoulder to shoulder in a gesture of resignation inspired by my stupidity: and what about plastic bags with bombs in them, and the many other means of killing him that even he himself, without being a killer, has thought of?

8

For also, in Pollux, another difficulty: **that he has far-reaching ideas.** What far-reaching ideas, and how far-reaching? A single one that he succeeded in exploiting to the maximum degree, on the bad advice of the Buryat's black heart. I do concede that the idea he had in his laboratory in the Urals was far-reaching and unique. For the first time in history, color diamonds that bore no trace of having been manufactured. A far-reaching idea? All right: one far-reaching idea, I grant that. But then led directly afterward, by hand and mouth, to small ideas, to the infinitely despicable and minuscule idea of the swindle that had ended in their precipitous departure from Russia.

Any **good idea** I could isolate, stop in midair, and approach to study in detail was always your mother's. Such as the idea of hiring a tutor because you were missing your classes, because on certain days she'd found you reprogrammed, with nothing in your eyes but tiny purple and green figures chasing each other at top speed across your irises. A good idea: and then me here, my consultation of the Book. Not to mention all the good ideas I generated after the day I crossed the threshold, following Batyk's scrawny back. The way my knowledge of the Book allowed me to recognize the bad ideas immediately, bad ideas such as Batyk's incredible mistake with the antigravity machine, which I will presently proceed to describe.

Nor is he **just, humane, control**[ling] **himself and his passions** either. A man incapable of mastering himself, who would fall into deep depressions, whom I saw walking through the house at night, unable to sleep, **a defeated man.** Or rather, to use the whole phrase: **on his back, eating bread, a defeated man.**

Here: someone with nothing to do, without plans or goals, without obligations, no reason to cross the city from one point to another, to go to a meeting. Shackled like a Laocoön in his silk robe, enchained in the storied initials embroidered on his slippers. Or like a large animal with grass heaped up in one corner of the cage, always a little dirty, dejected by the hard asphalt onto which he slowly brings down a cloven hoof that opens out beneath the weight of the enormous leg.

Vasily: after Larissa, his lover, after the ephemeral delight of the Mercedes and the gold Rolexes, after the absurd luxury that was nothing but the incarnation of his wickedness and deceit, now **defeated** by fear. Imagining all the things purchased in his insatiability and bad taste rising threateningly into the air, the remote controls from atop the little marble table, the silver spoons, the fake samurai swords, all that was least blunt, all that was sharpest and most piercing, pointing at him, silently revolving, telling him: stop **eating bread,** stop **eating bread.** Leap to your feet! Make yourself Czar!

Eighth Commentary

I

For it was as if he, Batyk, were—you know?—a bad writer. Attributing to himself an as yet undemonstrated ability to hold forth on the most unlikely subjects with the greatest aplomb. Sweeping everything aside at his passage, all that he touched with his poisonous tongue. A toad stewed in vile potions, a sponge soaked in venom, a repugnant man living under a stone, lurking there to stain everything with his absurd and uncalled-for commentaries. Adhering the suckers on his tentacles to any topic, with the unctuousness of the charlatan, the security and false erudition of the hack writer, convinced that simply by pointing at things with his finger, "telling it like it is . . ."

I'm contradicting myself here or appear to be contradicting myself, but that's not the case.

A horror of a man, a man who would never take his hands off anything and spewed endless torrents of mistaken concepts, such as the notion that one can continue to wear nylon shirts decades after their appearance and apparent triumph in Europe, subsequently to be displaced, as we all know, by a return to natural fabrics, Egyptian cotton, Swedish linen. An inexhaustible source of interferences, a piece of ferrous metal, an ax beneath the compass, a block of confused signals sinuously dancing nearer, polluting the ether. And I incapable of finding one sensible word or commentary in this rain of ions, furious, white with rage or impotence, wondering at every step whether this wasn't the way—his way of speaking, lifting his chin with utmost insolence—that I, too, should speak: "getting right to the point."

And I, I repeat, who admire and ponder the Writer's straightfor-wardness and steadfastness and wish for just such straightforwardness and steadfastness in any primary writer, any writer worthy of being qualified as such, could not cease to abhor and hate that man and the type of bloviator or pencil pusher he represented here, in your father's court. Forever giving erroneous advice, a vision of the world that was incorrectly simplistic and fallacious buzzing in my ears like some in-digestible substance accumulating in layers at the entrance to the ear canal. Until finally I was deaf, watching him open his mouth and re-pressing my desire to jump on him—you know?—and reduce the flow to zero by exerting pressure with both hands on his stupid glottis, watching him inflate below that point, swell up like a toad with his lies, mistaken ideas, and stupid strategies. Like the plan to elevate Vasily, your father, on an antigravity shield—never! never! never! His bony elbows, his ready-made phrases. All bad, as in a bad writer, primary or secondary, what does it matter. Bad, bad, bad.

2

To the point that Batyk had come up with the most idiotic, delirious, and ridiculous solution, one that violated the strict security measures he himself had so zealously forced us to observe: not to allow any unknown person into the house to break through our protective barrier and endanger the life and security of all Miramar.

So imagine how I jumped, adrenaline rushing up my neck, the afternoon I came back from the beach (without you, your mother had again forbidden you to go down) and heard the dogs barking and knew they were barking at a stranger.

My first thought: Kirpich (and then, Raketa), his silhouette outlined against the glass sun porch, come to negotiate the handing over or reimbursement of the money (I still imagined them wanting their money back, demanding restitution of the swindled sum). And I moved like an Italian cardinal in a court full of Frenchmen, to keep them from noticing me, to avoid alerting them to the presence of another person (never forgetting the night of the slaughter), an invisible witness who could testify to the strange visitor's way of eating, his hand opening out in a fan over the plate from which he took not one nut or two but a whole fistful, which he threw into his mouth with sinister avidity.

No, not Kirpich or Raketa, but an accomplice of theirs: a man in a ridiculous checked suit worn-out at the elbows, bending over the plate of nuts with the debasement of having spent many years without eating as much as he wanted, little things like that.

But don't they have lots of money, these mafiosi? Don't they drink in bars that offer stylish ceramic dishes filled to the brim with assorted nuts or some variety of *fritto misto di mare,* on the house? Motionless on the grass, my back against the house wall, eyes on the swimming pool. Disbelieving my own ears: the most absurd and senseless plan.

That I would not have believed, Petya, I repeat, if I hadn't heard it quite clearly as I stood there in the garden. A character straight out of a traveling medicine show, a fraudulent inventor (fraudulent two centuries ago, not today!) come to his king to sell him the secret of manufacturing diamonds: carbon and graphite in the heart of a cannon, the flame fanned unceasingly. Or another scientist, who in the solitude of his lab had determined the feasibility of the *perpetuum mobile,* a loom weaving day into night without stopping. And three days after it was set in motion, full of admiration for the machine's autonomous movement, the vizier rushed to the royal chambers exclaiming loudly: "Yes! It's true!: without effort and without expenditure, HRH! In appearance and, I must affirm, no less in reality. The shuttle has not stopped moving; Professor Astoriadis's machine hasn't paused for a second."

Then he would bow obsequiously, thrusting forward his massive shoe with its enormous buckle, face toward the ground, his chin lost in his ruff. And now, here he was again centuries later, leaning on the living room table, the torso's whole impulse and vectorial spin aimed at the small plate of nuts. A pettiness outdone only by Batyk himself, his way of pondering his kilims and the entirely mistaken explanation he gave of the professor's idea, while Astoriadis—a patently false surname—never saw fit to shut him up or correct any point of his error-riddled presentation. Chewing without pause, the professor, nodding with the tranquillity of an Oriental in a teahouse who walks toward you thinking nonstop about how he's going to swindle you.

And Vasily, to my infinite astonishment, falling for it. Thinking something like: if I, against all expectations and the jeering comments of my colleagues could make colored diamonds, then this man Astoriadis, also a scientist, perhaps true what he says about the annulment of gravity. Amazed by the flexible disk that would hold him up without bending beneath his weight, spinning at light speed **like a top** (the Writer notes in this passage, enchantingly), nibbling away with absolute efficiency at the gears of gravity. The user (he chose that ugly word) would perceive nothing at first; the very thin disk would be slipped beneath the user's feet, spinning at the speed of light. But before long he would notice that the lipstick falling from his wife's hand, the makeup case, the powder puff, were not dropping to the ground but remaining miraculously suspended in the air, free of the ties that bind us to the earth and, in the end, bring us down: Vasily, triumphant over them! No.

3

I perceived with clarity that a wave of indignation (these were lies! lies!) was welling up in me and moving forward out of the years when I was younger and more upright, only to lose its momentum in the subaqueous crags of my soul, without my managing to say what I was thinking, reveal my perspective, without my lips articulating a single word. Beneath the thick layer of oil which, in those adventure novels the Writer tells us he read as a boy, they poured out by the barrel to calm the angry sea and send out a boat, a whaler. Floating beneath that dense film of oil, the iron grip of its tiny molecular hands, watching them argue, the veins of the neck swelling, rocking to the rhythm of the waves, the tranquil viscosity of a jellyfish many kilometers long, swaying and dancing smoothly on the surface.

Thinking.

A danger to turn all the work in that direction, in terms of physics: to endow it with a mass that was difficult to steer when set against the infinite and far less tangible effect of an imposture. An intelligent man, Vasily, very intelligent! But far too attached to the high flame of bunsen burners, to alloys of iron and tungsten—which could not easily be replaced by the sale of small portions of colored air, easily transported in carry-on luggage, shaped at will.

Thinking.

It will be science, nevertheless, that places a new monarch on any throne from now on, whether in Russia or in Portugal. No one will have any objection to a scientifically distilled monarch, whose capacity for command we understand with scientific precision. A certain interior disposition that obliges a king to raise the napkin to his lips in a certain august manner, to sweep the room with august eyes. Without anyone having a second's doubt about his capacity to reign. Not politicians—you know—party leaders, gobblers of greasy doughnuts, swillers of beer. Something in the last gene of the sequence that would move him to lift his arm in an unrepeatable gesture, a penetrating vision that would enable him to throw his gaze across the mass of problems and find, always, like the knife the Writer (Chuang Tse) speaks of, the most recondite interstices, without ever blunting the blade, the sharp edge. Simple, clear solutions where everyone else sees only the murkiest obscurity. Moving forward with grace, deactivating them, one by one. The ascendance and power of the one who knows.

And since his other talents would be known as well—that of growing diamonds, for example, gem-quality stones—there could be no doubt as to his capacity to rule. Like the man who, in Byzantium, from the depths of an encamped army, strode out onto a hillock and crossed the camp beneath a beam of light that shone on him from the zenith (and that light later passed into legend), to take command, to strip control from the Basileus, who was weeping and shivering. And no one—for they'd been raised to know that not all men are created equal, that there are superior men—no one ever doubted that he was the one.

With absolute certainty, inspired science. At one glance. Walking down a hill beneath that light, the last hill before the tent with the imperial flag, and then entering that tent to grasp the reigns of Empire, like Michael the Stammerer or Phocas the Usurper: men rough in aspect as they rode roughly across Asia Minor but who awoke one day suddenly knowing themselves to be kings.

And now: that certainty clarified by science. Because, I repeat, there would be or would exist some such genetic tendency or predisposition, blockages in their brains that would finally rearrange themselves one day, like an equation whose solution takes years to become clear, and then appears to them, lights up blinking in their minds, and they leap to their feet and stride outside to meet the army, the Empire, that awaits them.

Not the arbitrary process of the Tibetans who seek traits or certain signs of the Dalai Lama in the round faces of many babies. Until they find one on which they can stamp, by common consent, the mental image of a king. Though that works. They've been doing it for centuries, and it's never failed!

A boy, a pure soul, a tabula rasa, who ends up reigning over them and they yield to his government with gratitude and wisdom. Without any sort of certainty or scientific evidence playing a role in the process, only such inexact techniques as smelling the breath, inspecting the urine, scrutinizing an iris. And without their ever being mistaken, neither with Lama two nor with Lama five, the favorites of Lhamo Thondup, the current Lama. Differing among themselves, each one capable of making his own mark.

Think now, linger a moment over a dynastic selection in which the electorate consists primarily of the scrawny-shouldered (in a manner of speaking—your papa is not scrawny of shoulder), and this selection, in the depths of the laboratory, delivers an unobjectionable result: the finest one. Not a group of the best and the brightest—the finest one of all!

4

Or as if a young dramaturge who once hailed from Stratford-upon-Avon were to appear miraculously right now and place three tragedies on the table during the meeting of a theater company in England or anywhere else. If only the people in the meeting knew how to read it, the professors, the trustees, should it happen that they were able to read it as I do, with the simplicity, the appreciation or perception of its entirety, the certainty that comes of being in the presence of a master-work, as when (I remember it perfectly), at the age of nineteen (so early an age), on the semicircular front stairway of my school, I opened the Book and set my eyes on the first sentence of that volume (*Swann in Love*) and knew immediately that this was the Book, and that its author—a unique writer—was the Writer. That day. Like someone who finds the solution to a math problem.

Suddenly acquiring, over the course of just a few pages, the certainty that assaults you definitively as an adult, that now we'll never love anyone else. At least not with a love like that. That we won't fall in love again with the force and the intensity (and the abandon? and the abandon) with which we fell in love that one time, years ago. Never again. And without having lived much at all at that point, only seven years older than you are now, Petya, I perceived that truth. And yes, I have fallen in love, I have had loves, I have admired other writers and allowed them to enter my eyes and my soul. I've lived inside them, studied some of them, but have always gone back to the Writer, in the end. In the same way, if the trustees were to see two plays, two tragedies, three comedies, appear on the table next to their cups of steaming coffee, they wouldn't be able to go on drinking their terrible coffee, they would sit stock still, as if struck by lightning. The government ministers, the doughnut-gobbling presidents, the owners of country estates, the false connoisseurs of Russian literature, the ridiculous opera-lovers, they would all stop in their tracks if their black souls permitted, to prostrate themselves before a king as the thing most healthy and natural to their hearts, acknowledging and proclaiming that not all men are created equal, that some are superior. And yet they are hardened, bad; they pretend to be equal. Equal to whom? To Shakespeare? To the Writer?

5

You had conceded, after a certain time, and without thinking it necessary to tell me in so many words, the reality of the story I'm telling you. Understanding that however fantastic it might appear, having heard me out to that point, it was entirely factual: names like Kirpich and Raketa existed, as well as the two scientists, old friends, who had imagined the most harebrained scheme, given proof of the most insane imagination, forced the limits of the credible, carried the plausible to an extreme. And you assimilated that, as well, you let the pages with fistfuls of diamonds pass, in Ophir, the Solomonic kingdom of Ophir, millions in stones, bezants, and florins flowing between your fingers into the gilded mouths of coffers. Luxury and wealth, Petya, to that degree. You'd heard me out, followed and believed up to this point, hadn't you?

You didn't even stand up or dismiss as impossible something that, in view of your young age and so as not to affect the balance of your tender and childish mind, I kept from telling you until the last moment. Your father: Emperor of Russia . . . This, too, you accepted and allowed, though with an understandable expression of amazement, making space in your mind for this new and implausible plot twist: your father, King. On behalf of which I had to present arguments to you, supported by much evidence taken from the Book. An explanation you were skeptical of at first, and I, too, had had to give in, adding 1 or 2 percent more spandex to my mind's barrel staves, making room, putting my schoolmaster's satchel on my knees so that your father's other body could fit into the carriage that was now ready to flee, his symbolic body: the ridiculous little crown at the back of the head and Vasily smiling in embarrassment as if begging our pardon for not having a normal body like any other human being but—as the Writer explains and argues—a double body, the two bodies of the king. Fine like that? Comfortable? Let's close the door and finally be on our way.

But not, for all that, to accept, now, the absurdity of antigravity.

To imagine it feasible for men to fly. That? No.

And your mother complained of it bitterly. Why on earth expose us to ridicule, risk everything, the truth of our story, with the absurd idea of antigravity? Undermine our plan with something like that, Psellus? What reader in all the earth would ever believe such a thing? Refutable, moreover—added your mother, to my astonishment, for she was right—by the simple experiment of a falling apple, if such a thing were necessary, if there were a need for empirical refutation. "You see?" She would say to that gentleman (she was referring to Astoriadis): "You see? I drop it, and it falls!"

Good, Nelly. Correct!

"You, Psellus, had brought your good sense and wisdom to bear, we had a plan—and only to endanger all of that now with the ridiculous idea, the childish notion, of levitation? A petty and fatuous fairground attraction, what is it but that, Psellus? Which he claims will sell for a billion or two to the president of General Motors, to John F. Smith Jr., at this autumn's Salon de l'Automobile in Cannes. He hasn't stopped pestering my husband about how the country will rise again, how to recover the money that Nicholas loaned to the British, how the nation can overcome the crisis and reconstitute its union into a single happy family of Bashkirs, Tajiks, and Buryats."

6

Thus spoke Nelly, as if the Writer were speaking through her mouth. Turning against that repugnant and empirical being, a man who loved nothing more than rooting around in the mud of the physical world. All that Batyk imagined, the delirium that the vision of my success at court, my rise from tutor to Royal Councillor, gave rise to in him, stirring the bile of his envy. And he had cast caution to the winds, the security measures he'd so zealously forced us to observe. He started going out more often, to Puerto Banús (where he went to spy on me in Ishtar). He begged God to send him a solution, and one night he seemed to have come up with one and brought that man home with him, a stranger, a Russian, someone who might perfectly well have been an accomplice of Messrs. K and R, murderers. A Trojan horse, with his very strange way of moving, sneaking around next to the walls. The fifth column that would run out to draw back the bar on the gate; he was more of a traitor, that man, than a whole squadron of Saracens.

It hadn't taken much effort to find him among the many Russians who visited Marbella, who came so far south to observe with their own eyes the life being lived here and how well set up they were here, those who robbed most. That it was true: all the Russians here, all the money. He invited him in, allowed him to move his things to the Castle for an indeterminate stay. The only profit in this being that any visitor who might come to see us, in the hypothetical case that such a thing might occur, would observe that our household was growing: two liveried lackeys now instead of just one.

Continually moved, it didn't take long for me to realize, by the need to fill his belly, that Astoriadis. No thought of spying on us or alerting anyone else, that at least. Repressing with some difficulty—each time I found him on one of his nocturnal journeys to the refrigerator, closely studying its interior in front of the open door, valiantly stamping his many legs—my desire to jump on him, shouting: "The door! Haven't you, a scientist, heard about the ozone layer?" God! How I would have liked to hit him. With the Book, if I'd had it at hand. Quite certain of the result, for it's right there in the Writer: **When a head and a book come into collision and one of them rings hollow, is it always the book?**

What? From the Book, Petya? How could the sound come from a book? Is this a joke? Yes and notice, too, that he doesn't speak of a physical book or a physical head, he refers—had you grasped this?—to the obtuseness of certain minds, calling our attention to the fact that there can be heads that are hollower than the emptiest book. The danger and senselessness of levitation illustrated, moreover, by the influence of Jacques-Étienne Montgolfier with such nefarious effect for the monarchy; the example of ascension, the mechanical ascension of goats and dogs in 1783, or, in successive demonstrations, of any hatter, however mad, which inflamed the French, filling their breasts with the absurd ambition to fly, the belief that they could go higher than the sun, higher than their own king.

Quite the contrary, in reality: never could there be flight, never could anyone ever fly as Astoriadis claimed, levitating, as we fly in our dreams. Vasily atop a wall, his hair tousled by the land breeze blowing out from among the orange trees, the sun now very low, his feet illuminated by the light that after traveling through space without interruption for eight minutes has come to collide against his laughable little shoes, suspended in the air by the grace and effect of Astoriadis's ingenuity and that of the antigravity shield. The air, the emotion on his face turned to us down below: I'm flying! I'm flying! **I see the air and walk upon the clouds!**

To approach his ear, pressing myself into the spiral of his ear so my words would reach the soft mass of his brain and rescue him from his error. He landed gently on the grass, moved his feet toward me, raised his head. "It's false, Vasily, no such thing as a gravity-blocking shield exists. It's false. Can't you see?"

(If, as the Writer affirms, the external world is pure phenomenon, that is, something that appears before our senses and whose appearance is constructed by us, and if, as the Writer never thought, that phenomenon is a pure projection of the self, a shadow with nothing else behind it, then the world is a fable and so is the sphere in which the will to power is exercised.)

7

I surprised him when I cried: "Majesty!" He shot me a look, raised his eyes, both at once, and since he was too far away to scrutinize my eyes and cheeks millimeter by millimeter as was his custom, he wondered if I might not be pulling his leg. He was eager to get up, come over to me, and drill his eyes into mine with the same intensity with which, in certain primitive Italians (Masaccio, for example), Jesus gazes into the traitorous eyes of Judas.

He wasn't yet a monarch; there was no majesty in him. His far too expensive shoes peeked from beneath the hem of his pants as if placed there by a clever caricaturist who knew his trade well. All the absurdity of his repressed movement was concentrated in them, his need to cross the room and the manner in which he had to do it. A comic figure, or at least his pants fit badly. He should have paid only half the money he'd shelled out for that Versace to a tailor who could have cut him a good Savile Row suit with no gold-toned buttons, no fake monogram on the chest.

He stood there like that the whole morning, incapable of covering the distance that separated us, the sun shining through his translucent eyelashes. He had wanted to ask me: Is there something about this in the book you spend so much time reading? But my words had taken him by surprise, my brazen outburst, and now he would never dare ask me the question. Which I did not regret. He'd been needing a blow like that. To keep him far away, all the better to handle him with the long pole of the Book, maintaining the distance, exactly three and a half meters, that separated us, I calculated, looking down at my feet and lifting my eyes toward him as we do before snapping a photo.

I didn't pretend to have been mistaken or to have used the word lightly, but with perverse purpose, rather. He was a smart enough man, but I had to manipulate him like a puppet, an animated figure in a theatrical presentation, that alone would get us out of there with our lives (get them out, get me out, with the money). I had simply assigned him to a role, as when we were children and would sing out: You? Cop! You? Robber! The game about to begin.

Slowly he began to understand, at the rhythm at which a splash of sunlight made its way across the floor: I in my study, he eternally at the window. When finally the sun had moved quite a way across the sky, he seemed to have understood. In his face began to appear, along with the greater darkness, the signs of an intelligence of his new role. It didn't take him too much time, which says a lot for how clever he was: a test of anyone to accept a role like that, fallen from the sky, so quickly. To go from the white-collar worker one is, from the lowliest engineer on the project, from a doctor to His Imperial Majesty.

He seemed to understand, he no longer hesitated, but then he wondered: why now, we two, alone, in this room? And the public? The people before whom to . . . ? To pretend?

You must pretend for yourself, Vasily, play the role for yourself and not abandon it ever again.

He understood finally and was about to move his lips but the sun went into hiding at that moment and the two of us stood in the dark.

I end here: the curtain falls. The show is over. As you like it.

8

It didn't bother me for a second; the word didn't cause any change in my expression. It rose to my lips in the most natural way; my heart expelled it in an uninterrupted column of air, and it broke with a click as it detached from my lips, calling out happily to your father: "Majesty! Prince!" For he was a superior man, whom I approached with the serenity and peace of mind of one who has discovered voluntary servitude. Never would a black soul, a mediocrity like the Commentator, a man suffering from a mania for precise adjectivization, understand this or understand the soft and delicate air of that morning. Never would he place on paper or accept those two adjectives which, in that air, were simple and true. Only those, nevertheless, did I permit myself, those two adjectives.

I floated on that air and through it drew close to Nelly. I saw Vasily walking toward the car, pulling hard at the door. And that air, soft and delicate, brought me the sound of its slam, Nelly's friendly grimace and the angular elbows of Batyk who was running at top speed to feed him a lie without being able to address him as I had learned to do: Majesty! Prince!

Traveling now with Vasily to premiere his royal dignity, a place where he could stage a tryout of that other life (with symbolic intent? With symbolic intent). Approaching, across fields withered by the sun, the glittering isle of a shopping mall that we saw floating on the line of the horizon. Everyone in the car happy and dressed up for the occasion, you like a little boy in an engraving, wearing suspenders and ankle boots, your mother in her red dress, your father's three-piece Armani suit.

Only the Buryat's attire was out of sync, for he could never be convinced to change his fringed doublet, made of a striped cloth that was in very poor taste, suitable only for Cockneys or contemptible lackeys. Or, as the Writer calls Morel, **the shadiest of secretaries.** A man capable of splashing ink on all your papers, of muddying the most distant wellsprings of a day, who intuitively, among so many fine fabrics, had chosen this one with its very broad stripes, broader than good taste and decorum permitted (for no one had worn such a thing in public since 1975). He'd held it up against his torso and seen in satisfaction how the lines of the cloth perfectly matched the horrible lines on his face, and it's here that the Writer exclaims: **"Is it thoroughly clear to you that, if there be evil in your heart, your mere presence will probably proclaim it today a hundred times more clearly than would have been the case two or three centuries ago?"**

A piece of intelligence, an astute observation, that was more than applicable, as well, to the fraudulence that encased Professor Astoriadis's whole body, codified in his execrable table manners and the strange way he had of walking, lost in thought, while making two of his fingers, the index and middle finger, wiggle like a trolley car's antennae. A trolley car deep in thought. His legs articulated at many points in addition to the hips, knees, and ankles of normal human beings, at least five more points, which made him totter as he moved, staggering in disarray, as if his energy were frequently shut off. Luck had decreed that he would meet up with Batyk: the two had approached each other, recognized each other, Batyk listened to him and conceived the notion of taking him to your father with this far-fetched and repellant— or rather, implausible and impossible—antigravity idea.

An idea that fell, I already told you, as music on your father's ears and that I tried to negate with this excursion, a chance to go out and show off his royal dignity for the first time. It struck Vasily as a beautiful plan; he hesitated at first, but then it struck him as beautiful. He had hesitated: wouldn't it be too much of an exposure, an unnecessary risk? But no, your mother convinced him, with Psellus nothing will go wrong; he'll be our guide and translator.

To go out, Petya, and see for himself that the world outside had changed in the same way as the world inside him, that to the new arrangement of his cells corresponded a greater outward brilliance, at last identifying the new melody the wind drew from him as it blew through his altered reticular structure, the birds that flew into his chest, each seeking a hollow spot to stop and twitter in, as on a cliffside or a rock.

That solid.

9

Or with what the Writer calls **the crushing force of monarchy.** Hunching his shoulders now, Vasily, preceding us down the glass-enclosed gallery. Stopping in front of the shop windows that advertised sales, poking a thick index finger toward a pair of sweatpants (for what? your papa never played any kind of sport or went running) or a stereo speaker identical to the ones he already had throughout the house, bought in Cyprus or wherever he lied to us about having traveled. Like a Minotaur in a labyrinth of stores with Chinese wares, ill-suited to his dignity, and not knowing how to reach them, for the monster was unacquainted with the brittle nature of glass. How easily he could have made his way through the walls, lowering his head and neck for a second while the glass cascaded around him, crashing through like a giant purple automaton and carrying everything off with him: wireless phones, juicers, garlands of colored lights for the garden.

Hesitating between the symbolic intent of the journey and his desire to go in and listen to some very expensive speakers, importuning the salesman with questions about their frequency response (from twenty to twenty thousand, Vasily, your ears wouldn't hear anything beyond that). Taking him aside most respectfully, without ever going nearer than the five steps he had required between himself and me, attempting to steer him away from his disproportionate interest in tabletop fountains with whispering waters, clocks that project time onto the ceiling, an enormous copper gong complete with a felt mallet, to announce visitors.

And in front of the window display of a store completely identical in every respect to another one several passageways and five turns behind us, he stopped to inspect some sneakers for his tired feet, for his son and his wife (for me? no thanks), sneakers with which to outfit themselves like those families whose every member wears identical shoes on Sunday afternoons, purchased in one fell swoop, scooped up during a foray into the depths of enemy territory, ripped from the saddlebags without dismounting, and then happy as children, raising them to the sky, inspecting them beneath the ruddy splendor of late afternoon. And through the glass, his gaze refocused on the brightly lit interior of the shop, your father saw that a small drama was being played out on the carpet, at the front lines of the combat between distant Taiwanese companies and all the gullible consumers in the world.

A small drama, I noticed it as well, because of the disposition of its participants in front of the row of chairs: the young salesgirls with long braids holding a sneaker by the heel. Opposed to and divided by the axis that the sneaker scored in the air from a colorful group of people strangely and miraculously grasping the other extreme of the sneaker, its toe, the hands of the whole group, or one hand and one arm, pulling on that sneaker. Motionless at the moment when His Serene Highness raised his eyes, perhaps in the intention of studying the interior of the store, finding a seat there in which to frame the calloused hillocks of his backside and point from within toward the window, the tennis shoe or sneaker that had caught his attention among the many on display there.

In front of which he continued to stand without taking his eyes from the tableau. As a principal and organizing element now of the gazes of astonishment and admiration for his incontestable distinction. Some not so admiring, some looks of hatred in the eyes of the crowd confronting the shopgirls. Where—Vasily is wondering—does Juan Carlos of

Spain buy his sneakers? This is the type of small detail we've got to work on . . . The boy paralyzed at the center of the group, the gypsy boy (because no one else, etcetera), had managed to put on and was wearing one brand-new sneaker and the one he was holding was the right sneaker, interrupted on its way toward his unshod foot. And the ones in the shoebox were not, on closer inspection, new sneakers, but a very old and worn-out pair.

Vasily occupied the door frame for a second, sending a wave of silence out before him, an electromagnetic pulse that closed the mouths of both salesgirls and gypsies the moment it reached them. Their eyes could not sustain the force of his gaze and rolled back in their sockets just as children look away into space before breaking into speech. Before returning to the person in whom they discovered immediately, before Vasily had said a single word, an arbitrator. Either an inspector from the Better Business Bureau or a still greater personage—without, naturally, their being able to imagine his true rank: an Emperor.

Vasily gazed at them with the tired air of one who can easily imagine himself on the other side. He placed his hand on the shoe, a gesture that had the effect of deenergizing the group, which released it the moment that the force, which they instantly perceived, was transmitted. But with their hands freed from the physical effort necessary for hanging on to the sneaker, they quickly rechannelled that energy to their throats and began shouting at the referee.

The narrative of the whole story broke into little fragments that flew at him and accumulated on his shoulders and arms, on the hand he was still holding up in the air. He stopped to look at them for a second, at the words that were covering him as fast as the gypsy boys could release their lies and the shopgirls could try to catch them with open palms but without managing to keep them from adhering to Vasily with a slight click, attracted by the magnet of his body and his charisma.

Configuring on his chest the false story of how they had gone in—in all innocence!—to try on those sneakers, keeping their eyes on the door they planned to escape through and where the salesgirls had caught them.

Vasily understood it all, blood pumping through the muscles of his neck, making those lies jump with the relaying pitter-patter of an electromechanical telephone switch. He placed both hands on the sneaker and allowed a current to rise through his arms toward the thieving boys with the following message: **Hammurabi, the perfect king, am I, the king who is preeminent among kings. My words are precious, my wisdom is unrivaled. The perfect king am I.**

10

Such a message, such a sentiment within him. To make justice flow not toward the gypsy boys, as many in Sweden or perhaps in Norway would have wanted, and which would have been wrong, but to the shopgirls. Without proffering a word, with the muteness of a king settling a dispute in a remote region of his kingdom where he does not speak the language. Making the balloons of his words float throughout the store. So that everyone could see them rising to his lips and read them as well, without need of any interpreter. I was the one who, on seeing them emerge and discovering the spatial disposition of those bubbles in the air that floated off into the most distant departments of Marks & Spencer, identified the words that the Writer places on the lips of a king, through a secondary character in the Book, and which mean: **"I am the king preeminent among kings. My words are precious, my wisdom unrivaled. The perfect king am I."**

I was not the one who built the jets flying overhead across the skies of Marbella, my index finger had not followed their fuel and pneumatic lines, rendered in blue and red, across the blueprint. I overcame my fear each time I had to board one and fly in it across the firmament. And a jet would never stop in midflight or on the verge of takeoff, to open its mouth, lift its chin to the sky with these words on its propeller-lips, this absolute confidence in its own capacity for flight. **"The perfect king am I."** Not a good king: **"the king preeminent among kings."**

"Like Lufthansa?"

Better yet. Not a single accident in centuries, dynasty after dynasty, dynasties falling and rising, materializing in midflight. Why wouldn't we entrust our lives to them? He was a new kind of machinery, your father, with less physical structure than a jet, but with the same instructions from centuries past, borne out in practice. The gravity and aplomb of a colossus who contained in his breast, packed tightly within him, all his servants, the whole crew, his blue warriors and their orange jumpsuits. Ready to propel with their own feet, should the fuel source give out, the dynamo of their king, make him advance, move his arm from right to left.

The visible fact, Petya, that leads us to the invisible one of: king.

Ninth Commentary

I

We can deny the real existence of all that falls outside the Book: swimming pools, for example, which the Writer never mentions and that are hard to read for that reason, because they don't figure in the Book, don't glitter in a single passage of that vast work; the Writer never had the faintest inkling or notion of them and it was up to me to stretch the thin film of the text, trying in some way to make it cover them, to comprehend them.

Views, elements of the landscape about which, undoubtedly, he did not write. Had they escaped the machinery of his sight or was it just that he didn't see everything? I paused to regain my balance, bent down over those little gaps in the stiff tarp and discovered the blue and red bubbles of plastic balls (for he never spoke of plastic either, impossible). The balls broke through, sticking out here and there, smooth and shiny, and only with great difficulty did I managed to cover them over with a passage that mentions balls—whether made of oilcloth, rubber, or natural resin (the Book does not specify)—round and multicolored, played with by children on the beach.

And nothing about swimming pools, either.

The very large and beautiful one in your garden, its notches of light, the submerged flank of an enormous blue fish, the scales suggested by the illuminated semicircles that crossed and segmented its whole belly, breathing down below. None of that anywhere in the Writer. How, then, to comment on it? Certain things, certain visions of the days?

I stretched out the edges, my fingers pressing down hard on the polyvinyl (not that either!), running to some distant place, some province in the vast empire of the Book from which to fetch back, copied out on my pupils, a fragment about the sparkle of the sea on the awnings of Balbec. I placed it carefully against the gap of the pool, trying to convince the boy, managing at times to bring together the jagged edges of the opening, without ever covering it entirely.

And through the uncovered holes it continued to rise, I observed as if hypnotized by the (new?) effect of the light from below. He hadn't seen it? There were no pools in that house near Balbec that belonged to the Verdurins? The water of a pond, a hollow amid the reefs, didn't produce the same effect? Or was it only visible if one is strolling in a swimsuit alongside one of those California swimming pools (or one as large as the pools in California), probing the water with a thumb, breaking through the golden scales that cover the back of the animal, the enormous pike down below?

I raised my eyes, assailed by the unease of a teacher who hasn't spent much time preparing the class and faces the children's expectant faces knowing that he will lie to them without allowing a shadow of doubt to cross his face, wringing out the text to a maximum degree like a fraudulent exegete. I plunged in and began to swim, breaking up handfuls of the surface's changing prisms with the fury of a man silencing voices of discontent in the mayhem of a saloon, distributing blows with flailing arms and absolute perfidy. Now the light no longer found that smooth surface on which to refract: only my back. An opaque medium swimming obstinately from one end to the other, swift as a shuttle, roiling the waters. To keep anyone from glimpsing the dimensions of the gap, as large in the text as a swimming pool in the ground.

2

Or the way the Writer encourages us at a moment of equal bewilderment and discouragement. **Onward, dear reader! Who has ever said that there can be no true, faithful, and eternal love in the world, that such a thing does not exist? May that liar's tongue be cut out!**

Full of life at that moment, bursting with submission and devotion to her, ready to leap to my feet and do battle. Agreeing fully with the Writer that in any work one part must serve others, that a palace must have passageways. Very well, but through this passageway at a gallop: high and wide, two men on horseback can pass, or myself and your parents, our capes fluttering in the wind. Beneath chapters in which nothing happened, long strings of pages in which time seemed to have stopped, to emerge into fur-strewn salons, castles at the edge of the sea, the thronging banquet in the perfumed garden through which all the characters in the story move (and dance).

Following, in this, I commented to the boy, the Writer, who starts a party on the 1,001st page of the Book, where he reunites all his characters (and all the plotlines! And all the plotlines). The great final chords of a nineteenth-century symphony, no less thrilling for being long-awaited. A party to which we would invite Simon of Bulgaria, Leka of Albania, Duarte of Braganza, all the crownless monarchs who, for some obscure reason, chose Spain as their place of refuge.

Though not really so obscure: didn't Spain exert a magnetic attraction on them, Madrid, the unparalleled example of the Spanish royal house with its affable king? They would be able to recognize and understand our plan in a second, they would take the book for the Book. The volume in quarto that all the kings of Europe would receive at Yuletide, sent from Russia, and which they would open by placing a jeweled index finger (that of Harold of Norway) beneath its cover of gold, silver, and marble. And he would sit down to read it, instantly forgetting the ambassador of Grenada, the chancellor of Laos, allowing the full and reasonable meaning of the Book to enter in through his eyes, a text that requires no commentators, no false scholars heaping up commentaries at its mouth like gangs of miners. Its readers able to interpret any passage without strain, no need for any gloss to aid the comprehension of those for whom the real possibility of the new royal house of Russia would be obvious, clear, and feasible.

For the difficult passages, which the Book certainly does contain, are not necessary to an understanding of the message in its entirety, and furthermore I'm here to explain them to you, Petya. For example, at one point in volume 3 the Writer says **Princess Demidoff.** And this is a mistake (though a minor one, certainly), just the type of mistake we must avoid: this name has never existed, there has never been a Russian house that ended with that double *f,* a thing that would take aback any even slightly knowledgeable adult, a professor of Russian who, putting on his thick plastic glasses (nails stained with nicotine), about to leave for his class at the Mendeleev Institute (that family name, yes, in Moscow), would give a start of indignation: no such family exists; never have there been, in the nineteenth century nor at any other point, any Demidoffs, etcetera. The base and pretext for an exhaustive and ill-timed survey of the history of heraldry.

No genetic analysis either to decant with great finesse between a Trubetskoi and a Romanov, or between a Kuropatov (Vasily's own family name) and a Romanov. This many *X*s on that back (tattooed there by fire) and this many here: the numbers don't coincide! We would steer around those reefs into a world without the sharp-edged crags of physical resemblance, an old lady, a Romanov, who would howl, poking her bejeweled finger into his chest: It isn't him! We would condense seas, we would conjure up vessels, we would imagine reaching land without our minds projecting the crag of DNA onto the physical world for one second.

Only the Writer's enameled prose, his Versace prose. Functioning in all brains, entering into all ears, bearing to all central nervous systems the order required for the reorganization of their internal structure: to believe us. A prose adorned with veers and curlicues, an art nouveau prose, organic, vegetal, gleaming.

3

But here's another apparent triumph and another apparent truth of the Commentator, Petya: the conduct of the travelers in the train that took me to Madrid. The commentaries a young woman was delivering while continually looking out the window. The words she repeated again and again, the way she pursed her lips, rolled her eyes and said: "Can you imagine? She said to me. And I said to her." Indefatigably. An argument from the day before that was able to nourish a commentary many kilometers long, the changing landscape, the first houses at the outskirts of Madrid, a hillside covered with hideous multifamily housing units and her words, her commentary, still flowing from between her pursed lips, a series of gestures representing the entire incident. How that woman had come over to her cubicle and had come out with it the moment she arrived: such and such a thing. And she, could her friend imagine, not knowing how to react, taken by surprise, the steaming cup of coffee at her lips.

But she'd thought about it and an instant later was able to come up with a response. She'd put down the cup without taking a sip (moving the little telephone away from her lips, from which I inferred the matter of the coffee cup) and shot back: "But who do you think you are?"

Everything revolved around that, all misunderstandings: around who other people thought, erroneously, that they were. And it was necessary, from time to time, to correct them, put them in their place. To ask, "But who do you think, who have you believed that you are?" And the other party never reacting appropriately, always proceeding from the false position of the person she believed she was and not from the real and insignificant one of a person who was in fact a nullity.

A nobody!

And once the subject had been addressed, the incident acted out in a pantomime that was invisible to her interlocutor but transmitted to her through changes in the voice, pauses, the points of inflection of the altercation, once the whole matter had been explained and delineated, then and only then did the commentary per se begin. In the first place, opening with: who in reality this person was. An analysis that she could base on many factors, for even prior to this incident she had noticed: the horrible apartment the other woman shared with her mother, the hideous clothing she bought, the hairdresser she should have gone to but never did, for which reason she tied her hair back with a two-cent bit of elastic. All of this gone over in her presence yesterday in the office, details she now wanted to comment upon over the telephone so her interlocutor would understand, would finally manage to grasp the message, just as her enemy had finally grasped it the day before.

The train stopped. The cylinders in the doors released air. The woman in the red shoes stood up, the telephone still at her ear, her lips shaped into a pout from which words continued to fall into the receiver as from a cornucopia. She stepped uncertainly down to the platform and then walked along it with her head very still, listening now to the words of Ana or Inés, commentaries on her previous commentary or on a similar situation with the same person or on a similar incident with an equally unbearable person, perhaps she, too, stepping out of a train or, having waited throughout the whole conversation with one hand free, now parking her small car at the other end of the city.

It's no longer necessary to wait to see each other once a week in order to comment upon the offenses that are inflicted upon us every day. They can now be commented upon on the go, only minutes after

the coffee grew definitively cold and you had to get out of your seat—
all because of that idiot!—and go warm it up in the microwave, taking advantage of that time to begin elaborating the principal points of
your commentary as you watch the little cup spinning: but who does
she take herself for? Who does she think she is?

4

I left the invitations in accordance with the procedure described by the Writer: **To myself I seem, when I have dealings with other people, to be, despite everything, the worst of them all, and all seem to take me for a fool, so much so that I tell myself: "Well then, I will in truth play the clown; your opinion doesn't matter because all of you, from first to last, are more vile than I am!"** Words that support this gloss: myself dressed as a lackey, with the diminished volume of such an individual, the sunken chest, the elbows, small hands folded in front of me, obsequious. Moving forward with little skips of my dancing shoes, a smile of placid stultification. All that in a quick message to their retinas and nervous systems. Entirely false and contrary to my true self (and feelings? And feelings. You know). Maneuvering among the currents of distrust I saw emerging from half-open doors, the spying maid or butler watching me advance from the front gate to the house. Applying my whole weight to it, pressing the trap down against the floor, without neglecting it for a second, fearing that it might suddenly spring free, give a leap and catch my throat in its toothed jaws. In Spanish, but as if it were a foreign language, masticated, slow and torturous. Romanov? No, not Romanov. (Like a second-rate artist who's always being confused with his competitors: Yes, you are Fili! No, I am not Fili, though I know and admire his work. What more do you want? Uri Geller, at your service. Though of course not Uri Geller either.)

Leaving those houses with the air of a beaten dog, a lackey (of Russian imperialism now), muttering poxes against them, who did they think they were? Doddering representatives of the doddering houses of Europe, little old men who went out to take the sun like those decrepit ancients in the Writer whose withered faces peer out over a courtyard, studying it with utmost care, its uneven flagstones, fearing it as they would a stormy sea where they might easily and, to my enormous rejoicing, break a leg, hearing their weak bones crunch, watching them fall to the ground from the height of their absurd belief that they might some day be called back: to rule! A thing that never in all of history! Ridding myself of this thought at top speed, unwilling or pained at having to concede that Batyk was correct. Who in his right mind, Batyk had laughed at us, at your mother and at me: what country would agree to acclaim as king someone invested with divine power? What country? In what possible way could you speak of sacred royalty, of the Davidic lineage of the kings of France or the lineage— what?—of the czars of Russia? How to retreat from the current state of triumphant and exemplary democracy to a state of abject (that's what he said: abject) subjugation to a king, to the caprices of a king? To betray, to turn away from the hard-won equality of the people (or, if you like, of the Russian people) with such an elevation, and establish, outside the law, beyond the reach of the law, a king?

How absurd an ambition! False kings, oh yes, gentlemen, a King of Pop or a Queen of Love Songs with the same credentials, pure falsity, knowing it to be pure falsity. And I the accomplice and spokesman of this absurd claim. Just a young schoolteacher, in fact, one who would never forget his humble origins, an immigrant myself, who would never treat a foreigner as those heartless kings had, Leka of Albania, all of them as if hiding out there in Madrid, their black hearts drawn there by the resplendent example of the king of Spain.

The servants and grooms who burst out laughing when I announced myself. The sixth? How many czars of Russia does that make this week, Ramón? And they didn't stop laughing as they rolled me down the stairs, delivering (this is true, Petya, absolutely true, it happened in Madrid) many blows to my back. These lackeys, unleashed and encouraged by their masters upstairs, dabbing at their lips with napkins of batiste linen and turning back to the *Financial Times,* not to *Hidalgia,* the (Spanish) magazine of nobility and weaponry, not to the *Gotha.* Coldly calculating the moment when a crisis in their countries would bring their people's patience to an end, after which they would go back, acclaimed as the legitimate heirs to the throne! Carried aloft on a wave of popular fervor! To restore the monarchy. Though we were not seeking, I thought at the time, my back aching terribly, we weren't trying to restore anyone. Ours was a better plan, more modern, less vulgar: a dynastic election.

I didn't manage to explain it because I didn't get past a single vestibule. I was not allowed to place our plan on the table, for which purpose I would have requested, with the greatest respect and consideration, that His Excellency move aside the plate bearing the Hohenzollern coat of arms (the china saved from the rockets of the T-34s in '45, in Bucharest). And at other houses I only managed to leave invitations— without a seal! I realize now, without a coat of arms!—in the mailboxes.

A despot of that kind, deformed by centuries of rule and consanguineous marriage, centuries of despotic power, how to get him off your back, Batyk had asked me jeeringly, how, without elections?

Easy, I could tell him now, without having dared to answer him then, neither I nor your mother, but now, full of hate: easy. I myself guiding the plotters through the dark passageways of the palace to Michael of Romania's quarters, smoking torch in my left hand, katana in my right, to bring an end to his absurd claim in one fell swoop.

5

Imagining and understanding Plato's wrath in Syracuse as he watched the coast of Sicily recede, his eyes burning with tears, all hope of a Philosopher King gone. Well, not that idiotic Dionysius; not in Syracuse. But a philosopher or scientist king somewhere else: why not? A physicist such as Louis-Victor Pierre Raymond de Broglie, a blood prince with deep knowledge of quantum mechanics, discoverer of the undulating nature of matter: why not call upon him to reign?

Still attempting a solution. Imagining there might be one toward which to direct my steps. Until chance put it in my path, without deep thought or meditation. A solution that at first I believed to be outside the logic of the Book, but then I came to understand that no, steered by it as if along iron rails. Because I saw, Petya, when I left the Marbella station and headed out aimlessly along the Paseo Marítimo, a sign high atop a hotel toward which, when I had read it, without knowing what was guiding my steps, I began making my way with entire and perfect confidence.

Knowing that only thus: the only solution. That the Russians, in Russia, would have noticed the same hotel I'd just noticed, placed their index finger on the glossy photo of the hotel, at the level of the sign several feet high (but diminutive in the photo), certain it was the best, the most luxurious. They from bad taste: it was the Grand Hotel. Me from the taste instilled by the Writer: the Grand Hotel (of Balbec).

Easy to convince those tourists to attend a party very close by, along the beach, after the day's heat had diminished.

And I entered the lobby certain I would find them there, my future guests. But this was what I found, Petya.

6

I found a man—it's unlikely that he was a gentleman—standing in front of the reception desk who attracted my attention powerfully the minute I walked in. His blond hair and awkward bearing, the ponderousness of a nouveau riche who must constantly give to understand —with his manner of stopping to scan an empty spot between the armchairs in the lobby or speciously consult his watch with an expression of irritation or complacency, depending on whether he was on time or running late—his new status, the importance he's gained in his own eyes.

The way he speciously straightened the lapels of his raspberry-colored blazer, bringing his chin down close to his chest, his neck tormented by a wide tie that was out of place and out of climate.

And I felt attracted by that unknown face, unknown though familiar —in its general aspect? Touched by a vulgar and predictable taste, smiling through the fluorescent light. I crossed the lobby for a chat, friendly. They always find it odd, let me tell you, to be addressed by me. They are my friends but don't know it; they deny me and my friendship. Together, I would say to them, in the trenches of socialism! How's that? In the trenches! The trenches of socialism! But now, almost next to him, I changed my mind, his face clearly illuminated by the massive gold watch that slipped forward on his wrist as he raised the tiny telephone, little blue screen to pink earlobe. The gleam of his too new shoes, unmarked by wear (small and overly elaborate coffins are what such shoes always remind me of when I see them, unworn, in stores). I walked past him and limited myself to calling: Sasha!—a name invented on the spot, any name. He turned in surprise, reached within that beam of light by my call. And without taking the phone from his ear he studied me from head to toe and spat back: *"Nu, i kak banani v etom godu v tvoem Gondurase?" Well, how are the bananas this year in your Honduras?* (Or wherever it is you're from, he meant.)

The cutting phrase, the tone. To the point that I regretted having addressed him. He himself in a rush to abandon the Asiatic depths, little taste for fraternizing with a former ally, all that. Vast zones of his past totally clear to me: breakfasts of cheap sausage not three years ago, hard-boiled eggs in the train's café car for the two-day trip, a mother and a father back in Russia.

I pretended to have mistaken him for someone else. I said: "I've mistaken you for someone else." And he let it go, knowing I was lying, conscious that my retreat was due to his harsh response, the bulldog hostility he had turned on me.

You don't want to? Then I don't either, I explained to him, my eyes fixed on the elevator.

"Kirpich?"

7

I had calculated: a *garden party,* the effect of fair-haired aides-de-camp fluttering across the grass distributing pamphlets which candidly recounted our plan, your mother's and my plan, the speed and simplicity with which leaflets can recount and explain the world: the Russian tradition of and love for monarchy, the fervor of a people who despite the errors of an entire century (or of almost a century, almost a century is better, Nelly), that despite the many errors (and horrors! And horrors) had not—ever!—stopped loving and venerating their czars, the imperial family. Who acknowledged the monarchy as the clearest and most natural and most perfect for a country, indisputably identical to the authority of a father.

An inaugural ball, the snobbery such a thing would awaken, that we could churn up around an inaugural ball. The reporters we'd have from many TV channels—guests passing by in the background smiling idiotically at the cameras, so much nonsense to talk. The dresses to describe, the celebrities who'd pose for a photograph with the new king and queen or czars of Russia, the men in tuxedos, the women in long gowns, the hairstyles of the Duchess of York and Athina Onassis, the impossible hats on certain ladies, strange as antigravity engines. The enthusiasm the celebration would generate across the world, the early-morning dash to the kiosk for the front pages, something with which to fill up and structure an otherwise empty Sunday. With this: caravans of Mercedeses (or of Rollses, I'd have to exchange the Mercedes for a Rolls), a policeman's gloves holding a bouquet of roses, in black and white on the *Tribune* and in color on the *Sun*, the miraculous absence of security measures because so beloved a king, because the Russian people, so many years without a king. How enchanting it would be, the enthusiasm it would give rise to, how marvelous it would be to restore the imperial house of Russia.

Now if a true Russian noble had appeared before them he would have struck them as false. Like a young, virginal, and untalented actress who can't manage to be convincing in the role of a young, virginal girl. We wouldn't invite the Grand Duchess Maria. The Russian people wouldn't understand her: a good lady, but a little bit, perhaps just a tiny bit fat, the lumpy figure of the lady in number eleven who goes downstairs to get her milk every morning. Vanquished by Nelly's breathtaking beauty, very much in the Russian tradition, Petya, your mother, the beauty pageants that Ivan Kalita (or the Terrible) organized in 1547 and in 1561. A great deal of intelligence in that idea of Kalita's, an absolute sure thing, a solidly historical detail: girls, vestals from across Russia, a beauty contest in all rigor, parading in bathing suits, wreathed in smiles, standing up to Kalita's interviewers (or Kalita himself) with political platitudes, embracing the winner with false affection (nails long as spears ready to bury themselves in her back), the tears of happiness of the newly chosen czarina. Unerringly the most beautiful and intelligent woman—what doubt could there be?—in the whole country. A strictly historical antecedent, the intelligence and subtlety of the northern Slavs: only the most beautiful queens, only the wisest kings.

Which would all be received with understanding because of the total madness of the Russian people. The TV program I watched one night, my mouth gaping, not believing what my eyes were seeing: an imbecile, an idiot, an impossible man, who was passing himself off as the grandson of the last Romanov! And all Russia was supposed to believe this on the basis of a single test, a laughable demonstration in a TV studio. Do you know what such and such a word means in Greek? Such and such a word in German? Oh! Excellent! And I have written here (the host consulting his notes) that you know . . . how to tune a piano! Perfectly! Am I right or have my assistants misinformed me? Yes? . . . Excellent! A piano! To the studio! Though without your tools . . . It's a long process . . . Some other time. Better yet, why don't you say something to us? Something in Slavonic, old or ecclesiastical Russian.

The fact that the person who claimed to be a Romanov spoke many languages fluently had seemed to his children, crowded together at his feet like the children of a miller (in the Writer), to be the final and convincing proof that their father was the son of the last emperor, miraculously saved. Who had survived and triumphed over his hemophilia and the terrible eyes of Yurovksi, the gaze of deepest hatred cast on him in that cellar, where he knew enough to lie still, Alexei, while he saw the bullets that were nearing him turned away by the force of the years that remained to him to live. His sisters no, Anastasia even less so, and not his parents, Nicholas and Alexandra, either. The bullets that flew past him and buried themselves in the sodden wallpaper at his back like the rays of a distant star which, through the effect of the gravitational lens, Petya, bypass the sun and end up shooting into your eyes, the day of an eclipse, in 1919. The same year when Alexei recovered consciousness in the middle of a forest, got up, walked, asked for help at a peasant isba, the memory of his former life as heir to the throne flowering colorfully in his mind, placing itself between his eyes and the sole of a shoe that had to be nailed down (such was his adopted father's profession).

Wasn't it enough to make you die laughing? A madness like the one Larissa had laughed and jeered at, and rightly so? We had to elude, to leap over it: not a restoration or an inauguration. Neither would I tell them that the invitation was from the czar and czarina of Russia (too much, no?). Better to say a party thrown by some nouveaux riches . . . How rich? "Very rich, believe me, I wouldn't lie about a thing like that." Looking them straight in the eye: "Very rich, you know?"

8

"Kirpich?" Of course not. Why would it be Kirpich? Just some Russian or another, an old pal (said with irony).

The sinister man I had to pass on my way into the elevator and whom I forgot instantly, intent on seeking out my guests across the hotel, the Russians who in all certainty were now populating it, after having discovered this one example who was, in any case, impossible to invite to the party. At least not dressed like that, in the blazer with the gilded buttons. Without having resolved what I would do, almost happy about the failure of my trip to Madrid, the impossibility of the party, free now of the obligation to sell the stones in order to come up with money for musicians, flowers, and caviar.

Without any result whatsoever, not one tourist in the hallways, not on nine and not on twelve, upon quick inspection (holding open the elevator doors), traveling back down. But when I'd returned to the lobby and the elevator doors opened again, without yet having taken my hands from the nickel-plated rail or made a clear sign of intent to get out, I saw a radiant face come in, a face that filled up the space in front of me. A woman with red hair and Asiatic cheekbones, the transparent skin of her throat. Filling the space of the elevator from wall to wall. I blinked and weighed more for a second or two, felt that I was sinking because the elevator was rising. The new passenger took a step toward the glass, seemed to go into ecstasy at the sight of the glass wall, growing as well, her torso and her legs, more visible and coming into focus. The freckles on her face, the incredible mauve of her eyes glowing more intensely.

"My God," I couldn't restrain myself and exclaimed in all sincerity, wanting to warn her, "you can't go out in the sun with that skin." And, eyes squinting, I pointed it out to her, the sun, round and flaming on the other side of the tinted glass.

This woman, the tourist, dressed with impeccable taste: the blue silk blouse forcibly containing her breasts, the string of chalcedony across the fresh skin of the clavicle, the same red color illuminating her shoes, with absolute (Western) elegance. So much so that I pointed once more to the sun and to the freckles on her face because for a moment I thought that dressed like that, with such good taste: not a Russian. Perhaps only from the north, from a place without summers, going south every year to toast in the sun.

"Well," she answered, "in just the same way, in a hotel near here, a nice, friendly young man like you, decently dressed . . ."

(I was a bit more than decently dressed, I wanted to tell her, the laughter dancing in my eyes until I heard her: the horrible confusion.)

"They talked, agreed to see each other and . . . just like that! He had stolen her purse."

Such a bad beginning, Petya! Me as a hotel elevator thief. I'm almost ready to let her go, I let her go, so disconcerted was I: the doors of the elevator opened and her face and legs, her tattooed ankle, disappeared. Impossible to overcome such ill will, so much suspicion. Having descended to the lowest point of my mission, at zero. On such a bad footing. A Lancôme consultation! My ridiculous Lancôme consultation!

The breath of perfume she left behind: violets. The sun warming my arms, my feet slightly sinking into the carpet, a horrible hotel carpet.

But something curious here, some kind of fate: I'd forgotten to press the button, and no one had summoned the elevator from the lower floors (there's no elevator man in hotels nowadays: you do it yourself). The elevator cabin stopped there, the air-conditioning blowing on my neck. The elevator bell rang, I heard it ring from a place as far away as the sun and felt the doors slide open at my back. The distant hum of the cocktail hour reached me once more, snatches of music, the bartender's unbearable banter, some vulgarity in reference to the unknown lady, the Russian: "Did you get a load of that chick?" Or "Pretty hot, isn't she?" something like that. Not that vulgar myself, Petya, I would never have said or shouted that as the man carrying a tray through the lounge chairs did.

Very impressive she must be indeed, I said to myself then (I knew that, I'd noticed it immediately), for this waiter with so many women, so many Swedish girls (though, why Swedish? Not particularly pretty), so many Italians . . . And I felt a slight, oh so light, almost imperceptible oscillation or feeling that the floor was giving way and the red of her feet, the kid glove, the tattooed ankle entered my field of vision once more. She put her hand on my back and gave me a friendly pat: "Don't be upset," she said. "Not every girl is as smart as I am. You'll be able to fleece some of them. Anyway, I like your shirt. Do all the swindlers in Marbella dress as well as you do?"

9

(Everything that is written has an author, and every author, an intention.)

I didn't turn around right away, Petya. I don't like being treated like that. I do like being treated like that. Certain women: the lapis lazuli trinket on her wrist. What to say to her? I have seen it—you know?—your plastic purse, made of that hard transparent vinyl with a flowery print: do you think I imagine money in there? Do you think I don't know there's only sunblock, face powder, lipstick? And anyway, how much money, ever, in the purse of a Russian woman? I didn't say that but thought it, and then I had to say to myself: look how she's dressed, stupid! More money on that woman, more money has passed through her fingers than you've seen in your life (well, there were the stones, that's true, the diamonds in my pocket—but they were fakes!). I studied her mauve eyes once more. Security, confidence, confidence in having seen me from behind: an inoffensive lad, crestfallen, there in the elevator.

"What do you do, apart from . . . ?" She didn't finish her question, laughed (apart from stealing she'd meant, jokingly, now knowing or now almost sure that I didn't steal).

And here, Petya, I knew that I would have to begin from so far back, go back so far and so implausibly that I desisted. How to say to her—you know?—"I work for the emperor of Russia?" Or present myself, with a click of the heels: "Jacques-Bénigne Bossuet, tutor to the dauphin"?

And what had seemed so easy to me, to spread word of the simple idea of the party among the Russian tourists, struck me at that moment as clearly impossible. And still more so with a woman like that, very refined, her eyes cleanly delineated. Nearly thirty (younger than Nelly, one or two years older than Larissa), at the point in her existence when gravity comes knocking at her door, to suspend from her cheeks those heavy weights that, in advertisements, pull them down. Terrible. And lovable and pitiable.

The elevator doors slid open. I held them back with my hand, gallantly. I said: "I know what I said about the sun was stupid. Something you know or you must know, of course. But the sun is very strong here."

It was then that she asked: "But, who are you? What do you do?"

I hadn't foreseen this type of question. I mentally reviewed a great number of professions, placing them before her eyeballs like an oculist trying out lenses on a patient's eyes. I placed a thousand images there: myself as a dancer, with thick gold chains or without them, as a painter of seascapes (on the Costa del Sol), a specialist in quantum physics. I was tempted to tell her a marquis (like Gumpelino), but no, impossible. I paused then at the portrait of the talented schoolmaster, adopted the air of an old-fashioned tutor so that she'd be able to imagine me in close-fitting pants and a frock coat. I explained, thus attired (at least in my body language): my life in your house, my classes for the boy, and more recently, just yesterday, the matter of the party. She gave me a shrewd glance, understanding it immediately, my plan. Her lips grew then and moved to tell me something, and her eyes shone, a brief shudder ran across her from head to toe while her forehead, her hair, and her chest swelled and grew, swelled and diminished in a second.

Don't fall asleep, Petya! Such a woman!

Claudia was her name. I would have offended her if I'd shown her the letter Nelly and I had composed the day before to their throneless Majesties. No need for that. She asked me some questions, lingered over a couple of points. I explained them to her in detail. She played with the collar of her blouse for a moment, rolling it around her finger, letting it go. She conjectured: about twenty in our group, ten, maybe, in the other, the next hotel over.

To convince only her, to tell only her the story and the nature of my mission. That would be enough. I followed her weightlessly down the half-illuminated hallway, the force and intelligence of her calves lit from behind, the perfect equation of the curve at her waist. We stopped in front of her room, she went in, and turned to close the door softly, smiling all the while. We'll see each other two nights from now, she said, this Friday, no? and closed the door with a pleasant click and turned the lock, without appeal. Three rooms farther down an absurdly fat woman and a horribly fat man, a matrimonial alliance of obesity, came out into the hall, walked toward the elevator. The inadvisability of inviting people like that, tourists in shorts, people like the man I'd met down below.

10

Because I had, and this was the worst of it, Petya, what weighed on me most in that hallway, to put my plan into practice. The need to go ahead with it, the fatigue of all my past failures. Seeing it with absolute clarity, and not only in the Book: the only possible path to money, the most logical way of escaping from that situation without having to steel myself to enter the shop, then stroll around the jeweler's glass display case, studying the jeweler himself without him realizing it, wait until there were few or no clients left inside, then step forward to get his attention, preparing myself.

To sidestep in one swoop such a moment of discouragement, plunged into the most violent gravitational oscillation by the apparition of this third mass, large and luminous as a gigantic sun, like the sun of Aurora (in the Writer), not ceasing for a second to think about her, about Claudia, the beauty I'd just met. I knew it! I knew it! I knew it! I shouted to myself on my way back down to the lobby.

I had imagined it, the beach, its hotels, full of women like that. I would like, I told her, I would be enchanted, I explained to her, to dance with you. Waltzing smoothly through the garden after nightfall, though can there be a *garden party* by night or only during the day, with illuminated tents beneath the floodlights, the white, cropped jackets of the mariachis, their trumpets burnished with toothpaste?

Certain that the confusion would only be multiplied if I spoke to her of the Book, of my love for the Book. As on that occasion, newly arrived at your house, with your mother. I preferred, and it is something I advise you most earnestly always to do, Petya, to lie. I led the conversation far away from my (real, Petya, real) past as a smuggler and Saint Petersburg dandy. I hesitated a second, paused before answering her, because I didn't want to be a tutor in her eyes, a failure, it's the truth, without money. Who to tell her that I was, then, after so many years and in such swampy circumstances, on so viscous a sea? The watermark of a black past, the hologram that, seen in the sunlight, would give away the hidden traces of my existence? Finding all of my carefully set traps empty: nary a wolf cub nor a baby bear, not a coin earned in years; no money and no fixed occupation. I had planned to live only in the knowledge of the Book, never looking back, and this had seemed a more distinguished occupation, but not even: now here I was, plunged into the murkiness and opacity of your parents' swindle.

Because I asked myself the same question you've wondered about, son: Couldn't they, wouldn't it be easier to sell the car, mortgage the house, just get out of there? Why get in any deeper?

"No, they'd catch up with us wherever we went," Nelly explained. "That's not the solution."

She'd pondered the question deeply without allowing anyone else to interfere—Batyk, for example, with his stupid ideas. A different and unique solution each time she threw the dice of the story into the air, the possible paths of escape. And they fell with iron logic: imposture, the delirium of imposture (even she herself saw it that way), because otherwise, no matter where they went to hide: the outpost of German cheesemakers in Chile, an abandoned mission in Paraguay, or even, spinning the globe, bringing the finger down on another sea, the ex-hippie colony in Goa.

Tenth Commentary

I

The Writer awakens, opens his eyes in that grotto brimming with gold and jewels, and exclaims: **Oh, Wonder of Wonders!** Richly attired: the Malay *kris* at his waist, the turban at whose center the Koh-i-Noor, the Mountain of Light, glows ineffably. Toward the fantastic territory of the Book, where no one will ever be able to dethrone him, revoke his authority, cut him down to size with evidence. No principles to undermine, no evidence of his spuriousness to accumulate. No one, mounted on his shoulders, will be able to see any farther, as idiotic people (and the Commentator) claim. Farther than what? Than a bird? Farther than its feathers, farther than its beak, farther than its being as a bird? There is nothing farther, no "territory beyond"—a human construct that seeks to supplant the succinct and diaphanous idea of the Book.

The force and the shattering wonder of the passage where Marcel, on an exploration of the Arctic Circle, discovers a new and unnameable kind of water, a liquid thick as gum arabic. The commingled astonishment and intense chill this marvel arouses in his breast. And throughout this passage, the first description, the origin of a new machine, for he imagines this water, Petya, taking on density, condensing not only in the Writer's mind but also in that of the most minor and insignificant technician. The household use to which we could put it: no longer laboriously excavating swimming pools, but erecting in any garden a beautiful cube of these calm waters **like the hues of a changeable silk,** says the Writer, in **every possible shade of purple.**

A Mountain of Water! Sparkling in the sun. Can you imagine it? Imagine it!

In which we would swim, plunging in without causing the structure to collapse, for it would hold its rectangular shape, its cubic constitution. We would ascend through it, our arms open wide, like birds in a solid patch of sky.

Quite a vision, isn't it: men flying through this water that has somehow, we don't know how, been condensed? Isn't it?

And behind every house, in every garden, such a cube would rest on the surface of the earth where a swimming pool was once dug into it. Having learned to hold your breath and accelerate within the mass of water, pushing off from wall to wall, calculating and controlling your momentum so as to stick only your head outside, gulping in a mouthful of fresh air, your hair dripping, the sun sparkling on your wet head. Coming out, breaking the film of the surface before the astonished gazes, one head still below—heads up, guys!—laughing and taking a deep breath, shouting out for pure joy, then plunging back inside the cube.

A prodigy, a fabulous invention, this marvel that we would examine, attired like a couple in an engraving of the World's Fair, the bowler hat, the tiny, unnecessary parasol stuck into the lawn. Or else both of us in shorts, young ourselves, turning our backs on the cube, grown accustomed to the miracle, however strange it may seem, for it's still a miracle even in 2049, a miracle, and so is my vision of the young men rising up through the cube, slicing through it like birds soaring across the sky. The undulating block on the green lawn. Have you seen it? Shall I turn off the generator? The force field?

No, leave it on a moment longer, please—I'm still looking at it. (You should look, too.)

2

Or what amounts to the same thing: I sold the stones without a second's hesitation, because the consequences that can be derived from the Book are more than clear: somewhere in the house, I could never figure out where, your father had a laboratory, a replica of the laboratory in the Urals. Let's say it was in the cellar, and that he went down wearing a leather apron, a jeweler's magnifying glass at his forehead, the straps cinched tight around his skull, through the graying hair. No pincers in his hands—though a scene in a movie would have required that—but I'm better informed about the scientific procedure: no pincers in my hands either. Unnecessary when you're growing diamonds as big as garbanzos, diamonds he tossed into a glass jar or an empty vase like candies in a pediatrician's office.

He would open the room, a dimly lit place, the shadow of his big body, lips opening in a smile that broke the outline of the shadow on the wall. Or else he would release the hatch on a sort of glass diving bell and step inside, wearing a waterproof suit made of rubber or asbestos. Then he would switch on the machine after priming the edges of the growth chamber with a paste made of enriched metal or whatever it was.

Your mother didn't explain it to me in detail and I didn't ask. Just this: a portable installation that Vasily took out from under the bed and took with him into the bathroom, or an enormous, stationary press installed in the depths of the garden or in the Buryat's room, next to mine. He could fabricate diamonds of any color, any number of karats, she told me. Sapphire blue, ruby red, emerald green, raising or lowering the flame on the Bunsen burner (in a manner of speaking: in fact the apparatus was much more complex than that), increasing or diminishing the inclusions with extreme precision, sometimes leaving defects that seemed natural but were in fact perfidiously calculated. Enormous gems, like the Eugene or the Coromandel, even larger. At will. Essentially indistinguishable from natural stones. Not cubic zirconia: this is cubic zirconia and this, too—easy to tell the difference.

3

My first thought was red. Red for royal crimson, for the red of the sun. But then I understood: blue. For the sky, which isn't blue, and for the sea, which isn't blue either, and because blue is the color of deceit, the other colors of the spectrum filtered out: blue clearly favored in the design. For some occult reason, a cause I cannot discern: because life here, beneath the celestial vault, is a dream? And if that's true, then make it a large stone, Vasily, blue in color and immense as an orb. Forget the small colored stones we could try to pass off as real. Lots of money in that, perhaps, but the immediate impact is diminished. A single stone, on the other hand, heightens it. At the very top of the scale that establishes in descending order the value of all the others.

For how can you think, even for a second, about an antigravity shield when you, Vasily, are the best and only one in the world, the best counterfeiter (or manufacturer—yes, manufacturer!) of diamonds? A man who could attract to himself—just as the metallic inclusions attract and allow to condense upon themselves, atom by atom—the wealth of an entire nation? The chaotic solution in suspension that is Russia today, reordered into a coherent grid of lines, structured around a king. Not at the top of a pyramid, not a pyramid: an immense sphere, a blue sphere, through which, traveling toward the center, descending toward the nucleus, the traveler from Vega would meet a king, a czar, you, Vasily, your lips carved in blue stone, illuminated like an orb.

Toward which we would conduct rows of noble electors, smoothing down the hair at their temples before entering, hats in hand, without any word floating before them, because we would have eliminated all commentary or text from their minds, anything that could possibly cloud the vision of that immense diamond, proof of the fathomless wealth of the man they must proclaim czar. Their toothless mouths, some with gold teeth, gaping open before the light and brilliance "of the largest diamond ever seen"—that, yes, easily. And that phrase, "the largest diamond ever seen," would go in first of all and clean out the spot in their memory where the vision was to lodge and then gently set the immense diamond there in that region of burned-out neurons. To radiate out from there, to shine like a unique idea, grasped in a heartbeat: our czar! His eyes retro-illuminated by the light in their brains, regretting having met his gaze, denying having read the scientific reports you'd mentioned to them in the garden, that treatise on the biological life of stones. "In which journal? I'm not aware of that paper. In which academy, you say? In the Urals? We never go to the Urals. Do you know Dr. Brunstein, of Philadelphia? He was the first scientist I heard mention what you've just, etcetera." All their impertinences, you know? Effaced as if by magic from their faces, first pale with an understanding of their error and then radiant at the opportunity to be among the first to serve you, to prostrate themselves before their king, to exclaim without a shadow of doubt: czar! rex! All would open their hearts to you, use their lips and the vehemence of their narration to elevate your figure, the story of your unique diamond and how they had doubted you at first and then thrown themselves at your feet to venerate you.

You'll say to me: at the mere sight of a stone? At the mere sight of a stone! Beautiful, of a brilliance, a resplendence never before seen, a stone that would have an entire vast chamber to itself in the palace of their memories.

4

I know it will work: it worked with the first of the Russian imposters. In a bathroom, where, humiliatingly but with dignity intact, he was serving a Polish nobleman, an unworthy individual, a minor noble in whose home he, Dmitri, had taken a position as a valet. And in the bathroom of that house, for the trivial matter—can you believe this?—of some water that was a degree or so too cold to the touch of his soft and cerulean back, he, that man, gave him a hard slap, a slap to Dmitri, the son of Ivan Kalita, miraculously saved from Godunov's knife. The emperor endured the affront, bowed humbly, and, with his cheek burning, said: "Sire, if you knew who your servant is, if you could imagine it, you would not behave so." The Pole, shivering in the tub but from cold rather than fear, replied: "Who are you? Who is it that I should not, in such a situation, my back placed in contact with water so unpleasantly cold, deal a slap to, my fingers delivering the message of my anger, etcetera?"

"I," Dmitri, still almost a boy, replied, "I am the son of Ivan Kalita, and my throat escaped Godunov's knife in 1591, for another child, put in my place, was the one who lifted his neck to the criminal flattery of the murderer when he said, 'What a lovely necklace you are wearing today, *Gosudar*,' or 'Show me that lovely necklace, Prince.' And innocently the boy raised his chin to show off his beads—to the murderer!—opening an interstice in the bloc of his physical being that the murderer instantly took advantage of to slice open his neck, and the poor boy fell, convulsing and bathed in blood . . ."

That said, Dmitri drew from his clothing a gold baptismal cross studded with gems and placed it before the eyes of he who until that moment had been his master, and who now sat frozen with shock in the bathwater.

None other, the Polish nobleman said to himself: none but the Russian czarevitch could wear such a baptismal cross at his bosom. And he leapt from the tub and ran to his wife, ordering her to prepare the table for a banquet and invite all the other minor nobility. He returned to the bathroom where the pseudo Dmitri was waiting and invited him to rise, placing one hand upon his shoulder and gesturing with the other toward the brocade robe woven with golden thread and freshwater pearls, the cloak of sable, the sword of Toledo steel with its gold-plated hilt. Then he pushed open the leaded glass window to show him the beautiful horses that had been made ready: their manes hennaed and braided, their legs wound with silken ribbons, pawing the ground, steam rising from their snorting nostrils.

5

The effect your father's diamond had on me was identical! Unable to linger over any of the shades of blue, not a sapphire blue, nor an indigo: not cobalt. Deep and infinite as the waters of a frozen sea. It fluctuated, though not like the sky's changing face at sunset, trembling in the air as the light goes down; rather like the waters of a pond whose depths are shot through with white stripes of caustic light. Greater and more beautiful than any you have ever seen, Petya, the serenity and beauty of a lake in the midst of a meadow, all the light of morning in it. Enormous, glittering. I said: "Vasily, I have no words! . . ." (Something like that, I said.) Not even I myself . . .

He had listened with attention, had understood to perfection: a diamond as grand and luminous as the very idea of a king. Patiently grown at the rate of 0.2 karats a day. Its growth uninterrupted, or interrupted only at the moment when, mathematically: the largest diamond. Ever.

Because understand me: all that he'd suffered, the depths from which he'd had to ascend. I hadn't seen it that way, Petya, and blame myself for that. The most absolute poverty, the deprivation in which his entire childhood was spent, the life he had dreamed of, believing that he was allowed to rob, to swindle, in order to attain it. So far in the depths that he came to imagine that never, in all his years, would there be things, small pleasures like orange juice at breakfast, you know, day after day. A trick, that, to dupe the gullible—it must be: there could never be enough juice for so many people. And once in the West, he discovered in astonishment the golden sea of orange juice in which the simplest country folk of Valencia were floating. How he wept in secret at what he saw in Rome and Vienna, the pain he felt remembering his childhood, the hard clay of autumn before the first snow. His father, deaf and mute, face raised to the sky, snow falling on his silhouetted figure. That pained me, Petya, that image. Did you know that? Your grandfather, deaf and mute, all those years.

He had felt swindled himself, so why not swindle? It had to have begun very far back, Petya, in the deepest depths. Desperately seeking a shortcut to the light, to the money that was beginning to flow swiftly into the whole country like a river rushing back into its dry bed. Until he saw it: to change the gradient and grow, layer by layer, the most perfect diamonds ever fabricated. Never, no one in the whole universe. And he saw all that this could secure for him, not money, no, not a con job, that came later: fame, honor, a place in the Academy which—ay!—would soon cease to exist.

Determined, on the morning he had the idea of passing them off as real—counseled, it must be said, by the Buryat's dark heart—no longer to be a small man, the character in the Writer who dies of anguish for having sneezed on a count's bald head . . . To be the count himself, gravely mopping his head with a silk handkerchief and murmuring, without turning around: "Don't trouble yourself, it's nothing." That was the transformation he had sought, none of your blinding blizzards or the catastrophe of an overcoat for which he had scrimped and saved his whole life suddenly torn from his shoulders.

We crossed the garden, I walked alongside him, deeply touched. I said: "I know what you mean, Vasily, I understand perfectly: you'd like to invite Larissa to the party but can't." He shot me the glance of a king hidden in a cart (in Varennes). Infinite sadness in his appearance, his bad eye gone out entirely or like a dying ember. He got into the car, leaned toward the dashboard, started the engine. The way the front wheels of expensive cars bolt forward, dig into the turn, rear back, and take off in a single impulse—your father, the king, at the steering wheel.

6

And in the same flash of insight that accompanied my recovered dignity I knew what heraldic device would best suit our House. A frank and pithy vindication of imposture: *Esse est percipi.* Meaning: if you perceive a king, if a man with the bearing of a king, the august gaze of a king, the eloquent reserve of a king appears before you, then do not doubt that you are in the presence of a King, a Prince. Who also, in the bargain, God willing, will float without sinking, *Fluctuat nec murgitur*, like Paris.

In the first quadrant: the sea, the happy days, or days we would remember as happy, by the sea. A wavy field of azure and upon it, floating, the Castle, Miramar, the many-dollared mansion. A simple escutcheon, the scant furniture of a new dynasty: rising sun in splendor over illuminated diamond . . . Forgetting the attributes of the old Russian families, the Orlovs' falcon, the double-headed eagle of the Paleologos. Just as Napoleon himself once wisely abandoned the fleur-de-lis for bees of gold on field of azure. The blazon of a new dynasty, that of the Pool, upon which I would reserve for myself the modest role of supporter: a moor or savage, a natural man, a long-haired American, one foot forward, my tutor's quill poised at the ready. And reading from dexter to sinister, facing me, an animal with human face, a monster. Not a unicorn, not a lion rampant, not a mermaid in her vanity: the head facing two directions, in symbol of its duality, jaws gaping, viscous tongue hanging out.

7

I had stopped speaking to him—for how truly the Writer affirms: **the earth is full of people who don't deserve to be spoken to**! To Batyk, that is, whom I ran into after having said good-bye to your father, having heard his tremendous confession. Stretched out next to the water, in the full light of the sun, his falsity all the more visible for that, like an ordinary lizard and not one from the island of Komodo. He saw me coming toward him across the grass, crossing the garden and about to pass him by. He stuck out his forked tongue and spoke.

"They move me." He was addressing Astoriadis, who was eating grapes (bought with my money) from a plate. "What we have here is two charming friends who have never failed to amuse me. A pair of innocents who imagine that someone, some time, will take their plan seriously, the absurd idea of an emperor . . . I've said as much to Nelly, I've insisted on smaller diamonds, for engagement rings: flood the market with them, sell them as real . . ."

It was something like that, what he said, Petya. Bragging, essentially, about his unbridled passion for lying. At a moment when we'd all decided to turn our backs on him, had understood that his was a false solution. But not Batyk. He returned over and over again to the same point: Lie, lie! he shouted. Never tell the truth, on the contrary: always lie. Never affirm or cite or even allude to the line about fooling some of the people some of the time but not all the people, an entire country, all the time, a piece of sheer nonsense to which no sentient adult would ever subscribe. A phrase which, correctly glossed (he was openly mocking my method, Petya), says—and he raised his finger, as I was supposedly in the habit of doing—but I don't do that, do I? I don't assume false scholarly airs?—quite the opposite: "Swear and perjure yourself, but don't ever reveal your secret." Here he laughed odiously, rubbing his thighs hard and looking me up and down in amusement.

To what a striking degree was Batyk's taste bad! How vulgar and plebeian of him to have replaced the eye he lost in a fight with that diamond! The dendrites of his lies, the metallic iridescence of their tangled web glittering hatefully on his chest, Petya, a very thin thread, almost invisible, which until that instant I hadn't noticed and finally perceived then only because of a reflection that shimmered across him as if he were a puddle of oil.

8

I didn't open my mouth for a second or unclench the fist in which I was hiding the Pool. I moved away without turning my back on him and went into the kitchen, still with enough time before the guests' arrival to implement the second half of my plan: something simpler but with no less impact (the description and operative principles of a bubble machine there in the Book). I built it quickly and effortlessly before Lifa's astonished eyes. I had only to assemble the parts and dip the perforated disk in the soap solution and the machine's blower produced a bubble in every orifice, the smaller bubbles rising more easily through the air, clearing the wall with greater agility, falling without hurting themselves on the rough asphalt, wisely adapting themselves to the sharp protrusions of this new situation, transforming myself into a different young man, a new me in the dark street. I would cast a final gaze over my shoulder: there's only one city in the world whose name corresponds to this condition, to a lighter, more buoyant soul: Los Angeles. Wasn't that a lovely name to dream of here in Miramar, knowing that all of us were heading toward the inevitable bursting of this bubble?

I went back to the living room, took one of the elephant tusks from its base and put the Pool there. I assessed the thickness of the glass with my eyes, and out of the usual fear of robbery and renewed disgust with Batyk, I thought, without taking my eyes from the stone, about how the Writer introduces an ostrich into the party in Kimberley, for, strangely, his characters travel down to Kimberley, to a drawing room in Kimberley (South Africa), where the ostrich swallows a stone that is on display, a diamond of incalculable worth.

I don't believe I need comment at any length on that passage for you, only this: in the ostrich's warm craw, the stone, mingled with the other stones the bird uses to grind up the grains it eats, survives intact, due to the thin film of grease covering it. Then months later, after being extracted and cleaned, the diamond explodes.

But before that, on the night of the party, the Writer's characters, gathered in the drawing room, don't realize that the diamond has disappeared, nor does the Writer himself, waiting in the library where he'd been ushered as the music played and as the ostrich, unremarked by the other visitors, was crashing the party, moving one leg forward—its thick ostrich thigh (they sell them in the supermarkets now) as yet unfrozen—in the direction of the stone's flickering brilliance.

Here in Marbella we ran no risk of an ostrich coming in; not one family here keeps ostriches.

My plan would work. We had successfully eluded the danger.

9

Whatever you want, I'd told her, whatever you want: the idiotic and absurd notion of a King, an Empire. As long as it made her bend her waist more supply, arching her back in my arms like a tango dancer, the two of us on the dance floor at Ishtar while her husband dealt with the ambassador from Martinique. Myself seen in profile in far more photographs than were necessary, my head rising above the feather boa around her neck. The most beautiful woman, I must say that: despite Larissa's splendid, cloudless complexion and Claudia's pink-tinged skin, the most beautiful. Beauties that were similar though resolved in different color schemes: gold and turquoise for Larissa, ruby and violet for Claudia, and marble and onyx for my girl. The way her hair fell between her beautiful shoulder blades, the soft curve of her neck, the most beautiful woman, Petya, and the most sensual, your mother.

The way your mother's behavior toward me gradually changed— rather unpleasant at first, during the early weeks when she would invariably call me "Mr. Lonelyhearts," and then that same Lonelyhearts began growing and changing in her eyes and her esteem, along the lines of **I am the king of Babylon who makes the light shine on the earth of Sumer and Acadia.**

I hadn't wasted a second on sentimental calculations of the number of years she had on me, the number that would go by before I was the same age she was now. As in those novels where a young man falls in love with an older women or even, in the Writer himself, with the countess of Stermaria. There would be more women in Moscow and in seaport cities like Bordeaux and Lisbon, their breasts which I would capture in passing in my capacity as royal secretary, the lineup of pale breasts like faces along a hallway. Down which I would advance, strongly perfumed, on the way to my office. To rubber-stamp signatures with my right hand without my palm ever losing the conical shape of those breasts and without ever being tormented, even for a second, by the fear of death. Launching into a dance with some of them, their bejeweled arms and bellies, when, in midafternoon, I tuned in to the carefree burble of a happy day, the amber light of the hour, reclining my head on the bosom of the youngest one, having her read to me, Petya, fragments of the Book.

Vats of chilled wine in that garden, rose petals in the illuminated water.

I hadn't stopped looking at her for a single second, a single day. There had been many nights when I came back from the discotheque and wondered whether to go up and find her, whether her prelude to a kiss on the clifftop might end in something more. Sometimes I paused in the middle of a class, raised my eyes from the page and walked over to the window to see if she was there below, swimming in the pool. Circling around her, moving toward her with the inevitability of a sphere rolling, falling, and sliding along an inclined plane. **But, soft! What light through yonder window breaks? It is the east, and Juliet is the sun**, etcetera, precisely as in Marlowe. Standing, Petya, beneath the illuminated window of your parents' bathroom, the lawn dappled with colored lights. Nelly, at that moment, smoothly slipping into the foaming water in the round tub, checking first with her foot to see whether it was too cold or hot, the soft curve of her foot like a swan's feathered neck. (The secret desire to see her naked, to spy on her while she preened in front of the three-paneled mirror.) And more! First me, Petya (**on some occasions it incites lasciviousness**), then her, the two of us sliding down together along the smooth porcelain. Or, if she was startled to see me in her room, I would tell her it was only to show her the bubble machine, that pretext. In the dark bedroom I pushed open the bathroom door, the panel smoothly pivoted, slowly glided back, opening, and a vision was revealed to me in sharpest clarity and left me speechless: the wings and breast and neck of a bird.

An enormous bird.

10

Its powerful feet clutching the edge of the porcelain in an iron grip, its thighs covered with feathers like the thighs of a Lagerfeld model. The luxuriant resplendence of a garment made from the feathers of a single gigantic bird that had first been hunted and caught, and then carefully sewn, its fabrication supervised by the strong, knotty hand of Lagerfeld himself so that it would adhere perfectly to the model's torso and extend to midleg, leaving the muscular calves visible. The way she moved, like a tigress (though in this case, a bird). Falling, letting herself fall onto one hip, then the other. Settling on one hip as if to stay there a long while, then switching to the other. Without advancing in any direction: a bird in your parents' bathroom, poised on the edge of the circular tub known by its Japanese name: Jacuzzi. Arms demurely at the sides, leaning forward, balancing, with all the strength of its expression aimed toward its breast. The chin—of its face! a woman's face!—against the feathered breast.

Thrown off by surprise, Petya, without knowing where on earth that enormous, soft monster . . . Was it the holographic image of an immense bird that some Professor Kuropatov or, better yet, Professor Caligari had created in his laboratory, going farther than anyone else in the world here, too, in this new field: household avatars? A phantom, a creation of air? But then how could it be so vivid and so real? Repressing the impulse to go in and embrace it, as when we drew closer to the television the better to see the lovely newscaster's face and bump against the glass, in love . . .

The bird opened its mouth, balancing for a second on the edge, and let well up through its breast, with no effort by the neck muscles, a first note, a prolonged sigh that flowed out long and uncontainably as it tried to open the hands that had remained trapped, slender and fragile, in the bones of its wings.

That song reached into my soul, lifting me above the house and above the entire coastline and bringing me back in one second. The memory of that vastness, the hollow or void of a feeling expanding my chest, its song crossing through me like the blade of an airy knife that twisted in my heart and lodged in all the chambers of my soul. And without knowing what I was doing, without understanding that the movement might give me away, I pushed the door farther to see her better. My hand swinging out over the tessellated floor, I checked the windows, swept the ground with my eyes to try and glimpse the projector or generator of that image, the woman, the bird (I didn't find it). My foot went to follow the hand and step out onto the floor's mosaic when a thought made me stop, this passage, flashing across my mind: **"Sperrit? Well, maybe," he said. "But there's one thing not clear to me. There was an echo. Now, no man ever seen a sperrit with a shadow; well, then, what's he doing with an echo to him, I should like to know? That ain't in natur', surely?"**

It was Nelly! And I realized this, as well, and right away, from the necklace around the bird's neck which I'd seen her wear so often when she swam in the pool, for she never took it off to swim. Radiating now from her neck as she sang and slowly turned her head, rays of light emanating from the stones dappling the walls, the windowpanes, the floor, with multicolored points. The echo of her song having prevented me, Petya, from making a false step, giving away my presence, having the queen raise her eyes and approach me speedily with the jerky movement of a running bird, setting down its feet or claws along an invisible line, to take out my eyes, harshly, with her beak, one and two (pecks), blinding the eyes that had spied on her, although she was not naked: only transformed, terribly transformed into a bird.

But what was she afraid of? What was she afraid of, that I couldn't be allowed to see? Toward what abyss were we sliding without my being able to see it, this song speaking to me of the danger that menaced us, her gaze fastened on her face in the water, the reflection broken up by her tears. Unable to rest in midflight, unable to glide calmly along with arms opened out in a cross through the indigo of the sky and the reds of the horizon, for this once in our lives, Petya. Because even in our flight . . . Furies, such as Batyk.

The gong in the entryway boomed: someone, an important guest, had arrived. A *daaaaa*, thick and violet-colored, came through the window, flowed into the bathroom. The bird raised its eyes to look at it and discovered me standing next to the door. It was about to tell me something, about to open its mouth, but first Batyk, down below in the drawing room, opened his beak and squawked: His Most Serene Highness Simeon of Bulgaria!

I ran downstairs. The party was waiting. There wasn't a second to lose.

"My mama?"

"Your mama."

Eleventh Commentary

I

. . . **a thoroughly good man, no more dreaming of the horrors in which he was entangled than the eye at noonday in midsummer is conscious of the stars that lie far behind the daylight.** This from the Writer.

Meaning that the young tutor, his frank face turned toward them, allowing the light that bathed their luminous figures to enter his eyes, was incapable of understanding where the currents of the plot were flowing, the afternoon's cascading red mane streaming toward the horrible denouement. The boy getting out of the pool, the Buryat invariably standing next to it (I'd never seen him swim and how could I not mistrust a man like that, a man who mistrusted water?): all of it evanescing, bodies made of smoke that vanish if someone opens a window or porthole; we see them lengthening, limbs pulled out in whatever direction the breeze or howling gale is blowing, breaking apart at a neck that stretches too thin, all of them disappearing into the same vortex, heads detached from torsos. The simple structures that, on a nuclear testing ground, represent a family, a house and its yard, all eradicated by the expanding shock wave, sucked up by the blast behind them.

And the tutor, in this scene of the Book, is unable to discern anything, makes no conjecture. Which the Writer alludes to in this surprising image: of a man no more capable of perceiving **than the eye at noonday in midsummer is conscious of the stars that lie far beyond the daylight.**

Can you imagine or conceive of, in all the literature of the universe, a better, greater image of unconsciousness, involuntary blindness?

No. And it will serve to illustrate—you understand?—any similar state of mind or equivalent confusion in any other man or tutor. Forever.

2

I didn't need days to understand it, to discover the monstrosity of her deception, the perfidy of her fingers caressing my neck, tenderly interlaced with my hair. Horror! I had been prepared to give up everything, to jeopardize my trip to Amerika, to endanger my life for a woman who had thought of nothing from the very start but deceiving me, lying to me. A woman most unfortunately in love with her husband (and not her son's tutor). Who every time she'd come to see me on the pretext of some interest in the (princely) education of her son—you, Petya—had stuck, through the half-open door, a head full of the blackest schemes to deceive me and make me a vendor of gemstones, the remainder of her husband's vast production of colored stones. Having failed and miserably botched all sales missions themselves, finding themselves stranded on that plain in Spain, amid the desert dunes, and without seeing in any direction, neither from ahead nor from behind (turning back to scan the arid landscape), a knight, clad in gold and silver, glittering in the sun, coming to their rescue. In a terrible impasse, and mistrusting and hating Batyk, without my suspecting it and without their ever making it clear to me, Batyk, whose idea it had been, as you know, to swindle the residents of Saint Petersburg, and whose even worse idea it had been to hide out in Spain, and, worse still, in the last place in Spain they should have chosen, Marbella, a city rife with felons and Russian mafiosi.

But not them: they're merely scientists and amateur swindlers.

And one afternoon (I already told you about that afternoon, described it to you) they'd heard the knock at the door, the timid scratch of this small **Holgersson** whom they let in without taking their minds off the problem for a second. Hiring this diminutive personage to save the boy or at least momentarily distance him from the insufferably plebeian and lowbrow Spanish television, without interrupting even for a second their tortured deliberations. Until I tugged at the hem of your mother's dress and forced her, tiny as I was, to bend down, look down at the floor, and pointed out to her with my index finger a passage of the Book, its illuminated plates, the many tableaux that began moving before her astonished eyes. Here, I said to her: a way out and a solution. To all your problems. And I straightened and grew larger the longer they bent down, and I saw them stooping beneath the weight of the Book's evidence, and myself there, resplendent in the center of the room, until we reached the solution: the king, to become king. They looked at each other; she and her husband swiftly exchanged a look and conceived of the idea of swindling me, harnessing the strength of my generous heart and my candid goodness to their own, shadowy ends.

Where it says, for example, **without my being able to take a step or rather drop to the ground, return to earth, my feet a handsbreadth above the carpet, then falling slowly back down onto it, still plunged in my astonishment.** Which acknowledges, this passage, and must be interpreted—as I had to explain with patience to the person who had made her take off her necklace that morning, to Batyk —to mean that on the contrary she must never stop wearing the necklace, must come down every morning to breakfast in it. That the necklace, the sheer weight of the necklace, would tilt the floor beneath me so that I would roll easily toward her, attracted by its sparkle; that only thus would they convince me to sell the stones, that I would not cease to orbit near her, spinning before her chest like a bird caught in the slipstream of a larger bird. Prepared to save her (prostrate at her feet), to find—at the risk of my life—the money they needed in order to flee.

But that doesn't matter.

Or yes, it does matter. Explained with absolute clarity in the sixth book. When old Karamazov says, in the most literal way, requiring no commentary whatsoever: **And I have been lying, I've been lying all my life long, every day, every hour. Verily, I am a liar, the father of lies!**

And then, where it says, where I told myself: that a diamond cutter, a jeweler, must see himself as a ray of light or, even more peculiarly, as riding upon a ray of light. Must imagine himself entering the gem astride that ray of light in order better and more fully to understand the effect of the light on its interior, the walls against which the light will rebound and through which it will depart, refracted, to wound the imagination and deceive the eyes.

How could a woman like that not have known everything or have failed to deceive me: a woman like that, a siren, a bird-woman? Can you tell me, Petya? Can you, dear readers? How?

3

All right then, it doesn't matter: I loved her. All right then, it doesn't matter: this Book is the greatest ever written. All right then, it doesn't matter: we would get out of there, we would figure out how to make my plan work. I love her, I continue to love her, Petya. Even if there are things that cannot be explained. Obscure passages that defy the imagination and put the reader's credulity to the test. I know that; it doesn't stop me. Because it's more than likely that the original text was corrupted by Humblot, that the same envious hand that rejected the original manuscript may have interpolated phrases that do not figure in the first version and whose meaning, Your Majesty, can never be revealed (this to Simeon).

How long have I pondered these words, how often turned them over in my head: **God has disposed, and I believe this to be so, that not all are to be rich, for God knows very well why he did not allow the goat's tail to grow too long.**

For at first, in my adolescence, when I was reading the Book merely as a work of fiction and had no awareness or only some vague intuition of the mine of wisdom it is in reality, I tended toward an allegorical reading that was contrary to its literal meaning. In the sense that a longer tail on a goat wouldn't be the sign of a few powerful chosen ones, but only a caprice of nature from which to draw no moral or human implications. But now, with the years, I've come to suspect that the Writer's intention was more literal, very different from that which might be attributed to a writer addicted to the vice of obscurity such as Theophrastus Bombastus (aka Paracelsus). For yes: a few powerful chosen ones. And myself among those few, and your father and your mother among the few, and the Writer, let me tell you, not among the few, higher than the few, from which it can be deduced that I couldn't apply to her, to your mother, the same criteria by which we judge an ordinary member of the public, that she, like Your Excellency (this to Simeon), operates outside of the normal boundaries and, in effect, is excluded from my wrath. For she may have had her reasons for having acted thus, and I, in my insignificance, was not the man to judge her.

"My words, Majesty, are not calculated to gain your sympathy. I say that this is so because I feel it to be so. To understand things once more as they were understood prior to 1793 (when Louis was guillotined) or even to 1649 (when Charles was beheaded). Or as if the interval between 1917 and today did not exist. The horror of the two wars erased, a time in which, from the porthole of my ship, I see no blue sky and purple clouds or planets below, only death, -isms, genocidal camps. Is that life? Yes, but not in human form. A pseudoformation, a gulf in time, a shoot or bud that must be eliminated. I've repeated this to myself over the course of countless nights, for if there are so few flowers and only one sun, then why pretend to be all of us flowers, all of us suns? And the ether in which they breathe and exhale their fragrance? And the branches, Simeon, that hold up the sun, which shines and revolves amid their green formations?

"Without lingering for a second, Usia, over the fallacious argument that such an idea is outmoded, that this is an anachronistic form of government, from which it could be deduced that more modern or advanced forms, methods for governing that are intrinsically better, or more progressive and advanced forms of government . . . That a community (European) is better than an empire (Asiatic), a president better than a king, that Francis Bacon's *Innocence X* (a commentary) is better than Velázquez's *Inocencio X* (the text commented upon). Placed at different points along a scale or hierarchy, and not as I see them: equidistant, equivalent, combinable. All the arguments in favor of a regime of direct or indirect representation also easily applicable to a king. Against Lucius Tarquinus Superbus, the last king of Rome, and in favor of Lucius Tarquinus Superbus . . ."

Batyk took full advantage of the time it took Lifa to reach us with the drinks. He seemed to materialize in discrete moments or pulsations of time: at the door of the drawing room, one; in the center of the drawing room (on the tiger-striped rug), two; next to the Pool, three; then next to us, to Simeon and myself. Unctuous as an usher, fawning as a vizier.

"You talk like a book!" he interjected, bowing low before Simeon. "You don't know how right His Excellency is" (this to me) "for there is already the basis for a terrible argument against republics in the single fatal fact that any monarchy can in twenty-four hours be transformed into a republic, while, on the other hand, no republic can, in twenty-four hours, improvise itself back into a monarchy. To return to nature, to fall into barbarity, to go back to the primitive state, is always very easy, because one need only let oneself go: nature is always there, in the background, lying in wait for us. What isn't always there is civilization: that is, work, conquest, discipline, time, and patience."

I could not believe my ears! I was about to say something to refute his ridiculous argument, but just then the Emperor, your father, made his entrance. One by one the swimming pool's lights came on. Inside, a light awoke the Pool.

4

I warbled sonorously, my chest rippling like a bird's: Vasily I, Emperor and Autocrat of All Russia, Moscow, Kiev, Vladimir Novgorod, Czar of Kazan, Czar of Astrakhan, Czar of Poland (*we'd see about that*), Czar of Siberia, Czar of the Tauric Chersonese, Czar of Georgia (*and that*), Grand Duke of Finland (*and that, too*), etcetera, etcetera, etcetera.

Nelly glittering at the top of the stairs like a real queen, a thousand times more luminous and radiant than Maha, daughter of the king of Thailand. The majesty and grace with which she swept through the crowd, the aplomb with which she allowed some men and many women to kiss her hand. How I approached her, my chest still palpitating, shaken by the vision of her torso transformed into a bird. The grace with which she turned toward me, came down to me, lowered herself to me as slowly as a goddess, the polychrome statue that comes to life in a fairy tale, miraculously bending at the waist, its painted wooden dress rippling as it leans down to you, kisses you. She said to me, she whispered into my ear: "I thank you for all of it, all your effort, Psellus: you will be rewarded." Laughing in amusement at my childish whim, for I was about to fall to my knees and kiss her hand, and she detected that impulse and placed her hand on my forehead. How she floated then across the drawing room and went to take up a place against the bluegreen background of the Pool. Nelly settled into her pose and fell still, hands clasped in front of her. She, too, glittering like a star.

Vasily, gleaming in his Savile Row, illuminating everyone else, the group of tourists toward whom he graciously swiveled his torso.

Sweeping them with the light of his infinite goodness as well as that of the diamonds studded across his chest and at the jacket's cuffs and the waistcoat's buttonholes. Blue and red gems covering his enormous body like tears of resin on a tree: a patch of night sky revolving majestically, stars glittering in the dark abyss or fathomless universe of his body. Stopping and bowing strangely, extending the hand—the darkness visible—greeting the assembly with full mastery of his voice, for your father had changed, dropped his cover, shucking off his petty carapace; he had donned the constellated suit of the superior man. He knew he must reign, do justice to the people of Russia, the vacationers from Irkutsk, the odious professor Astoriadis, the sublimely beautiful Claudia, revolve glitteringly above them with the serenity and parsimony of a star that brings well-being and mutual comprehension, a sun of justice.

You in your Pierrot cape, the fulfilled promise of an entirely new fashion in children's wear. Your dirty jeans cast aside for breeches made of some new material, an intelligent fabric that at a command from its owner enfolds him and rises, snaking up the entire leg, covering his body. The owner, standing before the mirror in amazement, his garment responding, corresponding, conforming to the mind's most delicate impulses, the most capricious sketches, the strangest arabesques, total personalization (and democratization? And democratization!), Hilfiger and Dolce&Gabbana surpassed and forgotten, a unique nanotextile prototype, the nobility and taste and intelligence of each one clear to all eyes, on display for all to see.

More brilliant than your mother's Rabanne, still more magnificent than your father's solar attire, the imagination of mankind, your subjects, captivated by it. To begin again, I thought, exactly where the previous dynasty ended: with the hand-tinted photos of the grand dukes on sale across Russia in the year '14 as well as the years '15 and '16 and '17. A publicity campaign using deaf mutes to distribute them in trains, interrupting conversations, the passengers' insipid chitchat. They studied the postcards devotedly, breaking off their inane and resentful commentaries, their faces illuminated by the vision of Nelly, your resplendent mother, of Vasily, emperor of gemstones, of you, Petya, like a child of the future, the image in platinum and titanium of the Doncel del Mar, the youth from the sea.

The whole country, the miners who crawl through underground tunnels dragging heavy pneumatic hammers behind them and then come out into the sun, their faces and lungs patched with black, getting blind drunk every payday because they're terrified of dying young; the nurse who accidentally pricks herself with a needle she's just used on an emaciated patient; the music teacher who takes out a wallet gone limp from use as she stands in front of a counter calculating that she only has enough for half a loaf of black and half a loaf of white; the master glassworker in Pskov, the gene counter in Perm: all of them would proudly hang the plastic reproductions of the imperial family on their walls and mutter to themselves, without taking their eyes from the tableaux or moving off to attend to other household duties: this one, yes, *Our Father*! He'll put things in order, he'll whip this country into shape.

5

And at this point the Commentator wonders, with an insufferable turn of phrase: "What does it seek to say? What message can be derived or liberated from the quoted passage?"

I answer: in the plainest possible sense, entirely contrary to any recherché or obscure interpretation, the idea of a king is simple, clear, and profoundly elegant, easily understood, perfectly coherent, spherical. And no one, ever, in Marbella (and why only in Marbella? In all Spain! You're right, in all Spain), no one has ever seen a spectacle like this one. Never. The enthusiasm, the transports of joy awoken by the blue stone, the Pool, the deep throb it transmitted to the entire gathering, the confidence it awoke in me: We're saved! My plan has worked!

The same miraculous transformation in the Verdurins, from entirely insufferable bores to the Prince and Princess de Guermantes. And in one-tenth as many pages as the Writer. Is it not prodigious? A miracle? Or does Simeon, present here, understand it as a farce, knowing full well that Vasily will never become czar, will never succeed in launching a dynasty?

Has Simeon read the Writer, who judges men's souls with such good sense and benevolence, who does not label this plan a senseless one and recognizes the tragedy of the scientist, the man of talent, the person who believed it was possible to swindle the mafia, an essentially good man who chose the worst possible hiding place, in plain view of so many compatriots, the tourists who were still squeezing into the garden, dressed in all manner of strange garments?

Only one of them was elegantly garbed, someone from the A list, the first version of the guest list which envisioned the uncrowned kings and international jet set coming to the house to form a princely electoral college. His attire selected with impeccable taste and an air of ineffable refinement, red silk handkerchief peeking out of breast pocket. Distinction and years of training visible in the crease of the trousers, the way they fall over the high gloss of the polished boots. Standing out like a peacock in a flock of sparrows.

Certainly not one of the tourists that Claudia seemed to have an infinite supply of: people who were—ay!—not fully equipped for a party like this one. Nor the clever imitation of a gentleman, the Italian "spurious gentleman" who, in the Writer, has a rendezvous with Daisy Miller in Rome. A true air of lordliness here, the look of one who on learning of our party, this unique opportunity, had given instructions to his valet, selected his suit with great care, and stopped by the florist's downstairs, next to the reception desk, to pick up a carnation for his buttonhole.

6

But the most striking aspect of the gentleman's attire, Petya, the part that most leapt out at the eyes and that I couldn't tear my eyes away from, were the two black lions he was leading on a leash and that were revolving powerfully around him, setting their heavy paws down on the grass, hating, it was easy to see, the yoke of their collars, advancing toward your father. And when your mother saw them and belatedly realized that what she'd taken for two large dogs, two mastiffs —the play of muscles beneath their silken shoulders—she let out a stifled cry and gripped my arm, white-faced.

I stepped back, the blood rushing from my face as well, and then there ceased to be a sky. How to explain this to you? There ceased to be a sky, the plane of the sky tilted away in silence, not even a faint crackle, as the vaulted roof of a stadium slides shut. No longer a sky: a broad red plateau at my feet and as far as my eyes could see: the red vastness of space in which floated or suddenly emerged, pushed toward the surface, the half circle of a blood-red sun. The rays of its dark light crossing all of visible space, powerfully illuminating it. The whole plane dotted with stars toward which—I had a sudden certainty—I could walk, reaching them on an endless but possible journey, never leaving the plane, across that two-dimensional world.

The silence of the empty air into which the laborious breathing of Simeon of Bulgaria suddenly erupted, rattling in panting acceleration like a diesel generator starting up during a power failure. And he blinked during the second or two before the lights came back on and grew brighter in brief bursts as they returned to their former brilliance, dazzled by the revelation, for he hadn't imagined this, he had stopped believing in his mission after so many throneless years in Spain, had never expected to see the lions again.

But there they were, he saw them with his own eyes, to his great joy, and understood. He thanked the man, the unknown gentleman, for his gesture. Alerted to the presence of a king in Marbella, this gentleman had resolved to put him to the test, bringing the magnificent pair of black lions to the party. The resolute way that Simeon took a step toward the lions and reached out his hand, without the slightest doubt, without fear.

The lions felt it, the rounded front of his strength. They approached him like gigantic dogs, their flanks rippling tamely, arching their backs before the king, the taut, gleaming skin of their shoulders, hypnotic. The backlit agate of their eyes fixed on him.

Then the horizon returned, a slow swell of sky, there was a sky once more. From which a light drizzle began to fall, it seemed about to rain, but these were only the bubbles from the machine, falling from above, exploding on my cheeks like light, swollen drops of a cosmic, supersized rain. I didn't forgo the pleasure of catching them in flight, watching them come toward me, iridescing in the night air. But Batyk's thick ignorance, his disorderly love of lies, made him open his mouth and allow these idiotic words to emerge: "We'll have fireworks." Because the purity of the test had been compromised by the presence of Simeon, a king, I won't say a true king, but of ancient descent, the House of Saxe-Coburg. And the lions, who never attack a king, crouched before him. Not before Vasily.

I was hurt by that, I didn't want to hear it. It was intended to blemish my happiness. Why fireworks? Why a false and inappropriate display of fireworks? I, who had triumphed, who had extracted and condensed the wisdom of the Book, overcome the dangers, woven the most delicate deception ever conceived by the mind of man, nourished its engines with the sale of the diamonds, conceived of the construction of the Pool, the diamond that would be seen, that would shine as the cornerstone of the empire, I, all this—fireworks?

I cut him off with a gesture, went over to the boy, and said (fully prepared to withdraw and let things take their course): "I no longer wish to speak." I said to you: **"'I no longer wish to speak.' You said, 'Master, if you did not speak, what would there be for us, your disciples, to transmit?' I said, 'Does Heaven speak? Yet the four seasons follow their course and the hundred creatures continue to be born. Does Heaven speak?'"**

7

But these words by the Writer enclose such wisdom that he himself, with his exemplary frankness, attributes them to Comenius: **When once you have tasted sugarcane, or seen a camel, or heard a nightingale sing, these sensations will be so indelibly engraved on your memory that they cannot be erased.** All three, the *sugarcane*, the *camel*, and the *nightingale*, are words applicable to my case and whose literal interpretation presents no difficulty whatsoever, because it explains and illustrates a certain fatal tendency of mine, the way I had of walking with bent body or gliding along the slippery plane of dance floors, my perverse and inexplicable—indecipherable, even with the Writer's help—mania for dancing.

Just when I thought I had overcome all obstacles—the incredulity of the tourists, the danger that Simeon would leave a party he deemed inappropriate to his royal dignity (he didn't, he stayed right to the end), the terrible unseemliness of Batyk's attire, the danger of the lions, the black cloak of their shoulders, their agate eyes—I was about to ruin everything by succumbing to an astutely planned blow, the most subtle way of undermining my efforts, the blackest of betrayals.

Batyk played his last card. He had doubted, perhaps until that very moment, the success of my undertaking, but when he saw that no one could stop us and witnessed the palpable victory of my plan, the last and final rusty partition that separated the somewhat less murky portion of his soul from the unfathomable reservoir of sewage in his chest gave way and the sewage broke through and flooded everything. And his eyes began to shoot out a grim gaze on which he came gliding in like a surfer, to put his blackest and most perfidious scheme into action.

The instant my ears caught its placid undulations on the wind, my feet tensed, the ears of my feet, for I have ears on my legs, one on each calf. Listening to and obeying the sound of that music and letting myself be carried in the sole direction of that diabolical sound, defenseless before it, Petya, without the slightest control. Such perfidy! Seen and imagined by me in that same moment, in vividly cinematic flashback: Batyk's curved hand, his hard white nails, how they carefully selected a disk with that music. And before that, seeking it avidly in every record store in Marbella. Making himself understood with great difficulty, waiting patiently for the salesman to grasp so unusual a request, coming from a person with his almond eyes. "Lumba? Lumba, you say?" "Yes, you know, lumba, like . . . Like lock, etcetera." Until the *r* took the place of the *l* and understanding dawned on the salesman from on high. All right, then, he must have said to himself: what times these are, a Chinaman (though in fact he was a Buryat) asking me for that . . .

And my feet were electrified by the charges that shot through them, ready to launch into a Saint Vitus' dance, to begin one of the interminable sessions over which I had no control whatsoever, unable to stop as long as the music played, destroying with my spinning feet and the arabesques of the dance what my hands, with such diligence and effort, had built.

My eyes wanted to speak to his, plead with him, not for myself but for Their Majesties, but they ran up against the metallic gleam of his iris, blackest evil from the deep cavern of his face.

I underestimated the malevolent power of this **Negoro,** the eternal bad guy—that's what I'm getting at. But to his machinations, Petya, I opposed the countermachination of the Book. With infinite subtlety, having, under my tutelage and the Writer's words, completely changed your interior. A proven truth in you, a gaze that could never be confounded, knower of answers to which no objection could ever be made. Just as you were finishing your journey through the vade mecum of the Book, best foot forward, shod in elegant sandals. Having passed through it under my guidance, moved your brain through its pages, your masteries interwoven in more complex formations than your father's oscillating ferrites, too easily oriented in the wrong direction. Discovering you to be, displaying you now: a radiant boy, a resplendent prince, a scholar of the Book.

What country, what democracy, incipient or adult, knowing what I knew, having meditated and reflected upon the question, with the knowledge or data my eyes had gathered from your bearing as royal boy, would not want you as its prince? Forty-two years of Pax Augusta, a richer and fuller life in the force field of your eyes.

The disk of the *Vinteuil Variations* in your hands, the music by which you'd sought to pacify your father's insomnia, this composition—by the greatest of musicians!—you had learned to love and appreciate as I did. I believed I saw this, I thought this. But immediately, when I saw what disk was actually in your hand, I understood what your advice was, how to overcome the test, and skillfully free myself from the barbed jaws of that betrayal. Your advice was to enter further into the music, these new versions, beautifully commented on: to culminate, in short, in a great dance.

Better a dance than the passive adoration of the Pool, far wiser to set them all dancing, so that they might better apprehend Vasily's cosmic importance, his very beautiful wife, the new Imperial House of Russia.

The way you approached the silvery stereo and pushed the play button, the way you turned toward me with the majesty and propriety of a king's son, requesting:

"Please dance, Master Psellus."

8

And this **Mourdant,** the eternal bad guy, paled dramatically beneath his mask, as on the night when he'd heard me recite whole passages of the Book from memory, long chapters, the text incarnate.

Need I explain to you why? The reason for his pallor? Certainly not, of course not—right? You know it and Batyk knew it, too, the instant he saw me move toward the center of the room, waltzing smoothly, arms extended toward your mother. His delicately tubular ears sensed it, understanding what I was preparing to do even before he himself did. Distancing myself here, suddenly, from the Book—not a single dance in the Writer! Understanding how much better an inaugural ball than a simple banquet, a party with exhausting word games, bons mots, the gathering of many pages. On the wings of an inaugural ball, how easily we could glide into Russia. All the pitfalls of legitimacy, the relevance of our project, popular support, neatly sidestepped. Your mother's understanding of the situation: not the slightest injury to her royal dignity, on the contrary. The way she awaited me with arms outstretched, stepped flawlessly into my spin, smoothly twirling backward, dancing as no sovereign of any European house could have.

New dance steps, a goldmine of new steps blossoming from within me with perfect ease, from forearm to arm, arm to finger. Redeemed of my wickedness, my low passion for your mother, firmly grasping the whole matter of the restoration. The Russian people bedazzled by the prodigy of this dance, our triumphal entry into Moscow to sit on the czars' empty throne guaranteed. Even if, when the music began, the reediness of the voices were perceived, even if it were discovered that the new royal pair weren't as good as the terrific production values made it seem, the miracle of the lighting, the luxury of their clothing . . . A product! Natural talent is unnecessary. I could, if I liked, place a monarch in every European country, or a single one over all Europe, whatever I'm asked to do. And it wouldn't be an undemocratic operation: as we poll public tastes, study tendencies, publish ratings, the monarchs would end up no less democratically elected than if voted in . . . And, yes, maybe he was a bit on the chubby side, the one playing the king, but my God! What an ostentation of wealth! What money! How intelligent he is, that man! Me, that is, walking straight toward the audience from the back of the stage to bow, dressed soberly in black. From Cuba—did you know?—brought expressly from Cuba for the occasion. Such expense! And not in vain. A success. Undoubtedly.

Enough to reign for three hundred years.

Or like the victory of Augustus at Actium, or that other coup de theatre in India or Asia Minor by Nicephorus Phocas, who had himself publicly levitated to impress Liutprand, bishop of Cremona, I told you about this already, in 949 (no small thing, this effect of liberating oneself, annulling terrestrial gravity!). All the pomp and circumstance of Westminster, of the Hall of Mirrors (in Versailles), but in the air, pure play of lights. Broadcast live, seen by millions of viewers. And the videos and the "behind the scenes" footage; a whole twelve-hour program on the new Imperial House of Russia. The only authentically exotic royal house, the most long-suffering of them all, an ideal candidate for relaunching, eighty years after its forced defenestration.

9

Regressing back to Babylon, to a Babylonian apprehension of kingship, however much we may resemble modern men, whatever we fast food eaters may look like. Changing the cut of the suits, widening and narrowing the lapels, still looking like pencil pushers and wives of pencil pushers, some of the women pencil pushers themselves, but with an inner transformation, the fine substance of a sense of hierarchy in their souls. Conscious of the many rungs that separate them, the abyss between the simple construction of their bodies and the more formidable fabric of a king. The futility of all movement understood, all pride set aside: just men, you know? What better thing than this? What better than to dance?

Me with the millions, finally. God knows I hadn't stopped dreaming about that money and God knows, too, how much it surprised me to discover it glittering there in the garden grass when I had told myself: you won't get it. Never. My failure with the butterflies, the fiasco of my education of Linda, which I'll tell you about someday. All that, in its moment, drove me across certain countries, uncontrollably or as if uncontrollably, not only toward the sea, as I told you, but also toward the reflection of the golden stone. And I had closed my eyes in resignation, saying to myself: an illusion, you'll never get it. I had accepted this and lowered myself to giving a few classes, earning a little money (never as much as I'd imagined), until the day I saw the stone in the garden and everything changed, the world turned upside down as I looked at it.

Nelly and Vasily dancing there among the azure sparkle of those final days of the century, in perfect awareness that those years were blue. I'd felt this, too, I had sensed it and adjusted myself to blue. Not gray, as in the Writer's life, or some shade of red, the inexplicable reddish orange of my childhood. The blue of those years that still have not gone by, your mother's metallic skin and hair gleaming among ribbons of blue. OK, fellows, God would say, floating overhead, the best you can do, the wisest: blue. Precisely what I had in mind for those years.

10

Vasily gravitating in the middle of the room with a slow and majestic air, augustly. Absorbing all the light that rushed toward him, all the objects and the party guests spinning around him. Bathed by the brilliance of the stone. Large as an outcrop of rock or a colossus. His mass augmented, but also, like a neutron star, infinitely dense. The party flowing around him, gliding downward with the smooth tension of a curtain of water as he watched, spellbound, approaching for a closer look, then understanding that the curtain, seeming to flow as it fell, was revolving around him in iridescent bands, slower and slower.

He gave an involuntary start of surprise. I saw it appear on his face, observed it from afar, unable still, in that moment, in the heat of the dance, to understand or explain to myself the expression of wonder that rose to the surface of his eyes. He understood himself, comprehended himself as an object of almost infinite mass beneath which space warped, around which the hours grew still.

(For this, Petya, is where the principal lines of the Book arrive at their confluence: that of gravity and that of time.)

Only now do I understand, only now have I succeeded in explaining to myself his figure standing motionless in the center of the room, his surprise as he watched everything spinning slower and slower: Astoriadis's fork poised in midair, Lifa's apple cheeks, Batyk's bilious eyes, and the tedium in yours, Petya, as you waited for the moment of your escape to the sea, the shock in his wife's face, the three phases or moments it took me to understand what was happening before my eyes. All of us going, diluting into a single gray movement.

He didn't run toward that curtain but conducted himself with unfeigned grandeur: he approached it in the natural evolution of its orbit, moving unhurriedly, with reserved, noble, majestic gestures. He put out his hand and broke through the iridescent sheet that churned around his index finger. He tested the substance it was made of, the thickness of that panel or curtain, and fully understood what was before him.

11

Time for the individual self or time in itself: biological time or physical time, the Commentator wouldn't have thought twice about fatiguing us with such matters. Whereas the Writer, in modesty and with infinite intelligence, didn't hesitate to return to an old title, a combination of words already used by another writer, and simply typed out: **time machine.**

The brief pastiche he inserted in the Book as a divertissement, a ploy, a way of charging that title, that phrase, with a new meaning. He imagined, he tells us, that a certain minor writer, a bourgeois by the surname of Menard (a Frenchman), understood one afternoon, after long meditation, how and in what way to repeat the work of the English author H. G. Wells.

But not by the procedure of imitating his life, reproducing his raptures over Morris's bibliographic gems, his rejection of the prolix *Jugendstil*, his calisthenic defense of Swiss gymnastics: all his manias explored, his every irascible thought codified, incarnated, in a word. A procedure that Menard (in the Writer) would reject as far too easy. "Impossible, rather!" the reader will exclaim, etcetera. Something richer and more brilliant by far was what the Writer had in mind, more worthy of his unique and astonishing imagination: the expedient of rewriting page for page, word for word, two chapters of that Book. So that now, easily legible, enclosed in that simple title, *The Time Machine*, we have the Writer's more subtle reading, different, brimming over with new meaning, dictated by a new and scientific understanding of time.

To read instead—where our Englishman had simply written *The Time Machine*—this combination of words: physical artifact, vehicle in which to cross through the puff pastry of the years in the ridiculous aim of quarreling with the Morlocks of the future, redeeming the Eloi and other such trifles. In the Writer's Menard this phrase assumes a new meaning, an unprecedented nuance: **time machine.**

In the mind of the reader who wonders: in what way is this machine of his constituted? What is its internal structure? How does this machine generate time? What puts it in motion? Readings far ahead of their time, the brilliant treatment of new concepts: *event horizon, spatial rupture or singularity, stalled light, unstable stars.*

12

I understand now that this is what was happening. But at that moment, in the midst of the party, my mind rejected this explanation as fanciful (or as too literal, you'll say). Though I took it in immediately, with a single glance, intuitively. I understood what your father was preparing to do, how he discarded the possibility of escaping, entering into this infinity that was opening out before him, time gliding by in ever more widely spaced stretches or portions, the hand-lettered panels of the centuries, the painted screens of the days, the rune-covered shades of the hours opening up, sliding silently on their oiled tracks, at every turn of the machine.

How in the end it slowed and grew still—time. Its panels came smoothly to a stop, floating and glittering before him like some sort of large window that he looked through and saw, in amazement, the dull gleam of nontime. The flickering doorway, the entrance through which he could escape, flee from the assassins, disappear as if by magic from the Castle, from Marbella, and he chose not to do it.

Worthy, I mean. Saved, I mean. His inner workings as a great scientist reassembled. A great scientist who rejects with profound repugnance the mere idea, the urgency of hiding. He renounced it because the slumbering king who dwelt within him had listened to me with utmost attention. The Book had done its work in his breast. The emotion I saw in his face, the triumph and the truth of the Writer in the cry he let out this time, the words he uttered, from Aristophanes: **I walk in air and contemplate the sun! I walk in air and contemplate the sun!**

13

The Writer's sumptuousness, the always noble characters who people his pages, the slow intonation, the poise with which he introduces the theme of rescued honor, recovered dignity, the skill with which he places it before the reader's eyes. The majestic style of that part of the Book, the fantastic final climax, its tone and vehemence demanding something more than a calm reading as you sit there in your armchair: demanding that you jump up, toss the Book aside, raise your eyes and say: I believe!

And again: I believe!

Fist and ax falling upon you, forcing you to exclaim that no other faith, no other Book: **For I testify unto every man that heareth the words of the prophecy of this book, If any man shall add unto these things, God shall add unto him the plagues that are written in this book: And if any man shall take away from the words of the book of this prophecy, God shall take away his part out of the book of life . . .**

Isn't it truly great and terrible, Petya? Don't you see the strength and conviction, all his passion in this? Not a book to entertain us, the kind of book the Writer says justifiably that he could write thousands of. A unique Book: **the book of life.**

And furthermore this: Margarita and the Master fly; Habundia, queen of the fairies, flies; the archangel Gabriel rises through the air. A certain dubious taste there, but the Writer never let himself be stopped by a minor and trivial obstacle like taste. What is taste? Is it in good taste for a Frenchman to spend twenty-seven years in prison and then emerge from that pouch of time to fall, immensely rich, among his enemies in order to kill and take revenge? Is it in good taste for a German, in the flower of his youth, to make a bargain with the devil, sell his soul to the evil one, and then flee and repent and rue the day? Is it in good taste to imagine a country in South America where it rains for four years without stopping and the dampness is so terrible that fish swim through the air in the rooms of houses and careen, gasping, among the cobwebs on the ceiling?

I repeat: the Writer certainly never let himself be held back by a minor obstacle such as taste. Am I to be held back? To open my mouth and introduce so petty and commentaristic a reservation at the very moment I felt my feet lifting from the ground, my eyes glued to your mother's, breathing through her mouth?

14

I caught a glimpse of you, Petya, during a brief pause in the party when the high tide of the dance grew still for a second and then diminished until it flowed out in retreat, washing the last guests out of the garden. I caught a glimpse of you in your scarlet moiré cape. Floating for a second next to the front gate, going, I instantly divined, toward the sea, having adopted—the Book in your heart here, too—the sea that inundates its pages.

To go down to the beach by yourself for the first time, the dark and roiling front of danger far away, my plan triumphant. Tomorrow, when the sun rose, we would stroll unhurriedly down to the city, stopping to chat along the promenade, and the bathers, at the mere sight of us: "the king of Russia, in Marbella . . ." And I was about to take my eyes from the door, but something spoke to me at that moment, a glint from the ring on her finger, the hand that Nelly ran along the wall, that she'd left for a second, herself already outside, on this side of the garden wall. A message I was late in reading, its elements late in settling into me: the blue sequined dress, the Rabanne she'd worn that night to conceal her inexplicable transmutation, in those pages, that part of the Book, into a bird.

But not yet past the gate. The rays of light that shot from her eyes when she came back to the doorway and looked through it; they seemed to seek me out, those rays, illuminating me in their violet color. The thread of light still trembling in the air as she turned back to the street and, the following instant, left the garden.

Transported or abducted by the force of that ray, the floor sinking beneath me, curving beneath every step she took across the striped awning of the earth, careful not to put her foot down on the white. On the blue, only on the blue, her fear of falling. Sinking with each step into the taut substratum of space, ripping it open with my weight, a path that could be taken only once, along which she could never return or find her way back. Sand flowing through the gaping holes in the fabric, me falling at top speed toward the edge, the abyss where the rivers plunge.

15

The immaculate white of her back, the resplendent white of her shoulder blades, and she, lost or pretending to be lost in contemplation of the sea, gazing in rapt absorption at the waves that came to bathe her feet through the dazzling gleam of her Pradas.

She, too, imprisoned by the passions that assail all mortal flesh, previously prepared, up there in the garden, to sabotage my plans entirely and stave off the twelve-pointed stars I'd explained to Claudia in the sky over Arles, Klimt's gilding on the trunks, orange trees spinning in the garden and in Calder.

She heard me out without turning around, my fevered explanation: never, Nelly! A mortal for a goddess? Never! The fine hairs on the nape of her neck assented, seemed to summon me: and? You don't see it? What are you waiting for? One second, two, without being able to believe it, I no less a child than the child, you, Petya, you who were very far off now along the line of the beach.

And I saw it at that moment, as I fell toward her, understood how she must have laughed about the plan for flight, for antigravity, with the strength of a woman who could gaze into the evasive eyes of a charlatan and peck them out, cleanly. For there was only one quality she kept in her heart. So many things that cannot be gained by taking flight! No Russian would accept a bird-woman as queen, never could she transfigure herself on the throne, in view of everyone. Like a dress purchased directly from Lagerfeld that you keep at the back of an armoire and know you will never wear again. Or else only at a reception with other birds, a gathering or parliament of the birds, the bird-women, all of them able, with the greatest lightness and ease, to lift off and halt two feet from the floor, as if levitating there. But so what? What could that solve? She could have—you must understand this—blasted away Antoniadis's arguments with a simple demonstration, a blow of her wings, and she didn't.

How not to see, given all this, how not to understand the senselessness of the Commentator?

16

How not to deplore her resistance, insistently negated by the reality of the girls the Writer describes toward the end of the Book, in the mysterious chapter set in a nocturnal Paris, in the house of ill repute near the Champ de Mars, or perhaps on Mars itself?

Girls at 0.38 terrestrial gravity revolving between floor and ceiling, floating there, awaiting clients, the newest arrivals rising toward them with no more than a slight jump, capturing them in the air. The laughing certainty of those girls, skilled at dodging the client's body, bending at the waist, spinning for a second before your embrace in the air.

And I, caught up in her spin, without a second's resistance, her lips transmitting the impulse of her whole body to me, pivoting on my axis with the speed of a mechanical device. Seeing the beach again, the sea, the base of the cliff again, the gray of the sea, and the path of the moon on the water. Rising in circles, leaving a trail of blue-green bubbles in the air, a double helix of turbulence. Gliding across the sand easily, lightly, gripping her shoulders, pressing against her. Strong and natural as an embrace in a corridor of the metro, your body against hers, a river of strangers at your back, a crack in the tiles behind her neck. Her eyes, a sigh. God! The longest kiss ever!

17

But not, as the Writer had suggested and I myself, as well, under his influence, when I said: **unfathomable quartzes.** That had been replaced, in her eyes, by a superdense gel, a trap for cosmic particles with which she gazed at the sky, all the light of the first days of the universe in that gel, the weeks during which she had not ceased to study me, that light transformed into rays that now emerged from her eyes with the power of a spotlight illuminating a field and the sky over the field, at the far end of the runway, the furrows in the grass left by airplanes. The ease with which I could read it, the clarity, despite the distance across the confines of the sphere: projecting itself around me against the screen of clouds. A book, a sea of stories emanating serenely from her eyes, and we turned on the slow rhythm of its waves like a body electric.

The men who lived in her eyes like inclusions in a diamond, the sailboat and the captain with gold braid on his sleeves, whom I thought I'd seen that morning as I approached the window of her eyes on tiptoe, moved by the suspicion of something, the far-off silhouette of a soaring eagle describing a distant arc across the back of her iris, over that sailboat, the house on the shore, the woman looking out the window.

And I hadn't believed my eyes, I had doubted that strange vision: the life she contained within herself. The pair of swordsmen who were now doing battle in her eyes on the circular stairway of a palace by the sea, first in sunshine, then in rain, engulfed in their capes, interminably. Killing mercilessly, then disappearing into the mass of men without the slightest sign of fatigue, leaving a trail of blood behind them that was visible from the sky, across the city.

And one of those men was me!

Me, Petya! Can you believe that?

But where was this city, where was this valley? Where was the palace by the sea? Was it Larissa who lay at the foot of the staircase, a purple bloodstain blooming on her dress? With whom would I have to fall in love now, Petya, in this new sequel? All in an instant, the vertigo of many paintings in a dark room, the second half of a film projected rapidly in front of us before we leave our seats and go into the street, exposing ourselves to the heat or chill outside.

Overwhelmed by the truth that such a thing could never be written, a work like that, a book infinitely greater than that of the Writer emanating from her eyes. However great my triumph might be, however clamorous my discrediting of the Commentator, there were more stories in her alone, in this woman, than in any of the books, an original sea in her eye with thousands of pages diluted in it. And I would never again take my eyes off a woman, never again settle them on the Book. Betraying, you'll tell me, the Book for the woman I love. No matter, Petya, God will forgive me.

The circles of the swimming pools very far below our feet like springs welling up from an underground river of light, their turquoise waters flowing from that reservoir deep in the entrails of the earth, ascending along those veins to illuminate the night, the silver and alabaster vault of the Castle, the gold and quartz of its battlements. The sky lightening, the rosy-fingered dawn coming in to illuminate everything around us.

Isn't it beautiful, that image: **the rosy-fingered dawn**? Isn't it? Isn't it true that what I'm saying is perfectly logical and makes sense? How astonishing and amazing it is that so much could be contained in a single Book?

EPILOGUE

Twelfth Commentary

I

"Oh merciless destiny, how sorely heavy hast thou stamped with both thy feet upon all the Persian race!" says the Writer, but when he says "Persian" it's only a manner of speaking: neither Nelly nor Vasily is Persian. It's simply that the Writer requires an ancient race, upon which, because of its antiquity, the weight of destiny will fall more visibly. How right one of his biographers is to affirm that all literary production prior to him "seems like a panoramic literature, a bird's-eye view." Because where another writer would simply have written "destiny," in the sense that destiny fell on Vasily, the Writer has destiny jumping up and down on him—and with both feet!

Those feet that enter our visual field as they descend, the large, heavy feet of Kirpich and Raketa in their swanky Ferragamos. Though they didn't trample on your father, that's not what gangsters do nowadays, or only in the movies, to provide a more precise visual idea of the humiliation endured by the fallen man. Same thing with the Writer, in this passage where he speaks so wisely of the Persians and a thing as ancient as human dignity, which he places on the same level as the antiquity of the Persian race, all in that brilliant prose of his that seems to recast the literary erudition of the West beneath the enormous weight of the years.

All possible hues of literature in him, all sensibilities: so great a Writer! For at times he writes with the force and parsimony of Franz Kafka in Prague, in books that fall on us like a stroke of bad luck and distress us as profoundly as the death of a person we loved. Or else with the terrible obsession of the possessed, the bloodshot eyeball, the bitter misanthropy of a Thomas Bernhard, an author who was, curiously, subsequent. Or the faint gleam of those parts of the Book where the enigmatic words of Confucius blossom, without being him! Amalgamated into his unique style, cast in gold and silver. Not a cento, not a florilegium, not a chain of commentaries.

I could enumerate a thousand reasons to explain this to you, cite you his words in infinite numbers to illustrate what can appear to be a miracle: the breadth, the cosmic coherence, the profound ethical sensibility of the Book. Easier and more credible if taken for a miracle, the fruit of a roll of the dice, than for the vision that the Commentator slyly insinuates. Of an astute flaneur strolling through the literary wardrobe of the West and pilfering as he goes along, an overcoat here, a vest there, a pair of velvet gloves over there, a hat here.

An image against which my entire being and even my common sense rebels, and therefore I do not hesitate to exchange it at once for that of a prince, a king, a great personage whom I watch make his way into the forest of the years. Inclining with infinite humility before its carnelian and lapis lazuli fruits, harvesting authorities: here a diamond in Aeschylus (this being where he includes, in an astonishing great leap backward, the Persians), there a ruby in Stevenson, there a precious blue gem in Poe.

But not even that, for this metaphor of the gleaner vanishes, disappears in the presence of the giant who makes his entrance at the very end of the Book, the surprising reappearance on its final page, five lines from its grand finale, of the king of Uruk, Gilgamesh.

Here, Petya, where it says: **like giants submerged in the years.** Like Goya's colossus, many leagues in height, who advances with the clouds around his knees, who keeps the secret of death hidden away in his chest. Moving toward that abyss that only he from his height can behold, the rest of us inevitably falling into it, without exception. A place from which no one returns, from which the only thing that reaches us is the distant uproar of battle, the clamor of a clash lasting for centuries, millennia, with a single foreseeable result: the crushing defeat of the human forces.

And men must rise up, rebel against such a fate, believe fervently in victory, discover that they could die without finding any secret behind the enchanted forest, knot themselves together into a single sheaf, conquer fear, prepare to die, no longer live **lying flat on the ground, like a defeated man** (tablet 12, column 4, verse 270).

The Pool stolen, and the glass jar where he piled up his diamonds as well; the press broken, which I saw for the first time and approached, intrigued, having suspected its existence, but seeing it that morning for the first time, strange as an engine that runs on ethereal fluid, unreal as an antigravity shield.

Someone, perhaps Larissa, called him at that moment. His cell phone trilled and lit up with a green light like a goldfinch with a mottled throat, a bird singing from his shoulder, the brilliance of its screen illuminating the helmet's visor, its lifeless eyes. I didn't take the call, didn't touch the telephone. I was the youthful page weeping inconsolably for the death of his lord, small and insignificant, the grass as high as my knees.

2

I required no proof whatsoever, had no need to turn to any kind of writing or for conclusions substantiated by any authority. I knew who had betrayed him, who had shown his killers the way. Here I can break the principle of authority, and I'm breaking it, Petya. I saw it with my own eyes, beneath the empyrean sky of my vision.

"But it isn't a vision? It isn't a dream?"

"What do you mean: a vision? a dream? It's a device, an invention, a mental experiment. Not even Einstein, a contemporary of the Writer (more than contemporary, didn't you tell me they were friends? Yes, also a friend of the Writer): Did Einstein *physically* carry out his experiments, in real life?"

Mental or imagined all of them, that of the lift falling in a building in Zurich when its steel cables are severed. Or the other one, still more astonishing, in which he straddles a ray of light and rides upon it. Mine, my vision of Batyk, the way he took Kirpich to the laboratory, your parents' bathroom, is also a mental experiment, though one based on investigation. And with a result no less immutable and trustworthy than C, the constant.

I watched the Buryat show the killers the way, I saw him moving silently up from step to step, one foot (carefully) behind the other (very, very carefully). The pantomime that the Writer describes with jocular and chilling precision in the passage devoted to the Art of Ascending a Stairway . . . Turning in an angle of the landing, raising his eyes to the skylight from which they could have let down a rope, though no need for that thanks to Batyk, who opened the door to them, who gave them easy access to the place where otherwise they could never have . . .

Vasily sleeps, exhausted after the long party, minuscule hand beneath enormous jowl, thread of saliva hanging from his lip . . . All in the Writer's aerial swimming pool, the cube of condensed water. I see them walking, Kirpich and Raketa, stopping in front of the bedroom, awakening him with a kick. Because they must have wanted to give him some final message. Something like: **Take that, you dog!** (in an infinity of writers). Or: **Did you think you could hide from us forever?**

The Pool in Batyk's clutches, Batyk who tries, at that moment, inappropriate as ever, to drum its blue surface with his claws. He smiles then, with perverse delight, letting it roll from his palm, furrowed by the deep lines of destiny, all of them fatal or obscure, into the simian hand or palm of Kirpich.

Your father pivoting his head like a basilisk, explaining to them between clenched teeth how much gold, how many jewels ("Fakes!" his killers exclaim in unison at that point, they can't help themselves, "Fakes!") he could give them, how many mines and factories in the Urals he could hand over to them.

And I imagine and see clearly in the condensed air how the two thugs laugh in his face, accusing him, like children, of being a liar, someone who **wasn't going to scalp them again**, this time they'd do it to him, in the sense of the phrase used by Fenimore Cooper, another author much admired by the Writer during his childhood in Combray. In that sense, Kirpich and Raketa promised to scalp your father.

Kirpich brought the butt of his pistol down hard on the Pool, which instantly shattered, the huge stone, the unique gem, transformed into a fine powder that blew across your father's feet. Vasily tried, with an automatic reflex, to catch the Pool, as if it had been liquidated, and as he moved forward, thrown off balance, shots fired by both killers entered his body.

I want to shout, to stop the murder, but I'm as powerless down below as a spectator before a screen, though the effect is incommensurably more vivid.

The shots resolve, visually, in curving, dotted lines, as in a naïf Haitian painting, which disappear into Vasily's immense bulk, lift him off the ground.

In the lower parts of the cube, next to the real or submerged swimming pool, a few of the guests from the night before are sleeping: you can always count on finding two or five drunks on the lawn after a party with Russians (and non-Russians! And non-Russians, Okay). Nelly is dreaming placidly next to the czarevitch, next to you, Petya, where she fell asleep after the stroll along the shore . . . And in the watery air above her head, something like a cloudy excrescence that surrounds her head like a nimbus and which, more closely analyzed by me, as I stand on tiptoe, turns out to be something material, tangible. The dream that her brain secretes **as the liver secretes bile,** as the Writer affirms in his *Against Avenarius,* a book prior to and lesser than the Book. There, in that cloud, the very bright red of a peasant blouse and the vivid green of a rustic skirt that is pleated for pure joy. A man and a woman on the bank of a river, its water suggested by the blue lines at their feet. A pair of lovers, their hands interlaced . . . I could tell you who your mother was, is, in love with, who she was with in her dreams, abandoned to her love without a second's anguish. A young man, not fat like your father, to whom she's turning in this tableau, in the cloud, and at whom her eyes are smiling.

And beyond the calm of the dream, beyond that haven, though still within the cube or blue block of water, the still larger diorama of the house, the darker cloud in which the Buryat turbidly moves. Rubbing his hands together in glee, the pink hairless little paws of a mole like the one who marries Thumbelina, the same type of horror. Without need for any kind of proof, Petya, without having to subject him to any interrogation.

I've reached this point, this construction, only by imagining his steps, mentally extrapolating the duplicity of his silent, cunning movements, the grim gaze of his almond eyes. Brought here, me, by something my heart tells me; he, by his black heart itself; me, to the discovery of his crime; he, to the crime itself, planned and committed.

A traitor. A betrayal.

3

Which I've not stopped pondering, studying as I leaned down over that cube of water, my light illuminated by that faint blue light. For I would never give you that advice, Petya, never tell you to let your feelings grow cold, to write from a healthy distance, to recollect in tranquillity, at your desk, the emotion that led you to love someone more than anything else in the world. For that day, the morning after the party, when I got up and peered through the Venetian blinds, I saw the Castle as the happiest place, the happiest existence, and thought of her. Of the hand I had kissed, the smooth, delicate skin on her hands, the tiny, fine wrinkles around her eyes. Desirable and lovable in all the fragility of her human form . . .

Me, guilty? Me, who with my stupid confidence and absurd party had ruined everything, cleared the way for and given easy entrance to Kirpich and Raketa, as Larissa has not ceased to insinuate to me, jeering at me, hurling it bitterly in my face? How to believe that even for a second, Petya? And Batyk, whose body, whose scrawny corpse never appeared? Whose betrayal was apparent from the very first, the way he put himself first, letting them in if they would promise to spare his life. Not Lifa, Lifa died, and so did Astoriadis, and the dogs. And you, Nelly, and I would have met the same fate were it not for the power of the Book, which turned the heavy steering wheel of fate, which took you by the hand and led you down to the sea, and us after you.

If we hadn't flown that night, hadn't kissed, if I hadn't watched her preening in the bathroom (But was that it? All you did was spy on her while she was naked, all you did was kiss her, Psellus? No, Petya . . . Wait. Or yes, what does it matter?). If I hadn't seen her naked, a vision that inflamed my passion and made me pursue her through the night, if the Book hadn't intervened, we'd all be dead, Petya, corpses, horribly.

How your mother wept, sobs that made her face puffy, how bitterly she lamented when we found your father's body on top of the shattered diamond. And when the police, the Guardia Civil, arrived at the scene, they had to walk across that iridescent dust and draw the body's silhouette not on the floor, the mosaic of the floor, as is usual, but on that luminous dust. And when one of them went to the window and raised the Venetian blinds, a torrent of light poured through the panes, which seemed to move and run like tiny ants, a whole army of them, with Vasily, your father, lying there suspended between the glittering diamond dust and the luminous uproar raised by the windowpanes at the sight of their owner, dead.

And me? And me? And the pain I felt, the rage, the stab to the heart? And how, like Vagaus in Vivaldi's *Juditha triumphans*, I shouted: **Furiae! Furiae!**

4

Her breast beneath the purple of the dress, her wings (turning her toward me). Kissing her back, the birthplace of her wings, the way she had of placing a colored stone on each of her moles, the way she would jump up in a single bound, her white thighs filling my eyes, the two panels of the armoire opening together. In the same impulse, because it was enough to open one and both would open, and she would take out the jar of colored stones and hold it up in the air. From which she would extract, from that red heart in the center of her chest, the gems she would place in my hand and with which I would cover, one by one, the beauty spots on her body, a bejeweled bosom, a breast studded with diamonds.

And nevertheless she left. And nevertheless I let her go, I said good-bye that same night, Petya, as you know.

In the darkness of my room I had caught the scent of the air of hers, like an animal, feeling it waft through the whole house. And read on that air, on the disposition of its volumes, that her door was open, that now was the time to get up, go down the dimly lit hallway, occupy your father's place at her side. Not because the obstacle of her husband had disappeared. None of that I would tell her, to none of those causes or base motives would I allude, but only bring to its culmination what the two of us had begun. Obstinately: bring her to the throne, make her Empress of Russia, demonstrate the correctness of our calculations, the unerringness of the Book. My right eye peering through the crack of that idea: the faceted columns of a chamber in the depths of the walled city, the ermine cape on my shoulders, bent over a terraqueous globe, frozen in that pose, playing the regent until the czarevitch attained his majority, feigning to be from Italy or Monaco, from a country that would make me more bearable to the Russian people. As if not only your mother were awaiting me with her door open, but all of Russia, my adopted country.

But when I had reached her, arrived in her room, I saw her sit up in bed, look at me once, only once, giving me to understand with that glance that all was lost and impossible, and dropping back to her pillow. I understood everything—it was the end!—and moaned with impotence in the hallway, gnawing my fists, quickly riffling through all possible responses, not prepared to yield. Wrapped in my bathrobe as if we were in the ancient Year of Our Lord 1997 and empires still existed, men who would kill to make room for themselves on a throne, who would poison their kings.

All that still true? All that still true, the air had sent me that message: to wed the young widow, become czar myself. A foreigner, but what did it matter? What about the other foreign emperors of Byzantium? Michael the Stammerer, Constantine the Filthy, Basil the Bulgar-Slayer? Just by stopping in my tracks or in mid-flight, returning to her eyes, caressing her slender hands.

Why didn't I do it? Or here, you be the one to ask me: Why didn't you do it? Little Mother Russia in the reclining figure of your mother, her alabaster thighs. Perhaps I was too young that day, I don't know, Petya. I probed blindly at the Book, the whole text, consulted it extensively and did not find, for the first time—that's how it was, Petya! for the first time!—a passage, words that conformed to my aims or served my purposes. I found things in other books, in certain great writers and even in minor writers, but I wasn't going to be the one to attribute phrases to him, or even whole passages, that were not his, that clearly and patently had not emerged from his pen, Petya. Not when the heart of the matter was me, my life, this Writer. I passed over good and beautiful pages that I discarded immediately because they were not by him. I couldn't tell myself what I had told you, Petya, couldn't deceive myself as I had deceived you . . .

"I knew it, I knew it from the first time you told me about the piano that mourned like a bird abandoned by its mate and the violin that heard it and answered from the top of another tree."

"But that *is* by the Writer! . . . It doesn't matter . . . I won't say now (though perhaps this is the reason): it was my life, it was my life that was at stake. Pusillanimous. No, it wasn't that."

"Listen: you could never have been our sovereign. Never!"

"I know, Petya . . . Piotr Vasilievich. You mean they never would have accepted me as I am? I never could have ridden into Moscow on a white horse? I know that."

5

"Well, yes, he *is* named Borges, J. L. Borges—how did you find out? I didn't want to tell you, didn't want his name embedded in you like the names of the philosophers in Diogenes Laërtius who are known only by the fragments he cited or commented on in his book, most irresponsibly, I would say. Such an honor for the Commentator were you to sit down some day, grown up, and write about the days in the Castle, exalt the beneficences of the Book and the intelligence of your tutor . . . You, Petya, who could easily write such a thing, a real book, a primary book, without commentary or citations in bold face, and without the dark gleam of his name, the Commentator's, contained within or casting its light from any page of your book or any of the folds of your adult memory."

There are names, experiences, upon which a good person, educated in the Book, must never set eyes or think of. Not in pursuit of greater knowledge, not in pursuit of cultural breadth. A culture and an erudition that are false!

A man—forgive me for insisting upon this point—incapable of thinking straight or of writing with the unvarying frankness of a truly great author, and who, on the single occasion he met the Writer, during a ride in an automobile, didn't exchange a word with him but only exclaimed, toward the end, with feigned astonishment, "Sir, you slow and accelerate the rotation of the earth at your pleasure: you are greater than God."

Greater than God? How could anyone claim to be greater than God?

The Writer never claimed that, or to have made any great scientific advance, discovered any practical application for his Book, for the fragments or blue stones of Time he holds in his hands in volume 7 and gazes at in amazement, for, having taken his sincerity further than any other Writer in the world, each time he has asked himself *What is time?* he has been able only to keep himself from lying, only to confess, to respond, wisely and with absolute sincerity, with Augustinian wisdom: **"If no one asks me, I know what it is. If I wish to explain it to him who asks, I do not know."**

Or, what amounts to the same thing: We must never imagine the solution of imposture, never pretend to be more than God. Better to entrust ourselves to our fate.

6

But I already told you about my blindness, when I mentioned to you and commented extensively on that phrase by the Writer where he says, quite rightly: **he was a good man.** And allow me to add: naive.

Who took some time to understand the slander that another man, a false youth, a gentleman of Germanic surname, Aschenbach, put out against the Writer. A jeweler in Santa Monica whom I saw reading in his shop, and who did not get up when I went in, but put down the book he was reading to attend to me, placing it facedown.

So that I could read, decipher the title in English, and shiver in wonder: What? You have the Book, too? You know the Writer, too? And read him with veneration? And I asked his permission to pick it up and examined it rapturously, Petya, not understanding anything in that language, but leafing through it in ecstasy, surrendering before it.

Until I heard him speaking of the Writer as a standard-bearer—you know, Petya?—and I came to realize. That he was reading it because supposedly only in its pages would he find a knowledge and a comprehension, an exact and inclusive portrait of all the colors of the rainbow. I was horrified to hear this. The Writer as a standard-bearer!

I would dedicate an entire book, years of my life, to demonstrate the falsity in that, to clean . . . Petya, I couldn't stop myself from leaping over the counter to beat him in rage, until his mouth was bleeding, the mouth that had spoken ill of the Writer and said those things, odious prevarications, never!

An *instrumental* use, Petya—as if the Book were some sort of manifesto. Never! I beat him until someone, an accomplice of his, his employee (Tadzio! I heard him call him, Tadzio!), must have hit me on the back and I collapsed unconscious on the floor.

7

The beating I got in my turn, the interrogation I was subjected to. The tooth I spat out at my feet: blood and saliva. The things I howled: Is he not an imposter? Is he not assuming the personality of another man? Is he not using his words? Is he not putting in the mouth of a single Writer the words of many other writers? Is he not eternally falling into the fallacy of amalgamating many writers into one?

On the floor of the police station, my body aching but without regretting for one second having assaulted that man. All of him false (his horrible teeth, like a young man's), propagator of those nauseating falsehoods about the Writer. Unable to bear so much deception, so many lies: as if there, so far from death, from the place where he must be, Batyk were speaking through his mouth. But why should it matter to me: I know your mother, I know your father, I know you, Petya— all of you are full of respect for the Book.

Quelle horreur that in America, horrible Amerika, the horrible Americans should devote themselves to staining and outraging the Writer's memory. And I leapt on him the instant I understood the ignominious intent of his words until someone, his employee, as I told you.

I wept that night on the floor of the police station but did not say, did not permit myself to say, did not sully my lips with the words of so filthy an accusation. The police unable to find an explanation or determine what had triggered (like a gun) my rage. What a child I was! How ingenuous my reaction! The shiver I felt, full of admiration, when I found him reading and saw what book it was. And how he displayed it to me in delight, believing me to belong to his cult, a worshipper of the same god.

They didn't understand a word, the police. They beat me all morning, powerless, a feeling of impotence growing within them. Hearing me speak in that foreign language, so obviously a foreigner (there's only one small territory on the globe where I'm not, and therefore I am a foreigner more than I am anything else).

Cuban? Cuban! I told them a thousand times. What does it matter? Cuban, yes! And I was dealt another blow. Why, then, does no one here understand you? Jorge is from Puerto Rico: Martínez, Pedro, they don't understand a word. And he slammed his broad fist, its fingers tightly clenched—let me tell you—into my stomach again. And the questions rained down again: "Who are you talking about? Who are Pierre Hélie, Hugues de Saint-Victor, Borges?"

I looked out at them through a single eye: they're all French, I told them, or no, from South America, from a country, I don't remember which one (I don't know why I thought that if I said Argentina they'd beat me with even greater fury). I woke up that morning on the floor of the cell, and through the window high above me, when I'd risen to my feet and hoisted myself up by the bars, I saw the sea. A wine-dark sea. I wept . . .

8

Exhausted now, like a swimmer who's abandoned all struggle and floats without reaching any shore, a man who on one afternoon of his life, full of strength, has the idea—in the Writer, in John Cheever—of crossing through the swimming pools of his neighbors, behind those gigantic Californian houses, and dives through their subterranean branches without finding a way out, the way home, lost in the labyrinth, dying there. Or like a swimmer in time, **borne up by the whole movement of the wave and down by the whole movement of the wave, without there being any merit in him.**

Up to the service of the last emperor of Russia. The happy days after the journey to Barataria and the successful sale of the diamonds (which I didn't tell you about), the night of the great ball, when the kingdom seemed to be at hand and I saw your mother as a queen, and flew with her over the blue and white Castle, its galactic blue glittering from the sky.

Down to that flat city, the entirely pernicious example of so many low houses, like a valid refutation of the idea of a king. And still lower, to the floor of the police station, beaten. All my efforts seeming to have led me to nothing, and left me without any desire, for the first time in years, to go down to the sea. The city awakening, its men and women breakfasting on enormous glasses of milk, steam rising from the plates that waiters held up against the sunlight as they came out of the kitchen.

(How to bring her back? How marvelous it would be to make the journey to see her, simply going down the stairs and standing on the lookout on Alondra Boulevard where the taxis pass by, having first lied to Larissa about where I was going. Waiting for one impatiently, getting in full of air, floating in the backseat like those balloons we take home from a party and push inside a taxi, riding along smiling, enormous, lips laughing, teary-eyed, happy because in only half an hour's travel through this low city . . . But she does not occupy any of the blocks of its grid; none is marked by having her inside it. I'd have to subjugate myself to the pressurization of an airplane, dragging my feet along the pavement toward its steel flanks. Cuernavaca is far away. There's no sea in Cuernavaca, I've checked on the map. Only green and brown on the paper, an abhorrent place the Writer never heard of, about which he never wrote, though about Los Angeles, yes, I'm sure.)

And pay attention to me here: there's only this one point I would dispute the Writer on, one thing I don't agree with: not **without there being any merit in me.**

I went, I leapt, it was I who leapt. In me, as in one of the Writer's heros, lies dormant the stuff of which a lord is made—*Tuan*, he calls it—and which finally organizes itself in the air before falling into that mud, in Patusan, **in . . . the trust, the love, the confidence of the people.**

Crowned on my voyage to the sea: at the center, Petya. Speaking to you from the center of the sphere. Assisted by a cloud of instantaneous beings or winged homunculi, the yahoos, **they climb high trees as nimbly as a squirrel . . . with prodigious agility.** Small and subjugated devils who would purge the horrible guilt of the treachery of their man Batyk in the court of their fathers, or like captive angels flying to the most remote confines of the sphere. To bring back, in their beaks, fragments and passages of all books, to hold them up in the air before me with profound reverence. All the wisdom of the Book, of all books, before my eyes, infinitely wise, fabulously rich.

Infinitely wise. The generative principle of the Book understood; adding further volumes to the seven initial ones about the Perfect King, confident that perhaps, at a distance of thirty centuries, they would amalgamate into a single book, my clumsy commentaries and allusions to the warm Mediterranean commingled with his infinitely detailed pages on the sea in Normandy. In a single book? In a single book!

And fabulously rich. Because what other proof did I have? What other way of confirming my young life to the emperor of Russia (but you, so young? Yes, me, so young) but the enormous wealth, the unimaginable sum in diamonds that I carried in my pocket like a voyager across time?

Not a flower, as the Commentator falsely states: imagine that, a rose as proof of a journey to paradise! For paradise, as is well known and sustained by the authority of John the Theologian, is thickly strewn with diamonds, the stones he cites with undeniable pleasure in the final pages of the Book: **jasper, sapphire, chalcedony, emerald, sardonyx, sardius, chrysolite, beryl, topaz, chrysoprase, jacinth, amethyst!**

What would you bring back, Petya, from a journey through time? A rose? Or diamonds stitched into the hem of your coat that—when the friends who had gathered for a banquet in your honor reacted with incredulity to your story, all you had seen and heard in China—you would produce before their disbelieving eyes, as Marco Polo did in 1295, the final argument of the diamonds he poured out from the unstitched lining of his coat or caftan?

So that those present opened their mouths in wonder and shouted: a million! Which is what that Book is titled, the fifth I cite here, in accordance with Valentinian's rule for commentary: no more than five authors.

Millions in diamonds! Just like me. The best and only proof of my journey through time. Remember when you asked me: What is the

Book about? What is its subject? And I told you, I answered: It's about money, about how to make money. But now I can tell you this, too—for according to an old saying in the country where I am now, *time is money*—it is also about time. In search of lost money? (No, that would be vulgar and loathsome. Better to seek time.) You're right, Petya. Time.

AUTHOR'S NOTE

Rex is the third and final installment in a trilogy that began with *Enciclopedia de una vida en Rusia* (*Encyclopedia of a Life in Russia;* 1997) and *Livadia,* or *Mariposas nocturnas del imperio ruso* (1999; published in English translation as *Nocturnal Butterflies of the Russian Empire,* 2000). A few clarifications strike me as pertinent. With all three novels, I've tried to go beyond the realism commonly associated with the autobiographical novel (which all three are), yet not toward magic or *magical realism,* but rather toward science and a kind of *magico-scientific realism,* if such a thing is possible. Everything in this book, strange or outlandish as it may seem, is strictly factual and was exhaustively researched, in particular the plot line involving the manufacture of synthetic diamonds. The same is true of the many references to quantum physics, including matters as remote from a child's mind as Bohm's paradox of the fish, and terms taken from black-hole theory such as spatial rupture, singularity, event horizons, stalled light, etc.

It is not by chance, either, that Petya is the listener and sole recipient of the story; the whole tone of the book derives from that fact. *Rex* returns to the free fabulations of childhood, and the tales of Psellus, the tutor, are an amalgamation of all the books he read as a youth or a child, out of which he improvises for Petya a highly adorned story of his parents' life, a story that otherwise, told in some other way, might have been sordid and terrible.

The primary human theme of this novel is the strategies used to overcome the terrible experience of totalitarianism. Like me, my characters are survivors of the totalitarian catastrophe. Therefore, *Rex* can be considered a post-totalitarian novel, whose characters are all profoundly disturbed. This explains their obsession with money, as well as their decision to embark upon the impossible adventure of imposture, their embrace of the surprising and implausible idea of relaunching the Imperial House of Russia.

As many readers will inevitably have noticed, the Writer so frequently alluded to after the Fifth Commentary is not, in fact, Marcel Proust, but an amalgamated figure, much like the one described by Ralph Waldo Emerson when he very rightly says: "I am very much struck in literature by the appearance, that one person wrote all the books; as if the editor of a journal planted his body of reporters in different parts of the field of action, and relieved some by others from time to time; but there is such equality and identity both of judgment and point of view in the narrative, that it is plainly the work of one all-seeing, all-hearing gentleman."

I believe it important to mention as well that the idea of using manufactured diamonds in a swindle alludes to a little-known work by Marcel Proust, which has only recently been translated into English by Charlotte Mandell in 2008. In a collection of his early writings, gathered under the title *Pastiches et mélanges*, the future author of the *Recherche* tells the story of Lemoine, a late-nineteenth-century adventurer who swindled the owner of De Beers and other leading figures in the diamond industry. They paid Lemoine considerable sums to keep him from causing the diamond market to collapse by revealing a secret method of manufacturing diamonds he claimed to have invented. When the swindle was discovered and the whole affair brought to light, a highly publicized trial took place that all Paris followed with utmost interest. Marcel Proust, whose family had a great deal of money invested in De Beers, was particularly caught up by the story and derived from it his idea for the "Pastiches," which tell the story of Lemoine's trial as a delectable series of stylistic exercises, composed in the manner of notable French writers such as Flaubert, the Goncourts, Saint-Simon, etcetera.

Finally, I think it may perhaps be useful to the reader if I include an (incomplete) list of the works cited in *Rex,* either explicitly (in boldface) or implicitly:

First Commentary: Marcel Proust, *Remembrance of Things Past;* William Shakespeare, *Macbeth;* Herodotus, *The Histories.* **Second Commentary:** Jorge Luis Borges, "The Approach to Almotasin," "The Mirror of Ink," "The Secret Miracle"; Fyodor Dostoyevski, *The Brothers Karamazov* and *Crime and Punishment.* **Third Commentary:** Molière, *The Imaginary Invalid;* Isak Dinesen, *Out of Africa;* Marcel Proust, *The Guermantes Way* and *Within a Budding Grove;* Stockton, Frank R., "The Lady or the Tiger." **Fourth Commentary:** H. G. Wells, *The Time Machine;* Lewis Carrol, *Alice in Wonderland;* Ivan Efremov, *Andromeda Nebula;* Chutan Tse, *The Thief of the Peaches of Longevity;* Marcel Proust, *Swann in Love;* Michael Psellus, *Chronographia.* **Fifth Commentary:** Ray Bradbury, *Fahrenheit 451;* Washington Irving, *Tales from the Alhambra;* Alexander Pushkin, *Ruslan and Ludmilla;* Gabriel García Márquez, *One Hundred Years of Solitude;* Robert I. Friedman, *Red Mafiya: How the Russian Mob Has Invaded America;* Victor Hugo, *Les Miserables;* George Lucas, *Star Wars;* Sir James Frazer, *The Golden Bough.* **Sixth Commentary:**

Voltaire, *The Age of Louis XIV;* Truman Capote, *Breakfast at Tiffany's;* H. G. Wells, *The War of the Worlds;* Homer, the *Iliad;* Charles Baudelaire, *Mon coeur mis à nu;* Franz Kafka, *Letters to Friends, Family, and Editors;* Appian, *Roman History;* Vladimir Nabokov, *Lolita;* Avicenna, *The Canon of Medicine;* Racine, *Mithridates.* **Seventh Commentary:** Anonymous, *The Song of the Nibelungs;* Erasmus, *The Education of the Christian Prince;* Anonymous, the Epic of *Gilgamesh.* **Eighth Commentary:** 1 Kings 9:26–28, 10:11, 22; 2 Chronicles 8:17–18, 9:10; Ernst Kantorowicz, *The King's Two Bodies: A Study in Mediaeval Political Theology;* Aristophanes, *The Clouds;* Maurice Maeterlinck, *The Treasure of the Humble;* Hammurabi, *Codex Hammurabi.* **Ninth Commentary:** Mikhail Bulgakov, *The Master and Margarita;* John Milton, *Aeropagitica;* Fyodor Dostoyevski, *The Brothers Karamazov;* Heinrich Heine, *The Baths of Lucca;* Thomas Mann, *Time Magic Mountain;* Isaac Asimov, "I'm in Marsport without *Hilda.*" **Tenth Commentary:** Edgar Allan Poe, *The Narrative of Arthur Gordon Pym;* Prosper Mérimée, *Demetrius the Impostor: an Episode in Russian History;* Anton Chekhov, "The Death of a Goverment Clerk"; Bishop Berkeley, *Treatise Concerning the Principles of Human Knowledge;* Jules Vernes, *The Vanished Diamond;* William Shakespeare *Romeo and Juliet;* Robert Louis Stevenson, *Treasure Island.* **Eleventh Commentary:** Thomas De Quincey, "The Sphinx's Riddle"; Fyodor Dostoyevski, *The Brothers Karamazov;* Saint Augustine, *Contra mendacium;* Theophrastus Bombastus von Hohenheim (Paracelsus), *Three Treatises;* Alfred Einstein, *Relativity: The Special and General Theory;* Garci Rodríguez de Montalvo, *Amadis de Gaula;* Henry James, *Daisy Miller;* Confucius, *The Analects,* John Amos Comenius, *Didactica Magna;* Jules Verne, *Dick Sand: A Captain at Fifteen;* Bishop Liutprand of Cremona, *Relatio de legatione Constantinopolitana ad Nicephoruni Phocam;* Saint John the Divine, Revelations 22:18–19; Jorge Luis Borges, "Pierre Menard,

Author of the Quixote"; William Morris, *The Water of the Wondrous Isles;* Alexandre Dumas, *The Count of Monte Cristo;* Gabriel Garcia Márquez, *One Hundred Years of Solitude;* Farid al-Din al-'Attar, *The Conference of the Birds;* Homer, the *Iliad.* **Twelfth Commentary:** Aeschylus, *The Persians;* Ortega y Gasset, "Time, Distance and Form in the Work of Marcel Proust"; Anonymous, the epic of *Gilgamesh;* Julio Cortázar, "Instructions on How to Climb a Staircase"; James Fenimore Cooper, *The Last of the Mohicans;* Vladimir Ilych Lenin, *Materialism and empirocriticism;* the Brothers Grimm, *Thumbelina;* Antonio Vivaldi, *Juditha Triumphans*, George D. Painter, *Marcel Proust, a Biography;* Saint Augustine, *The Confessions;* Thomas Mann, *Death in Venice;* John Cheever, *Stories;* Joseph Conrad, *Lord Jim;* Jonathan Swift, *Gulliver's Travels;* Saint John the Divine, Revelations 22:18–19; Marco Polo, *Il Millone.*